ABE

FOUR IN HAND

TIES OF STEEL
BOOK ONE

MJ FIELDS

Copyright © MJ Fields 2014

MJ FIELDS BOOKS

This is a work of fiction. All characters, organizations, and events portrayed in this novel are either products of the author's imagination or are used fictitiously. Any resemblance to actual events, locales, or persons, living or dead, is entirely coincidental.

1st Edition Published: 2014
Published by MJ Fields
Editing by: MJ Fields
Cover Design by: K23 Designs
Cover Model: Derrick Keith Shane Meacham
Photographer: Steel Shots
Formatting by: IndieVention Designs

ISBN-13:978-1506133300
ISBN-10:1506133304

10 9 8 7 6 5 4 3 2

This book contains mature content not suitable for those under the age of 18. Involves strong language and sexual situations. All parties portrayed in sexual situations are adults over the age of 18.

All characters are fictional. Any similarities are purely coincidental

This one is for the readers who loved Men of Steel and wanted more Abe.

To the chance we take when giving up control in hopes of gaining so much more.

To the F2 crew, you rock.

MJ Fields would love to introduce you
To some of her favorite new reads.
Check out the these authors and their work at the end of

ABE

Kink vs. Class
(Full Novella)
By:
BFBS

Merciless Ride
By:
Chelsea Camaron

The Waltz: Sexual Awakenings
By:
Angelica Chase

TABLE OF CONTENTS

BREAK

Spring break in Fort Lauderdale was calling my name. I had been there a handful of times when I was attending college at NYU, earning my Master's in finance and business. But I hadn't been back in a few years. I needed a break. I hadn't had time for a vacation since my job at Steel Inc. as CFO kept me busy, and the owners, my brothers by choice, kept me even busier.

Jase, my best friend and CEO of Steel, was back to being the man I knew he would someday be. He was married with one kid and another on the way. He was still a pain in the ass, but his wife, my cousin, had his ass in check—well as much as anyone could have him in check. The others were attached too. Thank God!

Normally I had a bro in tow, but not this time. I was going to lay my ass in the sand, check out the scenery, get drunk, and bring back whoever I wanted to take out this pent up sexual frustration on.

Drunken, mindless, no-holding-back sex. It had been awhile since I had been able to hook up with someone just because. Just because I liked her ass, or the way she smiled, or the little twitch my dick did when I saw something I wanted to be inside of.

Sex now was planned. Does she work for us? Does she work for someone connected to us? Will she be just about the physical, or will she be a creeper? No more random hook ups with someone

I could just bring home, rumple the sheets with, and see where it led. Now I had responsibilities, big responsibilities, and I wasn't about to fuck them up. I would never live it down if I did. I had to give the damn sexual harassment class to my bros on several occasions. It wasn't in the job description, but it was necessary to keep the empire from crumbling.

The past year I took to hiring escorts, and I'm not ashamed of it, either. Lines were not blurred; it was a win-win situation. I had a handful of favorites and a rotation. I took care not to call on the same one within a two-week period. I didn't need it getting around that I was a bit demanding in bed.

The more stress, the more demanding I became. In my job, stress ran through me like a contagious virus ran over a subway train's handrail. I caught it every time. I admit to being a little uptight. I micro-manage, but am working on relinquishing that control, a little at a time of course. I didn't want to fail. Who the hell graduates college and lands a position like this? Add the fact that I am bound to the owners, they're family. Stress, yeah, by the boatload.

So as I stand in the boarding line ready to step into the airplane I am struggling, but as my cousin Carly said when she dropped me off at the airport, "There's more to life than work Abe. You deserve more."

This was after she rid me of the laptop and tablet I had packed in my carry on. When I tried to take it back, she warned me further, "So help me god, Abe, I'm knocked up and Jase is treating me like I'm a porcelain doll. I'm frustrated as all get out. Don't push me," she growled, then cleared her throat and smiled trying to make light of her outburst. I wasn't about to argue with her.

Carly had definitely changed since she met my best friend. Gone was the awkward fun loving, go with the flow kind of girl I grew up loving. She was replaced by a woman trying to keep control of herself. A woman who had to try to control the uncontrollable. If I didn't know better, I would have thought she had grown a set of balls.

I sat in first class, fighting my inner control freak. I was going to have a damn good time starting now. As luck would have it, the sexy brunette flight attendant came up and asked if I wanted a drink.

"Scotch on the rocks. Keep them coming."

She smiled and winked, "Anything else?"

I didn't answer right away; I just looked at her, taking a moment to see if I still had any of my old charm left. Her face heated up nicely as I raked my eyes down to her perfect little protruding nipples. I still had it.

She glanced down and blushed.

I leaned over and whispered, "Short flight so that'll be all."

She swallowed hard and nodded, "Give me … give me just a moment."

I watched her hips sashay up towards the beverage cart and I felt a stir in my pants.

When she returned she smiled and set my drink on the fold out table, "Enjoy. If there is anything else please let me know." She started to turn and stopped, "I have a layover in Ft. Lauderdale. I could show you around a little if you'd like."

I nodded once, "I'm not looking for anything more than a good time."

"I'm not offering anything else."

I nodded again.

"I'll meet you outside gate twelve. I have a room at the Hilton airport hotel."

"Perfect."

She walked away. I was tempted to stop her and ask what her name was, but I decided it really didn't matter.

***

I stood outside gate twelve waiting for flight attendant, Delta. No, it wasn't her name, but for all intents and purposes, it worked. I had packed light, so I didn't have to wait for luggage. If I forgot anything, I could just buy it. It wasn't like college days when we had to scrape pennies, so I wasn't going to. "Fuck it" was my motto for the next week. Fuck the responsibilities, fuck the planning, and fuck anyone I wanted without concern for what tomorrow would bring.

I wasn't always like this, but things had changed. I was no longer delusional about needing to do the right thing by the woman I was about to be inside of. If they were game, so was I. I could decipher between those looking for a man and those looking for a body. I was gonna be that body, regardless of the inner conflict it sometimes caused me.

When she walked out, she was in a pink tank dress that hit well above her knees. Knees that I was hoping would wear the imprint of her hotel room rug very soon. She didn't try to make small talk, which I was grateful for. I no longer had time for bullshit and pleasantries. Fucking was fucking.

I took her bag and her free hand, like a gentleman, and we walked out into the humid spring Florida air.

I hailed a cab, held the door open as she got in, and then slid in beside her. She gave the address to the cab driver, and I immediately rested my hand on her bare, sun-kissed knee. I tested the water by running my hand slowly up to the hem of her dress and looked at her. She relaxed against the seat and I pulled her knee closer to mine opening her legs slightly.

I ran my fingers up her inner thigh and she took a short intake of breath. I continued my slow journey. Her eyes opened as I ran my finger across the silk fabric between her legs. She looked at the cab driver and then back at me. She was a bit nervous. I held my free hand up to my lips and whispered, "Shh."

I wasn't worried that he might see what was going on. There was no way in hell he could, and I really liked the idea of taking this woman out of her comfort zone. She was confident, which is a turn on, but I wanted to be on top, most of the time anyway.

I pulled her leg so it rested over mine and her eyes grew bigger. I sat back and relaxed as I slowly ran my finger up and down the soft, damp, silky material between her legs. She made little moans that encouraged me to continue slowly teasing her, working her up so that as soon as we entered the hotel room I could have her on her knees.

***

She opened the door to her room and turned to me.

"I'd like a shower. Care to join me?"

"I'd like a blow job, care to give me one?"

She smiled, and when I didn't return a smile, she swallowed hard. Just like she would be doing in about ten minutes.

She looked down and nodded, "You want to sit on the bed?"

I kept eye contact and said nothing as I removed my shoes and started to unbutton my shirt. She was only a beat behind me throwing clothes off all over the place. I really didn't like the mess. I laid my shirt neatly over the chair, then my pants and boxers were next.

She looked down at me, "That'll be fun to work with."

"Then let's not waste any time."

I lay on the bed and patted the spot next to me. She climbed up and immediately took my cock in her hands.

"You're not hard yet, honey." She gripped me a bit tighter than I was comfortable with and started stroking me too damn fast.

I held my hand over hers and slowed her down.

"This how you like it, honey?"

Damn, damn, damn, she was fine and all, but I really just wish she'd shut up with the *honey* already.

"Music?"

"Of course. What's your fancy, honey?"

"Whatever. Anything is fine." *Just please hurry it up already.*

She got up and turned on the radio. *Take You Down* by Chris Brown was playing. Maybe she'd get the hint.

She climbed on the bed and leaned in like she was gonna kiss me. I don't kiss. As odd as that sounds, it's too damn personal. We weren't on a date or falling in love here. She was gonna suck me off, shower, and then I was gonna nail her. This was a mutual exchange, a give and receive.

I held her cheek in my hand and rubbed my thumb across her lip, slowing her down a bit. Hoping she'd get the point, I pushed my thumb gently into her mouth. Now I was doing this for another reason too. If her beginning hand job was an indication of what she'd be doing with her mouth, I was a little bit concerned.

She was a licker. She lapped at my thumb like a dog does water. This may not be my preferred method, but it could work. Her mouth on my cock was all I needed right now.

I hooked my thumb in her mouth and slowly dragged her down towards my dick.

"You need this huh, honey?"

"Yeah."

She bent down and started lapping at me. I pulled her ass over towards me and started stroking her soaked seam. I spread her, and she opened her mouth and sucked my tip. *Okay I get it.* I pushed a finger in her, and she moaned with her mouth full of cock. The vibration felt damn good. I pushed in more, and curled my finger up and pressed the magic button.

"Oh, honey," she moaned with her mouth still full of my dick.

I thrust my hips up at the same time as I rubbed my thumb over her clit. She was lapping, sucking, and grinding into my hand. Two minutes later she came.

I wasn't sure if she liked it, or if she was pissed. She turned into an animal growling and bobbing up and down so fast I was a little concerned with my well-being.

"You like it in your ass girl?"

She stopped, just like I expected, and looked up at me.

"If that's what you want honey. Just. Be. Nice."

"How about we try it after your shower?"

"Mmm perfect," She said between licks. "Honey, does it always take you this long?"

"You can stop. Go shower. Relax and enjoy."

"Sure thing, honey. Can I get you a drink? A snack?" She waved her hands in flight attendant fashion, and I shook my head 'no.'

As soon as I heard the shower start, I jumped up and got dressed. I leaned into the bathroom.

"Something came up. I won't be able to stick around."

She leaned out of the shower and looked at me curiously. "Surely I should return the favor, honey."

"Damn it. I wish you could, but as I said, something came up. Maybe I'll see you around next trip."

"I'll look forward to it."

With that, I grabbed my bag and was out the door, dick intact. *Fuck!* This was not a good start to my relaxing vacation.

Thank god the cab was waiting. "2272 North Atlantic BLVD, please."

***

I walked into the rental house and was pleasantly surprised. The view of the ocean was amazing from the first of two master suites, and I'm sure the other two rooms were just as magnificent. I threw my bag on the bed and flopped down beside it. I stared at the ceiling and laughed to myself.

How the hell are you gonna learn to relax, O'Donnell?

I sat up, pulled my shirt over my head, stood and shed my pants. I reached in my bag, grabbed a pair of board shorts, and threw them on. The realtor said there would be boards in the garage and I was dying to get out there and ride some waves.

I walked out into the kitchen, and as promised, it had stainless appliances with granite counter tops. I couldn't wait to cook. I worked so much lately, that opening a take-out container was the extent of my culinary creativity. I grabbed a flyer from the counter and decided to order groceries and have them delivered. I was gonna surf, drink, cook, and fuck all week long. Out with the new Abe and in with the old Abe.

***

I sat in the ocean off the private beach watching the sunset. I missed this so damn much. Years ago, I won the Manasquan Big Sea Day Surf Contest three years in a row. It was basically a fundraiser for a group of local high schools surf teams; it was pretty damn cool. Hometown hero shit is what I miss when I'm CFO of a billion dollar business. A year in, and Steel is running like a top, but walking away scared the shit out of me.

I paddled back to shore and dragged the board up the beach. I put it away and walked through the gate, but stopped when I saw the pool. I decided to take a dip to rid my body of the salt water. I was proud of my Irish heritage, but genetically my sensitive, fair skin had to be babied or I'd break out, and that wasn't gonna happen. Five days from now, I'd be a golden tan and rash free when I returned to my office. I dropped trou and dove in. The water felt damn good, and alone or with someone, it didn't matter much to me. Nothing felt as good as being naked in the water.

I floated around enjoying my privacy. I couldn't do this shit at the gym or at the shore. Conservative or not, there was something cool about my dick being free outside of my home.

I thought I heard voices. When I opened my eyes, I saw three women standing around gawking at me. My ears hadn't failed me.

I quickly pulled my lower half under the water and swam to the opposite side of the pool. They all started giggling.

"Something I can help you ladies with?"

The blonde smirked, "No please don't let us interrupt you."

She dropped her towel and jumped in.

The blonde was laughing like a fool, and I tried not to look annoyed, but fuck, I was a little taken aback by what was going on. The dark skin brunette jumped in laughing, too.

"Howdy neighbor," she said when she surfaced.

"Neighbor?" I asked.

"The cottage right there is where we're staying. Shared pool, shared lawn, shared…"

"Fuck! This was supposed to be private."

"Nothing's private around here anymore," the blonde shed her shirt and jumped in.

"One of you ladies mind fetching me my shorts?"

"You go right ahead big guy, no need to hide it, we've already seen it."

"So that's how it's gonna be?"

They all passed around looks, and the brunette swam to the steps and got out as the other's continued giggling.

"Here you go." She threw them into the pool.

"Thanks."

"Need some help?" The blonde asked and they all started giggling again.

I pulled my shorts up, contemplating what the hell to do next, and I was at a loss. I could stand in front of a boardroom full of investors or behind a podium holding meetings for hundreds of employees, but this right here was way out of my comfort zone.

I swam to the steps and walked out of the pool.

"My apologies. I will straighten this mess out as soon as I can."

I walked quickly to the back door of my semi-private vacation retreat and slammed the door.

I walked into the bathroom and got in the shower to rinse off the chlorine. I jumped out and grabbed a towel, wrapped it around my waist, and headed into the kitchen to call the fucking realtor and ream him a new ass.

I jumped and nearly lost my towel when the blonde was standing in the kitchen setting bags on the counter.

"Hey big guy, the delivery boy came. Hope you don't mind I signed for ya and brought them in."

"Thanks…um…"

"Laney."

"Right. Thanks and sorry about earlier. Had I known I never would have … "

"Don't stress. You have nothing to be ashamed of … "

"Abe."

"Abe, cool. We are all here for a couple more days, so let's just not make a big deal about it, okay?"

"Sounds good." I reached out to shake her hand and caught my towel right before I exposed myself a second time.

She laughed as I wrapped myself up again.

"We're going to grill tonight, if you're interested."

"Not tonight, but thanks." The look on her face told me I was probably being a dick. "Maybe I can cook for the three of you tomorrow night?"

"Four."

"Excuse me?" I scratched my head.

"Four, our friend is coming in, so there will be four of us."

"Four, good. That's good. See you all then."

She waved over her shoulder as she walked out.

***

I had some cheese and salad before I decided to put this fucked up day behind me and call it a night. Tomorrow would be better.

I lay in bed and returned Carly's text.

Abe: Banner start to stress-free vacation. Exhausted. Going to sleep. Chat tomorrow.

I was almost asleep when I heard the neighbors giggling. I lay in bed trying to ignore the commotion. I had decided I should probably shut the window to give them some privacy when I heard the blonde's voice.

"No girl, we're not pulling your leg. All American boy naked as a jay bird floating around in the pool."

"Shut up," I heard a sweet voice giggle. I wasn't alone. Shit stirred under the covers.

"He is built, too."

"You guys are drunk." The voice sighed quietly.

"Drunk or not, the boy had six plus eight."

"Really?"

"Yeah, and those lines that make even the smartest chick lose her mind."

"I swear I would have licked down that V if he'd have asked."

"And kept right on going."

"Eight plus eight." The blonde purred.

"What?" The sweet voice giggled.

"Eight pack, eight inches."

"He wasn't even hard."

"Oh my god, you three are so bad."

Damn that voice was killing me.

"He's cooking us dinner tomorrow."

"We should tag team his ass." It was the blonde Laney.

"You three have fun with that. I'm going in to shower and get some sleep. Maybe tomorrow after some shots I'll be able to follow this conversation."

"Hell no, you just got here!"

Yeah, hell no, keep talking sweetheart, please, I pleaded in my head.

I heard a door shut and then the girls all laughed.

"Six months, do you think she's over him yet?"

"She's fine." The blonde piped in. "She deserves better than a douche that's gonna cheat on her. She'll be just fine."

They all stayed quiet and then I heard the door shut again. I closed the window, cranked up the AC, and fell asleep thinking about that voice.

SURF'S UP

I woke feeling better than I had in weeks. I wasn't going to let the past hinder what I was to become. I am a strong woman. Beautiful in my own way. That had been what I had told myself for the past five months since Steve and I had split up.

"Split up" was a nice way to put the hell that I lived for five months. How is it possible that two words – split up, break up, end this, I'm out –could have so much emotion attached to them? Those two words couldn't begin to describe what had gone on between us since I caught him in bed with a girl who had been not only my friend, but my college roommate for almost three years.

She was a Texas girl. She had been in pageants from the time she was five, always doing what her Bible-toting momma told her. Always lived to make everyone happy. Then Sally went to college. What happens when the straight and narrow go off to college? All hell breaks loose. Sally went through a phase where she was bringing home boys every weekend. Then she went through a period where she was sure she'd go to Hell and she ate those damn éclairs like there was no tomorrow. Girlfriend gained her freshman fifteen and then some. Her momma came up and the way she looked at her with contempt, still upsets me, and I'm no fan of Sally anymore.

Don't get me wrong, no one loves Jesus more than I do. Southern Baptist girl, here. Raised up in church and my extended family living with us. My Daddy is a podiatrist, whitest white boy on the planet. He met my momma playing piano at church and immediately fell in love with her. Neither one of my grandparents minded the fact that he was white and she was black. As my Granny Ivy would say, "It's a heart thing. Love isn't black and white, either is life."

Granny Ivy lived with us from the time Grandpa Isaac died. That's how family is supposed to be. Mom and Dad both agree. When Steve and I broke up, it was her and my mom that got me through it, "Love is a funny thing, not always good, not always easy, and not always meant to be forever."

Sally begged me not to move out of our room. She just didn't know how she would explain it to her mother. "Not your cross to bear," Granny said when I told her, but I only had one semester to go before starting my internship over the summer that would last through my senior year. I sure as hell wouldn't give Steve or Sally the satisfaction of breaking me. Momma taught me right. "Hold your head high and don't give nay-sayers the satisfaction. Grace under pressure. And when you just can't do it anymore, come home and fall apart. We're here for you sugar plum."

I lay in bed contemplating what was next. I would have rather not have come here before moving on to the next part of my life, but my parents insisted I go and have fun. So here I was, passing the time, hanging with my girls in Florida, who were doing the same.

I sat up and looked in the bed next to mine, Laney was still asleep. The girls had gotten pretty tipsy last night; probably needed to sleep it off. I walked out of the room and peeked in at Mel and Paige, they were still passed out, too. I decided to go for a walk on the beach.

The beach was beautiful and peaceful. Small waves rolled into the white sand beach. A few surfers paddling around and one in particular rode a small wave toward shore. The sun behind him made him appear to be glowing. I was glad I had my sunglasses on because I didn't want to get busted for staring at him. I couldn't help but stare. He was a vision, even from a distance. Tall and built very well, his shoulders squared. He looked so comfortable and confident, like he belonged out there amidst the rolling waters.

He hopped down from the board and into the water. I should've walked away, but I didn't want to. It wasn't like I'd see him again anyway.

He picked up his board and held it under his arm as he walked toward me. My god, he was even more beautiful close up. He ran his hand through his hair and shook the excess water out as he continued toward me. I looked left so that he didn't notice my stare, but I kept my eyes on *Neptune*; he certainly was a beautiful creature.

As he continued walking toward me, I began to feel uncomfortable.

"Hey." His voice was soft yet strong.

"Hey to you." I smiled. He stopped and stood his board in the sand.

He smiled. *Beautiful.*

"You number four?"

"Excuse me?" I laughed and he bent over and grabbed a towel that happened to be beside me. I hadn't noticed it before.

"You with the three ladies staying up there?" He pointed to the beach house and then began to towel off.

It hit me right then that he was the All-American boy who my friends had caught floating naked in the pool. I bit my cheeks so that I wouldn't laugh and he smiled and shook his head.

"Yeah, I would be the neighbor who uh," he stopped. "Well, let's just say I met them last night."

"Oh, I heard about you." I smiled, embarrassed.

"I'm sure I made a great first impression. But in my defense I had no clue it was a shared space."

"I don't think they minded much."

He tilted his head and looked at me like he was questioning something. Then he chuckled and leaned down to grab his shirt. He shook the sand off and threw it on.

"I offered up dinner tonight as a peace offering. You're welcome to join us, Four."

"I see." I smiled because there was not much else I could do. He gave off that kind of vibe. He had a warm, inviting smile, the kind of guy you could be comfortable with immediately.

"So, any special requests, Four? I only ask because I haven't embarrassed myself in front of you, so you're like the safe zone."

There was a moment of uncomfortable silence that he broke. "You surf?"

"Never tried it. You looked amazing out there though." *Oh dear, god I just said that out loud.* The corner of his lip curled up slightly. "I just meant…"

"Don't worry about it, Four. I know what you meant. If it helps, you look pretty amazing standing here on the beach as well."

Now I was the one smirking.

"I'll be back out here in a couple hours if you're interested."

I nodded and smiled. Then I kicked at the sand, *giddy*. Neptune made me feel like a giddy little school girl.

"I think I'd like that."

"I think you will, too. How long are you here?"

"Three days."

"Me too. I can teach you a lot in three days, if you're up to the challenge."

"I'm always up for a challenge."

His expression changed and his eyebrow lifted a bit.

"Yeah?"

"Uh huh."

"I'm gonna push you hard, Four."

I may have not been in the game for a few months, but he was flirting. "I wouldn't want it any other way, Neptune."

He bit his lower lip and looked me up and down. "You got a suit?"

"A wet suit?"

"No Four, please not a wet suit."

"I'll have to see what I brought. I'll surprise you."

"I will look forward to it."

He hesitated before grabbing his board and walking up the beach toward the house. I watched him. He looked great from behind as well. This man could be the one to pull me out of my funk.

I was still gawking when he turned to look in my direction. I wasn't gonna hide it. I was excited about the possibilities. This vacation just got way more interesting. I waved and he waved back.

Wow.

***

I walked up the beach, looked toward his place, saw his silhouette pass by the window, and smiled at the glimpse of him. I held my hand to my heart and laughed out loud. Over at our little place, three sets of curious eyes stared at me before quickly ducking out of sight.

I walked in and they all sat quietly around the table. I sat down and looked at them, trying to keep it together. When I couldn't stand it anymore, I smiled and looked down.

"You met the neighbor," Paige goaded, and they all busted up laughing.

"Shh, geesh he's right over there, keep it down already."

"Ooo, looks like Stella's about to get her groove back," Mel whispered.

"He's very nice-looking." I whispered.

"Nice looking? That's all you got? That man is H.O.T. hot." Laney whispered.

"Yeah, he is. He offered to teach me to surf."

"No way!"

"Shhh," I giggled.

"When?"

"Well, in a couple hours, for starters."

"Oh no. We have massages set up in an hour and a half." Paige interjected.

"I didn't know." I tried not to sound disappointed, but I kind of was.

"Ho's before Bro's," Laney laughed.

"Yeah, I'll just have to go over and let him know."

"Go now." Mel sounded a little bit too eager to get rid of me.

"Fine. I will."

I pulled my shades back down, walked out into the shared lawn and across the patio to Neptune's door, and knocked.

He opened the door with a towel wrapped around his waist. He didn't have sunglasses on and his eyes looked like the ocean, sparkling and light blue, something I could definitely get lost in. The towel was slung pretty damn low and I was stuck on the tattoo on his hip bone. That tattoo pointed to the V.

He lifted my chin up so that I was looking at him now.

"You have a tattoo."

"I do."

"It's nice."

"Thanks."

I didn't say anything and he smiled.

"What brings you by, Four, did you need a cup of milk, some sugar?"

"No, um no." *Get it together, Nikki.* "The girls made massage appointments so I won't be able to take you up on the surf lesson. I just didn't want to leave you hanging."

My eyes went down again and then quickly up.

"Four, you keep checking out my stuff and I won't be hanging much longer."

"Well, I only thought it fair that I got to see it, too. You know since the rest of the girls did." I laughed, trying to make light of the situation.

"All in due time, Four."

I laughed, "So, I'll see you around."

I turned to leave and he grabbed my bicep stopping me. His touch was gentle yet strong, and it felt good. I looked back at him as he slowly released my arm.

"Dinner for four tonight. Don't forget."

"I won't. Thanks … um … what's your name?"

"I'm kind of liking Neptune, how about we stick to that?"

I smiled, laughed, and walked away.

***

As we lay on our stomachs getting massages, I told the girls what the neighbor had said.

"He likes you, Nikki." Laney giggled.

"Like, *really* likes you," Paige said, in her sexy voice.

"It's an obvious attraction, not love." I laughed.

"Love, lust. Who cares? You need to jump on that one, get out of your slump." Paige laughed.

"I'm not in a slump. I'm just not a ho."

I could only imagine what the masseuses were thinking.

"See, girl, you need it bad. You're coming apart under poor John's hands." Mel laughed.

"Who the hell is John?"

"That would be me, miss." The masseuse chuckled as he continued massaging my left leg.

"Mel, good lord!"

"Magic Mike over here is hittin' real close to home." Paige cackled.

We all laughed, and once we got going, it wasn't likely we'd stop any time soon.

"You bitches better quiet down or my guy's gonna get a golden shower." Laney snorted, and that did it. We all busted up laughing like we had back in high school. Tears falling, some snorting, some cackling, and we all had to sit up to try to keep from falling off the tables.

When we had all calmed down, I looked at the four men in white trying to maintain their professionalism. Yep, my guy was John, his name tag said so. I laughed again and wiped the tears from my eyes.

"See, you need the big O so bad you're crying." Paige held her stomach and laughed harder.

"What I need is a damn drink if I'm gonna have to deal with you bitches for three more days," I laughed and looked at my girls, all of them looking at each other like they were hiding something.

"What? Spill it."

Silence.

"Come on, Laney give it up."

"We're all flying out tomorrow night … " Laney began.

"WHAT!"

"We told you," Mel spoke up.

"Like hell you did!"

"Well, when do you fly out?" Paige interjected.

"Three days. So I have two nights left here."

"The neighbor will be here. What's his name again?" Laney asked.

"Neptune."

"No, that's not it." Mel scratched her head in thought.

"That's what I call him. He calls me 'Four.' "

"Four?"

"Yep. He said Laney told him we'd have four for dinner tonight, so I'm four."

"I bet he'd like four for dinner." Paige laid down and let out an orgasmic moan. But I wasn't laughing.

"You guys are serious? You're really leaving tomorrow night?"

"Yep, sorry, girl." Paige looked over at me. "Check your messages. I'm sure it's in there. How the hell you're going to be organized at work is beyond me."

"Screw you. I know you said this whole week."

"Yeah, we have the place for a week but have to leave on day five. You showed up three days late, remember? Some of us have classes to get back to, not some cushy paid internship for the rest of the semester and all of our senior year."

"I needed to get the hell off campus."

"We get it."

I lay back down, nervous about being alone for three days and excited at the same time.

***

"There's a bar on the beach," Paige pointed to the left. "Let's go have some drinks."

The first round of frozen, fruity, umbrella-laden drinks was on me.

We sat and laughed as we drank and reminisced about our high school days and about the boys we left behind. When we were sixteen, we made a pact to love em' and leave em', to move forward and not look back. This decision came after our group of five became four. A high school friend Heather allowed herself to turn to drugs when her heart was broken, instead of her friends. Laney and I still tried in vain to get to her, still sent her messages, invites, Christmas cards and birthday cards for a year. Mel and Paige gave up after six months and that's when we made our pact.

We talked about how different college was from high school. The freedoms would have gotten a few of us in trouble academically if the others didn't push them back on track. We took college seriously. We all wanted to succeed in life so parties were minimal. We all played a sport, mine was track. We had plenty of time to hang out together. Mondays, we watch The Bachelor while we study. On Tuesdays, we discuss books we read for pleasure. Wednesday is our wine night. Thursdays was supposed to be our "date night" when we went out to dinner instead of eating from vending machines. Fridays were normally prep for a weekend of sports team trips or laundry. God, I hated laundry.

After each of us had bought a round, it was my turn to buy another.

"If you bitches are leaving me tomorrow, you'll think of me all day while you nurse a hangover. Drink up!"

***

We took a cab back to the house and stumbled through the front door. Giggling, drunk fools, we all peeked out the side window at Neptune, who was lounging and sipping a Corona in the courtyard. Music blasted as he tapped his foot to the beat. *A man with rhythm.*

"Okay, girl, if you don't go get that, I'm gonna. He's fine, fine, fine." Mel groaned.

"You leave him alone, she's got dibs." Laney slurred.

I laughed and waved them off as I walked into the bathroom and shut the door behind me. That man did things to me.

I leaned against the door and closed my eyes. Dibs and alcohol induced fearlessness. My reflection in the oversized bathroom mirror alarmed me. *Damn!* My eyes were bloodshot. I didn't make it a habit to get inebriated by … I looked at my watch, three o'clock in the afternoon.

"Oh well, Neptune, I got dibs."

At least I had enough sense to brush my teeth before making a complete fool of myself.

The girls were gone by the time I'd finished drunk-primping. My skimpiest bikini laid conveniently on the table, so I grabbed it. It was a little yellow one with white polka dots. *Ammunition.*

She wore an...

I spent the day surfing, drinking and thinking about Four. The way she'd looked at me when I answered the door, the way she gave it right back to me with that beautiful, smart mouth of hers. *That mouth.* I wanted it on me, to taste it, devour it. I wondered if it tasted as good as it looked. I wanted it to be mine while I was here.

All three were out at the pool, but Four wasn't. I watched the beautiful women swimming in the pool and laughing. I didn't remember any of their names and it didn't really matter, but I certainly didn't want to come off as a dick.

"Hey, Neptune!" The blonde yelled.

"What's up, girl?"

"You should come in, water's warm. Shed the shorts if you feel more comfortable."

They all laughed and so did I. "I'm manning the grill."

"You're manning those shorts, too, Neptune and we know what's hidden deep …"

The brunette pushed her under the water and I returned my attention to the smart phone I regretted bringing with me on vacation. *Fucking work.*

The sound of a door sliding open caught my attention and looked up at the vision walking out the back door across the expansive lawn. I took a long pull off my beer and pushed my shades down, to hide the fact that I was checking her out. Four looked better than I had remembered.

She pointed at the grill, "Need some help?"

"All set, but why don't you have a seat right here so I can put some sunscreen on you. The sun's hot, Four, wouldn't want you to burn up."

She sat in front of me, and I scooted up close. Maybe too close. I took a deep breath and squirted lotion into my hands, eager to touch her again.

"I don't want to mess up your hair," I went to pull it back at the same time she was doing the same. Our fingers touched and the connection caused her to tense up a bit, it also caused blood to start pooling in my groin. "It's gonna be cold, Four, brace yourself for impact."

As soon as my hands touched her she leaned her head to the left. "Don't forget my neck."

"I won't forget any part of you."

"No?"

"No." I leaned her gently forward, rubbed lotion across and then down her back, slowly touching every part of her back, and moving all the way down to that nice, round ass that was barely covered by the tiny yellow polka dot bikini she wore so fucking well. "You can sit back now. I need to do your front."

I stood and she tilted her head up and looked at me. "I can get the rest."

"You sure, I don't mind at all." I saw her cheeks turn a bit red and I took the opportunity to squat down in front of her. "Four, I have to do the front, your cheeks are already turning pink."

I squirted some sunscreen into my hand.

"No that's … "

"Head back, I promise I'll be a gentleman."

She held her breath and that was enough to rile me up a bit more, and the few beers I had sucked down while waiting for her to get back made it even easier to let the boss in me want to take charge.

I lifted her chin then started slowly rubbing lotion into the skin of her collarbone. I made my way up her slender neck. She let out a slow breath and a virtually silent moan as I held her chin in my hand. I pulled it down gently and then held her hair back as I rubbed the white cream across her forehead and cheeks.

"Wouldn't want those lips to burn, but this stuff won't do. I'm gonna share with you, Four. Don't move, OK?" I leaned in. She took in a quick breath, but didn't move. "Stay very still. Don't move."

I set my lips on hers and she whimpered. "Don't move."

I rubbed my lips slowly across hers. I took the time to breathe in her sweet scent and her entire body relaxed. I pulled back.

"Much better."

"Thank … you."

"You are more than welcome." I smiled, letting her regain control, before sitting back on my heels. "Do you like roasted vegetables and chicken?"

She cleared her throat and nodded.

"Good. Give that lotion a few minutes to soak in before you get in the pool to … cool off. Don't forget your chest and stomach. I wouldn't want you to be uncomfortable for the next few days."

I stood up and walked towards the grill.

Fuck, she was sweet. The only problem was I liked this girl. I didn't want to like her. She had to know what's up. This would be a vacation fling, nothing more. Stick to the plan O'Donnell.

I took the food off the grill and brought it to my kitchen. I dished the food onto a platter and opened the wine refrigerator. *Something light.* I found a *Moscato* that would pair well with the grilled chicken and mixed tomato, squash, and onion vegetable medley.

I grabbed two carafes out of the cabinet and filled one with water and the other with wine. I set everything on the table.

I grabbed four towels out of the bathroom and headed out the door.

"Ladies, dinner is waiting."

They giggled and one-by-one, walked out of the pool. I handed them each a towel and then finally she walked up the stairs. Her hair was wet now and the curls drove me—and my cock even crazier. I held the towel open and she went to grab for it.

"Four, I'm trying to be a gentleman here."

She smiled. I stepped behind her and wrapped it around her.

"Love the hair," I whispered in her ear. "Sexy as hell."

She turned and took a step into me and tilted her head up. She grabbed my face and pulled it down, her lips almost touching mine and I smiled.

"You are a very hot man, Neptune."

"Have you looked in the mirror, Four?"

She smiled and leaned in. I took her face in my hands and held my forehead to hers. "When we kiss, I won't stop at your lips. Contrary to what One, Two, and Three, over there think, I am not an exhibitionist. When I kiss you, it won't be in front of an audience. It will be my lips, your beautiful, hot, and sexy-as-hell body in a one-on-one situation. So go get dried off, come eat dinner, and then, Four, if you want to serve up dessert, I will gladly savor whatever you have to offer."

I kissed her forehead, stepped back, and turned away. Then with every ounce of strength I had, I walked into the house to wait.

After turning on some music and wiping down the counter, I pulled on a Polo shirt.

They all came in as I was laying out the silverware. All three girls were very attractive. And if not for the girl in the white cotton tank dress, I may have noticed them, but damn, she was the most beautiful woman I had ever seen.

When she finally looked at me, I noticed her eyes for the first time. They were the lightest shade of brown I had ever seen, like sand, so exotic and sexy. The contrast against her dark skin was stunning. Note to self: avoid them at all costs, or I would be unable to control the raging hard on I am about to be sporting.

The girls laughed and chatted about the massage. Honestly I heard nothing of what they were chatting about. I couldn't stop watching her smile and interact with her friends. I had to have her.

When we finished eating, I began to clear the table and she started to stand. I held my hand on her bare shoulder and shook my head, "I got this. You sit and relax."

Her friends were on their best behavior. I could tell they were a pretty classy crew. I kept their glasses full of wine and then I loaded the dishwasher. She held her hand over her glass and smiled.

I leaned down and whispered, "Your last three have been water, so have mine."

She smiled as she looked up at me and nodded. Damn, her eyes were amazing.

I sat back down, reached under the table and took her hand. She closed her eyes for a moment and inhaled a slow deep breath.

By the time the wine was gone, the three girls were yawning. As they lazily talked about their leaving the next day, and Four staying,

I smirked and sat back in my chair.

***

Each of them gave me a hug before they left. When Four hugged me, I held her a bit longer than I should have.

"See you later?" Her beautiful eyes widened and I saw a bit of fear flash in her eyes. *Damn. I was moving too fast.* "If not, that's fine too. Just figured you and I could spend some time together when your friends leave." I hesitated, hoping she'd say something. Anything. "If this doesn't feel right then that's fine. If it does Four, come back. Either way, I've enjoyed the little time we've had together."

"Thank you."

She turned and walked away.

What the hell just happened? Women didn't normally walk away from me. I paced around the fucking kitchen looking out the window for a half hour. When she didn't show, I headed outside with a bottle of wine, not sure whether to drink it or throw it against the fucking house. Instead, I grabbed a board from the garage and stalked out to the beach. I pulled the cork out and sat in the still night air looking at the ocean.

I laid back, looking up at the sky on this otherwise beautiful night and -- *fuck that!* I was wasting time. I had five days tops before I was back on the shore and I hadn't even gotten laid.

I gulped the rest of the bottle down, threw my shirt off, grabbed my board, and headed into the water. I paddled out and sat in the still water for a while.

Tomorrow, irresponsible, reckless, I-don't-give-a-fuck behavior awaits. I paddled back to shore ready to take on Ft. Lauderdale. As I got closer, I noticed a beautiful curvy body walking towards me. I paddled a little faster when I saw who it was.

I loved how the moonlight lit her face up.

I shoved the board into the sand and stormed towards her. Dick hard, heart racing, head buzzing, and not ready or willing to take no for an answer. I stopped when I was a foot from her and looked at her.

"Tell me your name."

"Four."

"Do you need mine?"

She shook her head, "Neptune."

"Do you know what I'm about to do to you?"

She nodded her head quickly up and down.

"Say it, Four." I knew I was gonna burst as soon as she did.

"Make love to me."

"No, Four. What do you want from me?"

She swallowed hard. "I want you to — fuck me."

I stepped into her and grabbed the back of her head. I held her so that I wouldn't knock her over, then pulled her by the hair, forcing her to look up at me. "Did you bring protection?" I was already out of breath.

"No." So was she.

"Are you on the pill?"

I pulled her dress up and over her head.

"We're in public." She tried to pull it down.

"Private beach." She let go and I pulled it off. I dropped to my knees and ran my nose across her white silky panties before dipping my tongue just under her waistband.

"Oh dear god." Her knees started to tremble.

"No, sweetheart, it's Neptune, god of the sea and I *see* exactly what I want."

I tore her panties off, grabbed one leg, and threw it over my shoulder. I inhaled her scent and rubbed my tongue between her moist folds. I had never tasted a pussy as good.

"Oh god."

"Mmm," I sucked on her sweet lips and then licked up her wet slit, deeper. "You need to lie down while I taste you, Four. Then I'm gonna fuck you so hard you'll need an icepack between your legs tomorrow and I won't apologize when I take you again."

"Jesus, oh god."

I cupped her ass with one hand, lifted her, and laid her on the sand, my mouth never leaving her. I plunged my tongue into her, licked up to her throbbing little nub, and then sucked until her body fell apart against my face.

She lay shaking and I kissed up her belly and took those sweet little tits in my mouth until she cried out.

"You been tested lately?"

"Yes, but ... "

I pulled myself free and rubbed against her opening.

"You STD free, Four? Because I am and I want in so fucking badly, I can't stand it anymore."

I licked her hard little nipple again and she yelled out the one word I needed to hear.

"Yes!"

"I'm gonna fuck you and come all over that sexy stomach of yours, sweetheart. Say 'yes.' "

I rubbed my cock against her still trembling nub and she screamed out again.

"Oh, please yes. Please."

I pushed into her a little.

"Fuck, you're tight."

I licked her tits, reached between us, and rubbed her clit until she pushed into my hand and cock.

"I'll try to go in easy, Four, I don't want to tear you apart. Just bruise you a little."

I leaned up and kissed her as I held myself up with one hand.

She moaned and I licked into her mouth further. I gasped when she bucked her hips up against me.

"I need in. Hang on, sweetheart."

I rammed into her and her pussy clenched around me. I stopped when I felt I was bottoming out.

"Ohhh," she whimpered.

"Can you take more?"

"Please. Oh please!"

That's all I needed. I pumped into her repeatedly. She dug her nails into my ass as I continued pounding into her hot little pussy until I felt her tighten around me and scream out her orgasm, again. I hit it harder and faster as she lay limp beneath me.

I stilled for a moment until I realized there was no way to stop the white-hot lightning from pumping out of my cock. I pulled out just in time to spill my cum all over her belly, marking her.

She lay panting beneath me. I picked her up and she leaned her head into my chest and held her arms loosely around my neck. I carried her into the water to clean off my cum, even though I didn't want to.

I knelt and rinsed as she panted against my chest.

"You'll stay with me tonight."

"Yeah," she whispered.

"You alright?"

"Yes."

"I don't know if I'll be able to control myself." I bent and licked her tits, pulling one of her perfectly alert nipples with my teeth. She whimpered. "There's no way in hell I'll control myself. You are so fucking beautiful."

"You too."

She nuzzled into me and held on a little tighter. I kissed her sexy full lips as I stood up and carried her towards the house.

"The board." She reminded me.

"Tomorrow I'll be eating your sweet wet pussy in the water as you're sprawled out on it. The board stays."

RUNNING

The cool ocean breeze against my heated skin caused me to tremble. He looked down at me and his jaw flexed as his deep, throaty hum swept over me. The sound vibrated throughout my entire body and made me feel completely out of control.

This beautiful man had given me more pleasure in the last fifteen minutes than I'd had my entire life. My body was still responding to him, and I was so afraid that I would moan or whimper making him even more aware of the power he wielded over me after just one encounter. I had never been loud in bed, nor begged a man for anything. My insides had never burned so intensely, needing to be filled. But with him, I'd lost all control.

As my feet touched the floor in front of the bed, I struggled to stand.

"Steady, sweetheart," he held my waist as I looked up into his beautiful blue eyes. "That's better."

"My dress."

"You won't be needing it for … a while."

His arm snaked around my waist and he pulled me closer to him.

"My panties."

"Destroyed."

His lips met mine, but he didn't kiss me, he just held them against me. Only now did I notice the alcohol on his breath.

"Four," he took in a deep breath through his teeth, "I've had a bit more to drink than I had promised myself I would have when you and I happened."

I attempted to pull away from his embrace, but he grabbed the back of my head.

"Don't."

His lips covered mine and immediately I was lost. The heat began filling me again, my body hummed as his tongue sought entrance into my mouth. I gave it willingly. His tongue stroked up and down my own, causing me to whimper and him to groan as he ravaged my mouth.

His hands now moved back down my body and came to rest on my butt. He squeezed and pulled outward, spreading me. I grasped at his strong shoulders trying to steady myself, hold myself together.

My tongue began stroking his in long licks, tasting him as he had done to me. He tasted of crisp wine and something else, me. Never before had I been as turned on to the point that I needed more in a kiss, not like this.

I bravely let my hand slide down his arms and then lower. I held his hips and then allowed one hand to make its way lower and I took hold of his rock hard erection.

He immediately lifted me, forcing my hands to grab his shoulders again.

"I need to taste you again, Four."

"I need .... "

"No talking, let me give you pleasure," he lowered me to the bed and knelt before me.

He spread my legs wide and looked up at me. "Your pussy is absolutely stunning."

I closed my eyes, embarrassed of being spread in front of him in the dimly lit room. His fingers spread me and his hum played to the most private and intimate part of my body.

"Look at me."

He lifted my leg and bent my knee gently as he placed my foot on the bed so that it was beside me and he pushed the other leg to the side spreading me even more.

"Never seen anything so fucking beautiful," he whispered as he rubbed his finger up and down my seam.

When he looked up, I knew he hadn't intended on me hearing those words. For a brief moment, his self-confident, sexually charged gaze gave way to something more, and in one blink of my eyes his mouth covered my opening as he sucked harshly on my sensitive flesh.

"Ohhh … "

He pulled away and looked up, "Watch me devour you, sweetheart."

His tongue plunged deep inside of me and his hands gripped my thighs forcing them apart even more. I watched because he said so and I watched because I had never witnessed, felt, or encountered such a hungry, sexual man.

His mouth worked me into ecstasy and a state of orgasmic bliss. His tongue caressed and then dove deep into me. His lips sucked and tugged at mine. Then a finger pushed into me and curled up and then another entered, causing me to take in a deep breath.

I held his shoulders just like I was holding my breath, fearing I would scream and fall back. Fearing that I would break the contact our eyes made. I couldn't look away if I wanted to. His eyes held mine captive as his finger pushed in further, curling, turning, touching every part deep inside. The sensation, the places he hit made me lose myself completely and fully. I fought, fearing another orgasm so soon would take my breath away. He sensed my concern.

"Let go," he commanded.

With Neptune, it was much more than pleasure. My breathing became erratic and my need to come was so — immediate. I couldn't hold back or delay my release.

"Oh, god," I screamed out as it burst, rippling throughout my entire body.

"That's it," his fingers continued torturing and pleasing me, "More. Give me more."

I felt my insides contract around his fingers and I couldn't stop myself from slowly falling onto the bed as I screamed out incomprehensible words of pleasure and praise.

His fingers slowed at the same speed my breaths did.

"Perfect," he whispered as his fingers pulled out of me and his hands grasped my ankles.

He gently rolled me onto my stomach as I continued lying almost lethargically, still falling like a feather from orgasm.

He cupped my bottom, not too hard, but not gently. His strong hands caressed and then squeezed, caressed and squeezed, repeatedly. After several minutes, the concept of time was lost on me. I started to move.

"Not another inch," his voice carried a soft demand. "Stay right there."

His hands left my body, yet I felt his eyes burning into my backside. I looked over my shoulder.

"Eyes forward," his heated gaze washed over me just like his command. "Not an inch. Do you understand?"

"Yes but – "

"No buts," he chuckled to himself and then he grabbed me firmly, one hand on each cheek and spread me, "Fucking beautiful."

And then he let go. I heard him walking out of the room and I wanted to stand, to cover myself, to do anything but lay there exposed. My modesty tried to overcome my body's desire to let this sexual god have what he asked for without getting anything in return, but it was in vain.

"That's a very good girl."

He sat at my side with a glass of amber liquor in his hand and a bottle in the other gazing over my body. He put the glass to his lips and threw it back, all of it.

"Drink?" He asked as he refilled the glass.

I shook my head.

"Are you alright?"

I nodded.

"Words, please." He smiled slightly.

"I am — alright."

"Good, then we'll continue, if that's alright with you."

He drank down the glass again and hissed when the liquor hit his throat. I've never been able to drink whiskey.

I started to roll over and he let out a chuckle, "No, stay just like this."

His hand cupped my chin and his thumb rubbed across my lip.

"Can you close your eyes this time for me, beautiful? Close your eyes and just feel every pleasure I'm about to give you."

"I don't know."

"No?" His head cocked to the side.

I didn't answer and he stood up and walked behind me. "Do you trust that I won't hurt you?"

"I did until just now," I answered honestly.

"Because of the question, of course, how stupid of me. I won't hurt you, Four." I heard him behind me, but I tried my best to focus forward, it's the least I could do.

He lay on his side next to me and rolled me onto mine. His arm snaked around me and he pulled me closer to him. I felt his erection rubbing against my stomach.

"You'll be okay." He kissed my head, "I promise."

I opened my eyes and looked up at him. He rubbed my back and kissed my forehead. "This should have been a sober conversation."

"I'm sober." I swallowed.

"You have me at a disadvantage; I am not used to that." He gently pushed my shoulder so I was lying on my back.

He held up a fisted hand that held within it something black. "Normally I'm better prepared, so this will have to do for now."

He opened his hand revealing a black tie. He held his empty hand out for me. I hesitated, unsure whether I wanted to play this game.

"Trust me," his hushed words were no less demanding than the ones used before.

"What's this for?"

"To help you focus."

"On what?"

He reached down and took my hand pulling me up.

"Pleasure."

I didn't speak as he bent down, resting his forehead against mine. "You are a beautiful woman, Four. By the end of our time together, I am going to show you just how much I enjoy you. This is nothing more than a tool of focus. You'll focus on feeling tonight. You won't see me as I eye fuck your perfect ass and your sweet pussy. This, Four, is a way for you to escape your inhibitions, a way to open up to me even more than you already have. For the next few days, I am going to use your body, take pleasure from your beauty, and give you orgasm after orgasm, pleasure after pleasure, and possibly delve a little bit further into the erotic unknown. For the next few days, I am going to own your body."

I should have said something. I should have objected. But before my jumbled thoughts could be formed into words, I was blindfolded and rolled onto my stomach. He pulled me to the very edge of the bed. As my feet touched the ground, he spread me again.

"What are your limits?" His voice was direct.

"What do you mean?"

I felt his lips touch the base of my spine and then travel down. His tongue rubbed at the peak of my backside's spilt.

"Is this alright?"

"No further," my voice squeaked.

"So no anal play whatsoever?"

"No." *Anal play, oh dear lord what have I gotten myself into. Boy next door? No, not even.*

His tongue dipped a little further and I tried to pull forward. His hands gripped my waist.

"No means no, Four. I won't touch there until I know that's what you want."

"I won't want that."

He let out a deep chuckle, "Okay."

He leaned over me, kissing my neck softly.

I felt him bite my cheek and then lick before his finger pushed between my folds.

I took in a deep breath and held it until I couldn't any longer. His finger curled up inside me hitting an unfamiliar spot and my knees buckled immediately.

He hissed, "That feels good doesn't it? Don't hold back on me, Four. I found your magic button."

I scooted forward trying to escape the pleasure and pressure building so intensely.

"Stop, please."

Before I could finish protesting, his finger left me, leaving an unexpected emptiness, and he pulled the blindfold off.

The bed dipped beside me and I looked up as his dark smoldering eyes stared into mine.

"I'm sorry." I didn't know what else to say.

"Don't be," his gaze drifted down my body and his jaw clenched.

I had disappointed him, and for some illogical reason, I too was disappointed.

He closed his eyes, ran his hands through his hair, and leaned back on his elbows.

"I haven't had time to date in a while. I am a gentleman, Four, I truly am. However, I want to do so much to you that isn't gentleman-like in the next few days," he stopped and took in a deep breath. "I won't hold back. I can't, not with you. You are the epitome of sexy. Your body, your face, your eyes, your taste, your response ... I want to devour you."

I pulled the blanket from the side of the bed and covered myself.

"I see," he whispered.

"See what?"

"You ... how many men have you been with?"

"Excuse me?" I squeaked out.

"I apologize if I offended you. I just don't think you're very experienced and now I feel like I'm rushing you. But, Four, I know exactly what I can do to you and for you."

He stood and pulled down the blankets, "Tomorrow, Four, I'll be sober and you'll remember everything I have given you tonight. You'll crave it. Tonight, you should rest. You'll need it for what I have planned."

Like a fool, I did as he asked. What the hell was wrong with me? Here I was in bed with a man I hardly knew, allowing him to blindfold me, torture me with pleasure and I wanted more, so much more that it scared me.

The Note

I lay next to her and watched her roll to her side, her back to me. Not the position I expected nor desired. I pushed her beautiful, thick, black hair over her shoulder and pulled her back against my chest. She didn't fight it, and after a few kisses to the back of her head she relaxed against me.

"Thank you," I whispered.

"You're welcome."

"Are you cold?"

"Not anymore."

"Glad to hear it." I reached down, pulled the blanket up around her, and pulled her against me even tighter. "You have a million tiny goose bumps right here."

I kissed her neck and her back arched, causing her to push her tight round ass against me.

"Four, I'm alright with you resting, but might I remind you my restraint is already being tested by your sexy body, add to that alcohol, and I am hanging on by a thread here."

"Sorry," she breathed out.

"Not yet you aren't." I chuckled.

She didn't respond. I assumed she was asleep so I decided to follow suit. Tomorrow was going to be one hell of a day.

***

I woke in an empty bed and thought I heard the water running in the bathroom. I was also sure I had a big fucking headache and wasn't ready to be awake. The sun hadn't even come up yet.

I looked down at the tented sheet and decided I needed to drain that before Four thought I was even more freaky than she already did. I hated calling her "Four." *Today we will be exchanging names*, I thought as I got up and made my way to the bathroom. I knocked and when no one answered, I walked in thinking she may have gone next door to see her friends off.

When I came out, I saw a note on the nightstand.

Neptune,

> *Thank you for a memorable night. I had to cut my trip short and return home to take care of a few things before I take my next step in this crazy journey called life.*

I didn't want to wake you, you looked very peaceful.

I won't forget you.

XOXOXO,

4

I must have read the note three or four times before folding it up neatly and shoving it in my bag because I didn't want to forget either.

I spent the next two days on my board and my nights sitting on the beach drinking and wondering what the fuck it was I wanted from my life. Was my role as CFO of Steel, Inc. worth not trusting in humanity? Questioning everyone's motives? Not allowing them to know who I am? I slammed another beer and decided right then and there not to doubt myself and not to let anyone in because I would not give up control. I was control.

The next morning, I called and changed my flight and packed my bags. I wanted to go home.

I didn't let anyone else know I was back at the shore. I didn't want Carly to get all crazy, or the Steel boys to think I didn't trust that they could handle the company. I knew they could. Never doubted it. The only thing I ever doubted was them handling their dicks, and well -- now I wasn't too sure I could handle mine. I must have scared the fuck out of Four. No other explanation for her ditching. Never had that shit happen before. Maybe it was Karma's way of kicking my ass for sticking up for my boys all those years. Or maybe she was one of those girls who just liked to fuck. Well, Karma and I were now on fucked up terms because I didn't appreciate that shit at all.

***

I walked into the pub and Pops was pouring a draft for old Sal, one of the locals.

"There's my boy," Pop's voice boomed through the air.

"You back where you should be, Abe? Ready to take over and let your old man retire?" Sal was always busting my balls. Telling me I needed to lose the tie and get behind the bar.

"Sal, you're looking good," I lied. The poor old son of a bitch was practically yellow, which was a big indicator that his liver was on the fritz.

"That your fancy suit wearing way of trying to shut me up, boy?" He hacked.

"No, sir, not at all."

I walked around the bar and gave my pops a hug. "How you doing?"

"Doing well, boy, doing well," he chuckled and hugged me back.

"Mom? How's she?"

"Still here. You should stop by and see her. Been a week, Abe. That's not like you, you know."

"I will as soon as I leave here." I grabbed a beer and stood against the bar.

"O'Donnell's Pub is a landmark, son," Sal was starting the same damn spiel he gave me every time I walked in the door. "This place has been here for seventy-five years. Not always with the O'Donnell name, but," he gave my pops the same look he always did at this point in the story.

"You ever gonna get over that, Sal?" Pops laughed.

"You should never have changed the name."

Pops chuckled, "I gave Shaw a choice. I either keep you, or I keep the name. I kept you."

Sal, honest to god, came with the place. He was a damn landmark and a legend at this establishment. Just ask him, he'll tell you.

"Next thing you know you'll be getting rid of corned beef and cabbage on St. Patty's day." He grumbled. "Got rid of the baseball team."

"No one wanted to play anymore," Pops chuckled.

"Brought in a lot of fine women folk on a Thursday night." He tipped back his beer and finished it.

He stood and pulled on his hat. "You should bring back the baseball, boy. The least you could do to help out around here."

When he walked out the door, Pops and I laughed, "You ever gonna tell him he's not Irish, Pops?"

"And break his heart? No thank you," Pops laughed.

I looked around at the empty pub, "Business been slow, Pops?"

"We're getting by." He gave me his generic answer.

"I make a lot of money, Pops. Enough to pay for … "

"I make enough money to take care of me and my Margaret."

"I know. You also paid for my schooling. I wanna pay you back."

"Your mother and I told you, you do well in school and we pay for college. You did well." He nodded.

"Things changed though, Pops."

"Nothing's changed son. We're still us."

I didn't want to upset him, but I wanted to do something. "You up to sponsoring a baseball team?"

"You don't wanna play ball," he chuckled.

"If you're not up to it, Steel can."

"You wanna play ball, boy, you'll play for O'Donnell's Pub." His face lit up. "You think you can get a roster filled up by Monday night? League starts Thursday."

"I can, and I won't just fill a roster, Pops I'm gonna win the trophy."

"I know you can," he laughed. "I know you can."

***

I walked into Steel on Friday, and no one noticed until I stood at the elevator.

"Good morning, Mr. O'Donnell." The receptionists yelled in unison.

"Good morning, ladies," I said as I walked onto the elevator.

I rode up to the fifth floor and stepped off. The floor secretary wasn't at her desk. I walked down the hall to my office and opened the door.

"Fuck! When did you get back?" Zandor hissed at me.

"A few days ago. What are you doing in my —"

"Nothing, could you give me a minute?" He looked pissed.

"Fuck you, Z."

"Abe, I am asking nicely," he said through clenched teeth, "Just a few minutes--"

There was a black heel sticking out from under *my* desk. "Don't you have your own office? Fuck, Zandor!"

I turned around and walked out of my office. *Fuck!*

I shot Jase, Cyrus, and Xavier a text asking that they come up to my office and immediately shut off the phone. I didn't want the "what the fuck are you doing back" texts annoying me any more than I was right now. *Fucking Steels.*

It wasn't long before Zandor and Bekah walked out of my damn office with his arm wrapped around her waist and her head buried in his chest, no doubt hiding from embarrassment.

"It's all yours, Abe," Zandor chuckled and Bekah's muffled giggle erupted from against his chest.

"Is there a problem with your office?"

"Variety is the spice of life, isn't it, Kitten?" Zandor ran his hand down her back and rested it on her ass.

She looked up at him. "I need to use the ladies room."

"A kiss first," he pulled her against him and kissed her. "Damn I taste good."

She giggled as she walked away.

Zandor looked at me and smirked.

"Don't do that shit again or so help me god I will be working at the Pub."

"Like hell you will," I heard Jase from behind me.

I turned and saw him, Cyrus, and Xavier getting off the elevator.

"I need a favor," I motioned them to my office. Before I sat, I looked at Zandor and he smirked. "Is it safe to sit down?"

"Yeah," he laughed. "Just don't reach under your desk. That sticky shit probably ain't gum."

I jumped up, "You better be fucking joking, man."

He laughed out loud, "Yeah, I am. Gotcha."

"What the hell is going on?" Jase asked.

"You playing in his office now, Z?" Cyrus laughed.

"He was supposed to be out of town for another week," Zandor winked.

"Is this gonna take long? Taelyn and I were gonna head home for lunch," Xavier looked at his watch.

"You should just have a picnic at Abe's desk, Z already did," Cyrus chuckled.

Zandor and Cyrus high-fived and I saw Jase's smug ass trying not to join in. He knew I was annoyed.

"Clear Thursday nights from six to eight. We're gonna play ball."

"Baseball pants?" Bekah giggled as she walked into my office. Zandor grabbed her hand and pulled her against him.

"That make you--" Z started.

"Alright, enough," I interrupted. "I don't ask for much okay, but this, I need this. Play ball for an hour and go to the Pub for an hour. Is that too much to ask?"

None of them said a word. They all looked at me like I had lost my fucking mind.

"Kitten, why don't I meet you in my office. I think I need to take care of Abe," he winked.

Once she left, Jase shut the door, "What the hell has gotten into you?"

"Nothing. I am simply asking for a favor."

"You know we're in, bro. Just chill, okay?" Xavier smiled.

"Why the fuck did you come back so soon, man? You need a fucking break." Cyrus scowled at me.

"I had enough relaxation alright?"

"Did you get laid?" Zandor acted like he was truly concerned and Jase laughed. "What man? Seriously, Abe, you need–"

"Of course I got laid. What the fuck," I shuffled some papers around on my desk. I didn't want to talk about this shit.

"Bad lay?" Cyrus tried to keep a straight face and I rolled my eyes.

"You wanna talk about it?" Jase asked in his most fake sympathetic voice.

"I didn't grow a vagina, Jase. There's nothing to talk about. I got fucked and then she went—wherever she lives."

"You don't know where she lives?" Jase gasped.

"It really wasn't necessary," I opened the drawer to my desk and grabbed a file that I could work on over the weekend.

I looked up and they were all staring at me, all looking concerned, which pissed me off.

"I'm out."

"Bullshit man, spill it." Jase leaned on my desk.

I knew I wasn't getting away that easy. "The house I rented wasn't private. It had a shared pool, courtyard, and beach access with one next door. Four girl–"

"Oh shit," Zandor groaned and sat at the conference table.

"No, Z, I don't play that way," I walked around my desk, sat at the table, and leaned back in my chair. "Number four, last one to show up."

"Was she hot?" Xavier asked as he sat.

"Hell yes, she was hot."

"What was her name?" Cyrus sat too.

"Four."

"That's a fucked up name," Jase sat next to me.

"We decided no names, just a vacation thing you know," I rolled my neck. "One hot-as-hell night. Perhaps I was a little—controlling and may have made comments alluding to the next three days that I suppose could make a girl--"

"Hot and wet," Zandor wagged his eyebrows.

"No, man. Scared."

"Scared?" Xavier laughed.

"She wasn't all that experienced," I explained.

"Did she cry?" Zandor asked.

"Z, what the fuck? No she didn't cry."

"Then what happened?" Jase asked looking at his watch.

"When I woke she was gone. Never got a name. She left a note saying something came up at home. I think that's bullshit. I think I freaked her out."

"Did she come?" Zandor asked.

"Fuck yes, Z, you writing a book?"

"Maybe I should. Called 'The Importance of Bondage' that way your chicks wouldn't run away while you're sleeping."

We all laughed, which only encouraged Z.

"You were like *Grease,* the movie. *Summer lovin' happened so fast–*"

"Shut up Z," I laughed.

"She Australian?"

"No," I laughed.

"Did you kiss her down under?"

"Okay, I'm done here. I'll see you Monday. You guys wanna get together to throw a ball around over the weekend?"

"Dude, just 'cause she left you doesn't mean we gotta play with your balls," Cyrus laughed.

Jase's cell rang and he answered. I was just about to walk out the door when he said, "Hold up."

I waited until he hung up. "You remember the newspaper, The Shore?"

"Yeah why, what's up?"

"All that media attention about us Steel boys being the most eligible bachelors?"

"Of course, what's the point, you're all married."

"No, Xavier isn't yet and apparently, Abe O'Donnell, CFO of Steel Incorporated, just bumped up to number one. They want an interview."

"Tell them 'no.' "

"We need to do something. They were following Taelyn the other day. Freaked her out so I kind of --"

"You kind of what, X?" *This ought to be good.*

"Caught up to them and when Taelyn parked at the grocery store, I pulled in and pulled the photographer out of his van."

"Why the fuck would you do that shit?"

"Why the fuck wouldn't I?" He snapped

"So we need to make nice," Jase interrupted. "Do the damn interview. It'll do us all a favor."

"And who knows, maybe you'll find one who won't run away," Zandor chuckled.

"When?"

There was a knock on the door and Jase flashed a big smile.

"I am not ready for this, Jase. I'm in jeans man," I pointed to my bathroom. "Give me five minutes." I walked away shaking my head.

I grabbed my spare suit, yes I keep a spare in the office, and threw it on. I combed my hair and wet it a little. *Good enough,* I thought.

When I came out, the woman was sitting at the conference table with her back to me. I walked around to the empty spot between Jase and Zandor and sat.

"Thank you for meeting with me Mr. –"

I finally looked up and into sandy brown eyes and a very stunned reporter.

I didn't say a word and neither did she.

"Sandy?" Zandor whispered.

"Danny?" Xavier chuckled.

This was not cool, not cool at all.

"O'Donnell." I nodded. "Abe O'Donnell."

"Right, Abe, uh, uh--"

"O'Donnell." She looked mortified. "And your name?"

"Nikolette."

"Your last name? I want to keep this professional." I don't know why, but I felt anger brewing inside of me. I kept my eyes locked onto hers enjoying the hell out of her discomfort.

The girl who left the note, Four, was here to interview me. Karma wasn't so bad after all.

UNWILLING SUBJECT

The way he looked at me made me squirm in my seat. I was lucky to have gotten this internship and if I messed up my first assignment, I would probably spend the semester in the mailroom.

"Bassett, Nikolette, err, Miss Bassett." I stammered like a complete idiot.

"Miss or Mrs.?" He asked and the others chuckled.

As unprepared as I was for this, I was determined to do my job and do it well.

"Miss. I'm an intern for The Shore and was asked to--" I stopped and looked down as I fumbled in my briefcase for something to write with. And paper, I needed paper, too. I looked up briefly and all four men were staring at me. "I'm sorry, I'm normally better prepared."

They looked skeptically at me.

"Inexperienced, huh?" One of the men chuckled.

I made eye contact with the one who laughed, "You're Zandor Steel, right? From the picture at the airport that brought this all on."

"Yes. The woman, Rebekah, in the picture is now my wife."

"Congratulations."

"Thank you." He sat back. "We'll make sure Abe goes easy on you, Nikolette."

Another one laughed. "And you're Xavier?"

"Sure am. You need to tell those motherfuckers if they keep chasing my fiancé around, I am gonna tear shit up."

"I understand how you must feel. I can assure you it wasn't The Shore who has taken the pictures, but with Mr.?" I looked over at him, Neptune, again forgetting his last name, which was completely embarrassing.

"O'Donnell. His last name is O'Donnell. He's not that unforgettable is he?"

"You're Cyrus?"

"The one and only," he nodded. "Alright, I am gonna jet, go see how my wife is doing. I'm sure I am leaving you in capable hands with Mr. O'Donnell, but if you need anything let me know."

And with that, he left, "I'm out, too." Xavier stood up and shook my hand, "Nice meeting you, Nikolette. I'll be leaving around *four*. Until then look me up if you need anything."

He walked out of the room chuckling. I looked quickly away and at the man sitting next to Mr. O'Donnell. "I'm Jase. Abe's best friend and business associate." He reached over and shook my hand. "You're pretty damn lucky to be in his hands and not one of those three characters. He'll take care of you. Abe's a gentleman."

Jase stood and looked at his brother, "Let's leave them to it."

As soon as the door shut behind Jase, I felt my whole body tense. Abe stood and unbuttoned his gray suit coat. I turned as he shrugged it off and threw it over the desk. He walked to the door with a different confidence than what I saw in Florida. But his body was no different. Long and lean. I knew exactly what was underneath and I--

"Miss Bassett," he interrupted my very immoral thoughts.

"Yes?" I asked.

"I'll walk you out."

He opened the door and I sat looking at him. "I don't understand."

"Unlike the *four,*" he paused, "men who just left, I have no interest in," he waved his hand flippantly in the air, "doing this."

"But--"

"Let's go," he turned his back to me.

It took several moments for me to organize the thoughts in my head hoping to make any sort of "Abe--" I pleaded. *Finally, a name.*

"Mr. O'Donnell." He turned and looked at me.

"Of course," I stood fumbling with the pad and pen I had just pulled out of my briefcase. I walked to the door he held open.

I followed him to the elevator, and he pushed the button to the ground floor a few times before his hands fisted and he shoved them into his pockets. He was angry and I was out of sorts. Once we stepped into the elevator, he pushed the button to close the door and then walked to the far corner, seemingly to get as far as he could from me.

I had to do something, say something. I wasn't sure which subject to broach first, the time in Florida, or the fact that I needed this interview.

"Mr. O'Donnell," I said as I turned to him. He leaned against the wall with his hands still shoved in his pockets. "I need this interview."

He said nothing, simply looked at me.

"I know this is awkward." I continued as he remained silent. His eyebrow shot at the word awkward. "Will you please say something?" I whispered.

The door opened and when he walked past me and out into the reception area, I followed. He walked briskly out the front doors. When I caught up, he stopped and turned to me.

"Nice seeing you again, Miss Bassett." And he nodded to the parking lot.

"Please just listen to me."

"I'm a very busy man," he started.

"Why are you acting like this?"

"I'm at work. This is a professional environment. And this, Miss Bassett, is not an act. This is who I am. I don't have time to spend answering questions about my preferences in what I am looking for in women and certainly not to you. Good day," he nodded towards the parking lot again.

"You keep speaking about professionalism. Have I given you any reason to believe I will be anything, but professional?"

"It's a bit more complicated than that now isn't it, Miss Bassett."

I was not sure how to fix this, but I couldn't walk away with nothing. I had two weeks to write this story and I was not going to fail. "Thank you for your time, Mr. O'Donnell, I will just go ahead and write it without your input."

I was calling his bluff and crossing my fingers that he would stop me as I walked away. I made it all the way across the parking lot to my car before I finally looked back and watched him walk into the building.

I observed the Steel Incorporated building, a place made famous by the infamous "Men of Steel" brothers I had read so much about. I couldn't understand how they had kept Abe O'Donnell a secret. The only pictures that popped up in any search engine were of him with shades and a ball cap on. I couldn't believe that I didn't recognize the man who I had dreamt about for a week. A man who had invaded my dreams and woke me up in the middle of the night feeling regretful over leaving his bed the way I did.

It was unbelievable that I would run into him the way I had. It was even more unbelievable that my future as a journalist would end before it even began because he refused to do this interview.

I had landed this internship and maneuvered my entire schedule around, begged professors to allow me to finish classes online, and gave up my entire summer in hopes of making a name for myself.

I was trying to break into a male-dominated world, sports journalism, and they handed me a vanity assignment hoping I would fail and they could pretend they had given me a shot. I had to do something.

I watched the entrance of the building, wishing I could convince him to do the interview at the same time as I tried to convince myself that my desire for his sexual dominance over me would go away. The draw was inexplicable. I was sure the more I saw the real man and not the laid back sexually charged surfer I had spent the hottest most fulfilling night of my life with, the more the draw would fade or at least become manageable.

Two hours later and I was ready to go back to my apartment and pack up. Then he walked out of the building. He wore jeans and a tee shirt, he looked so different, yet still so tempting. I watched him walk through the lot, pull a key fob out, and push the button unlocking the Land Rover in the row marked restricted parking.

He jumped in and backed out. I started up my little Elantra and nosed out of my spot, making sure I stayed far enough behind him that he wouldn't spot me. I was three cars behind him and at a light when he signaled right. I followed further behind afraid he would see me with no cars between us.

He pulled into the parking lot of an old warehouse type building and I pulled over and watched as he leaned over and hit a code on an intercom or security system. The large gate door opened and he pulled in and the gate closed behind him.

I sat and watched the building as the sun began setting. A cab pulled up in front and a woman in a black coat exited the back seat and the gate opened revealing a shirtless Abe O'Donnell in basketball shorts and bare feet. He greeted her with a kiss on the cheek and then he turned and walked inside a garage. As the garage door closed, I saw him grab her rear end and she looked up at him. Before what I assume was a kiss was exchanged, the door closed.

I knew something was questionable about his actions that night. Something too good to be true. He was not single and he was hiding it from the world. He had used me, well maybe not. It was just like he had said. A vacation fling, we didn't even exchange names.

When I realized that I wasn't able to not feel for him after the night we spent, I left. I couldn't face him the next day. I wouldn't be able to spend the next few days with him without feeling something deeper. And even now that I knew we were in the same area, even if he wasn't of the cheating kind, I would never allow a man to own me or my body, regardless of how unbelievably good it felt.

Experienced or not, I knew that to be true. When I discussed it with the girls, as I literally threw my belongings in my bags, they admitted to never have experienced a man like that. Although Laney told me I was crazy to leave, she did understand.

Two hours later and I was still sitting in my car watching the building as I looked at my iPhone and posted to the girls and my blog. I saw lights coming up the road and watched as a cab pulled up and the front gate opened again. He was handing her something. She gave him a peck on the cheek and turned around to look at her hand.

Oh my God! He gave her money. He gave her a stack of money. I knew it because when she pushed it into her bra there was a slight bulge that disappeared when she pulled her coat around her and tied it.

The gate didn't close this time and I was sure he was looking in my direction when another car pulled up, and yes, with a woman driver. Dirty bastard! It was dark, but a shorter woman got out of the car and he greeted her with a hug and kissed her cheek.

He opened the back door and grabbed a few bags and she took a few, too. Before the gate shut, he looked back toward my car.

I don't know what possessed me, curiosity I suppose, to stay for any longer, but after twenty more minutes I was ready to leave when the gate opened again. The Land Rover exited and headed my way. I sunk down in my seat until I was nearly on the floor while waiting to see taillights in the rear view.

I sat up quickly, turned on my car, did a U-turn, and hit the gas so that I could catch up to Abe O'Donnell. All the false feelings I had for him quickly turned to disgust and fear. I had unprotected sex with him. I wasn't an irresponsible girl, not ever, but I had made a horrible mistake and I would be damned if I didn't confront him.

He pulled down into a street that was off a main road and not as well lit. Dear God, where was he going now? Drugs, oh please don't let him be into that as well. He pulled into an alley and I slowed down so that I could look to see if it where a dead end or a pass through. To my shock and horror his reverse lights shown and he started to back up. I began to panic and drove faster as I watched in my mirror as he sped up. I looked up and the traffic light ahead had turned red.

Oh dear lord, please don't let him notice. I silently prayed as I tried to grab my phone off the passenger seat to call someone to take my mind off the chaos that I seemed to be causing.

A loud thump on my window made me jump and scream.

I looked over and saw a pair of furious blue eyes in my window. Oh why? Why, why, why? I thought as I rolled down my window.

"You care to tell me what the hell you're doing?" He snapped.

"Getting my story," I answered as calmly as I could.

"How the hell is that going for you?"

"Well, if you must know, I am pretty disgusted with myself and wondering if there is anything I should be worried about--"

"How about a harassment charge?" he spat.

My jaw dropped and he continued.

"Let's add stalking to that and throw in a little–"

I interrupted him when I looked in my mirror trying to avoid the furious glare of his blue eyes and saw someone get in the vehicle behind me.

"Abe--"

"Mr. O'Donnell," he corrected in a condescending tone.

I watched as the Land Rover peeled out around us.

"Is that–"

"You have got to be fucking kidding me. Move over, Miss Bassett."

"But--"

"Now, damn it."

I moved and he jumped into the driver's seat and his knees hit the dash. "Fuck!"

He peeled out and darted in and out of traffic as I pulled my seat belt across my chest snapping it just before he slammed on the brakes. He jumped out of the car and ran towards his vehicle now stuck between two cars at another red light.

I unbuckled and grabbed my phone and dialed 911.

When I got up close, I saw Abe, pulling the man from the driver seat by his black hoody. I saw the man pull something shinny out of his pocket.

"Abe!" I screamed, "Watch out he has a –Oh God!"

I dropped my phone and ran to him as he held his face and jumped back avoiding the next jab.

"You better do better than that next time, motherfucker," Abe sneered at the man.

The man looked at me and started towards me.

I froze then started to shake, "Nikolette, fucking move!"

Abe lunged at him from behind, knocking him to the ground as I stood still frozen. I saw the man reach for the knife he had dropped when he fell and finally I was able to move to kick it out of his reach.

"Fucking bitch," the man yelled and Abe's knee crushed down between his shoulder blades.

"You don't talk to her like that, shitbag."

I don't remember hearing any other words exchanged between the two of them as I watched blood pour down the side of Abe's face until the sound of sirens and other people talking surrounded me.

I stood as still as a statue as I watched the cops handcuff the man as another talked to Abe. He turned and looked at me. I tried to move, but I wasn't able to, not yet.

"Miss Bassett," Abe took a few steps to me. "You okay?"

I blinked and then finally nodded.

"She okay?" one of the officers asked.

I cleared my throat and squeaked out a yes before tears sprang to my eyes.

Abe looked horrified and I started to turn away.

"Hey, you're freaked out."

"I'm fine," I wiped a tear and he took my shoulders and turned me facing him.

"Miss—Nikolette, take a few breaths," he gave a caring smile. "Come on girl, before you hyperventilate."

As soon as the air filled my lungs, the shaking came and then the tears fell like rain down my cheeks. He pulled me against his chest and held me while I cried.

"You're alright," he whispered in a very calm tone.

After a few minutes, I stepped back and looked up, reaching up to wipe the blood off his face. The way he turned slowly away and closed his eyes was so different. He wasn't trying to stop me, it was something else.

"You're going to have to go to the hospital," I said as more tears fell.

He turned back and looked at me, his eyebrows turned in and he wiped my tears. "I'll be fine."

A detective walked to us, "You really shouldn't have run down a carjacker, O'Donnell."

"That's my vehicle, not his."

"We have a slight problem in regards to your vehicle."

"What?" he asked as he wiped more of my tears.

"There's a backpack filled with a bunch of shit that I assume is stolen and some drugs. I wanna take your vehicle in to make sure we get everything done by the book. This son of a bitch needs to go away for a while."

"That's fine, I have a car."

"You need a lift to your place?"

"No," his hands finally left my face. "I'm going to drive Miss Bassett to her place; she's in no shape to drive."

"Then head to the hospital?"

Abe rolled his eyes, "It's a scratch."

"I want pictures tonight. I'll ask you both to come to the station in the morning and file reports. Get her home," he said to Abe and then looked back at me. "Clean that up and if it's deep, make him go to the hospital."

"Okay, Miss Bassett," Abe took my hand. "Let's have some pictures taken."

And even after everything that happened, what did I do? Followed and did as he asked.

JACKED UP

When I finished with detective DeAngelo, I walked to Nikolette's car. She approached the driver's side.

"You shouldn't be driving. You really should go to the--," she stopped when I took her hand and led her back to the passenger side of her vehicle and opened the door. She looked up at me with those sandy brown eyes as she sat down. She was nervous and I knew it. Didn't like it, but there wasn't a damn thing I could do to change the opinion she had already formed about me.

I got in and shut the door. "I'm going to need your address."

"1273 Park Street," she answered quietly as she continued looking down.

There was no music playing and no conversation, all there was, was silence. The wound on my head stung and pulsing. Son of a bitch got too damn close to my temple. For whatever reason he missed and I was damn glad of it. My pulse quickened as I drove and thought about what had gone down, unreal.

When I pulled onto Park Street, I slowed to look at the house numbers. The buildings were all the same, older homes that I assumed many years ago were single-family homes converted into apartments.

"It's the next one on the left. You can pull in, my spot is all the way to the right," she pointed.

When I shut off the engine she turned and looked at me, "I'm sorry."

"Wasn't your fault," except it was. I got out of her vehicle, walked around, and opened her door. "You getting out?"

"It was my fault, Abe—Mr. O'Donnell."

"It's fine," I should have told her Abe was fine, but for some reason it wasn't. I liked her calling me 'Mr. O'Donnell.'

I reached in my pocket and grabbed my phone to call a cab, "Son of a bitch, could this fucking night get any worse?"

"Mine's dead, too." She whispered as she looked down at her phone.

"Fuck!"

"I have a charger inside. I should have gotten a landline, my parents tried to make me because--" She stopped and looked up at me. "Come in, it shouldn't take long."

I nodded and handed her the keys after hitting the button on the key fob to lock the doors.

We walked to a side entrance that was too damn dark and she unlocked the door and flipped a light switch. The light flickered on and then the bulb blew.

She looked over her shoulder, "It's the third floor. Maybe the next floor will be lit. If my phone wasn't dead, I could use the flashlight app."

"Does this happen often?" I took a step forward and bumped into her, "Sorry about--"

"It's fine. The handrail is here," she reached back and took my elbow and moved it to the railing, "Got it?"

"Yes."

She let go of my arm and I followed her very closely up the stairs. This was a very uncomfortable situation to be in. I was so angry at her for leaving Ft. Lauderdale like she did, for showing up at my damn office, for not taking no for an answer, for spying on me, and for fucking following me tonight, causing me to get carjacked and nearly stabbed. Even more fucked up was that it scared the hell out of me that the piece of shit tried to get to her and that she fell apart in my damn arms. It felt damn good to hold her, and that pissed me off too. She was after a fucking story. She was not interested in me.

When we got to the second floor, the switch didn't work.

"I'm sure it'll be fine on the third," her voice was shaky.

When we reached the third floor, the light didn't work.

"I can't believe this happened again," she groaned.

"Does it happen often?"

"I've only been here a week and it's happened twice," she grumbled. "If you put your hand on the wall my apartment door is right up here."

A bright light shone in our eyes, she jumped back startled and screamed into her hand.

I grabbed her and shoved her behind me.

"Nikolette, you okay, Hun?" I heard a male voice ask.

"She would be if you didn't just scare the hell out of her," I snapped.

"I'm fine, Mr.?"

"Thomas," he chuckled. "Looks like the lights are out again."

"I see that," she said trying to catch her breath.

"You buy a flashlight yet?"

"No. I didn't expect this to happen again," she seemed more relaxed and walked around me.

"Take mine, Hun, I have two," he handed her a flashlight.

"Thanks, Thomas. That's very nice of you."

"Oh, you don't have to say that, I would do anything for you, Hun."

This man was starting to irritate me a bit. "Nikolette, can we go inside, please?"

She looked back at me and shook her head, "Thanks again, Thomas."

She unlocked the door and we walked into her apartment. When she flipped the light switch, it didn't work.

"I'll find some candles." She said and then walked through the room with a flashlight.

"If there's no electricity the phone chargers won't do us any good."

She walked back into the room and set the candles on the kitchen island. "I hadn't thought of that."

"Do you know where the breaker box is?"

"The what?" she asked as she lit a candle.

"I'll take that as a no."

The soft glow of the candle light illuminating her was enough to make my dick twitch and my heartbeat a bit faster.

"You need to come over here so I can see your cut," she said as she pulled out a barstool.

"The paramedics cleaned it after the pictures were taken."

She shook her head no, "I said that I would look at it. That's what I told the officer. I promised him and--"

She was starting to sound nervous, almost panicky. "Miss Bassett, tonight was--"

"My fault. I know, it's my fault."

"Why don't you pack a bag, I'll put you up in a hotel tonight."

"I can drive you home," her voice broke.

"I don't think you're in any shape to drive me home."

She nodded as she took several deep breaths. "You could stay here."

I shook my head no, "A hotel is a much better option, Miss--"

"Nikolette. My name is Nikolette."

"Right, let's get a bag packed." I took the flashlight and shined it around her apartment.

It was nice, small, but charming. The kitchen was stainless and the island a gray granite. The walls were a rose color. "You like pink?"

"Uh huh," she said as she followed me to the other end of the open living space.

I shined the flashlight at the door, "This your room?"

"Yes," she sniffed.

Well, she certainly liked pink. The walls in the room were a very pale pink, I think, and the bedding was all covered in hot pink and what I think was white pillows.

I looked away and at her, "Do you have an overnight bag?"

She nodded and walked towards a closet to grab it. "This is unnecessary, truly."

"I don't feel the same. You're obviously shaken, there is no electricity, you have no phone, and a neighbor who's more than a little strange."

"He's nice." She said as she shoved clothes in her hot pink bag.

"Sure."

We finally made it to her car. I opened the door for her and she got in.

It was only a five-minute drive to the Hilton. When I parked, she was looking through her purse, "I can't believe I … I forgot my wallet. It has to be in here somewhere."

"I offered to put you up for the night."

"No, I can pay." She dug through her bag, pulled out her wallet, set it down, and ran her hands through her shiny black hair, "I can't accept that. But I don't want to be alone. Could I just take your couch?"

"I don't think that's a good idea."

"Oh right," her face flushed, "your girlfriend."

"Miss Bassett I don't have ... "

"It's Nikolette. My name is Nikolette, not Miss Bassett, not Four, not anything but Nikolette or Nikki." She was pissed and it was kind of fucking sexy. "I know it was just a stupid fling and I have no idea how I ended up being given this god forsaken assignment, but I can't mess it up. And I already have. After tonight, there is no way I could get you to do this for me. I even considered offering sexual favors, you know, Mr. O'Donnell, but then I see you with that one woman and then the one who lives with you and I realize what Florida was and--"

I got out of the car, not wanting to hear another word. When I opened her door, she scowled at me and crossed her arms. "Let's go get you settled. I have a slight headache and your ranting about who you think I am isn't helping one bit."

"I--"

"Let's go," I reached in and grabbed her bag, then took her hand and pulled her up.

She tried pulling her hand away and I took her by the waist, pulling her to my side.

"Let. Go."

"Then do me a favor, Miss Bassett, behave."

"Behave?"

"I am trying very hard to be a gentleman here. I am putting you up somewhere safe. You've obviously had a very rough night, albeit your fault, I am doing this to make you feel safe. Instead of acting like a spoiled little girl who deserves a spanking you should be grateful."

She gasped and I released her. I motioned for her to go ahead of me and she did.

I got her a room for two nights, allowing enough time for her building's electricity to be properly fixed. She didn't argue when I took her hand and walked her to the elevator then boarded with her.

"You're being awfully quiet, Miss Bassett. Nothing else to say?"

Her brows knit together and she looked down.

"Don't hold back, Miss Bassett, nothing you say or do is going to get you that interview."

"I'll write what I've seen."

The door opened and I took her by the elbow and guided her to her suite. I slid the card through the lock, opened the door, and walked in. I set her bag on the floor and turned to her.

"Is that so?"

"Yes. If you don't give it to me, I will do my own investigating and write a very detailed profile and story about *the* Abraham O'Donnell."

I nodded, "Very well, do what you need to do. Just do me a favor, don't leave out the part about your cum soaking my face."

"You bastard," she hissed.

"Or the part about you lying on a bed in Florida blindfolded as a perfect stranger gave you the best orgasm you have had, or ever will again."

"Get out," she snapped.

"Fine. Lock the door you'll be fine."

"Are you insane? One second you're degrading me and the next trying to play hero."

"I never degraded you, Miss Bassett. I was merely giving you some facts to add to your little story. And I'm not being a hero, I'm being a gentleman."

I turned and walked out the door before I took her; because I was damn sure she needed it.

***

I woke in the morning to a throbbing head and my intercom buzzing. I sat up and looked around trying to find my phone, and then remembered I had left it in the kitchen charging. I jumped out of bed and pulled on some basketball shorts.

When I made it to the kitchen and grabbed my phone, I punched the security app to see who was at my gate at seven o'clock in the morning.

I chuckled when I saw Miss Bassett looking into the monitor. I pushed the button, which acted like Facetime, and saw her look of shock when I appeared on the screen.

"Good morning, Miss Bassett, how can I help you?"

"I was going to give you a ride to the police station."

"Is that so?"

"It's the least I can do."

"I can manage, but thank you."

"I also have no idea where it is," she admitted, "Or what I am supposed to tell them."

"I will buzz you in. Use the side door. Make yourself at home, give me ten minutes."

I pushed the button giving her access and walked back up the stairs to take a quick shower.

When I came down, she was sitting up straight on the edge of the leather sofa with her slender ankles crossed. She stood when she saw me.

"Morning," I nodded and walked over to the refrigerator and pulled out my normal breakfast foods. Kale, eggs, blueberries, and Nutella.

I grabbed the Nutri Bullet and tossed the berries and kale in, then scooped some Nutella, and finally cracked three eggs and blended it together.

I was doing my best to avoid Miss Bassett's stare. I knew damn well she was after a story and like it or not, she was gonna do it. I sure as hell wasn't gonna help her out any. She clearly had made up her mind about me long before she washed up on the Jersey Shore.

While breakfast was blending, I put everything back in the fridge, pulled two glasses out of the cupboard, and set them on the counter.

I turned off the machine and poured the mixture into the glasses and handed her one.

"That doesn't look very good." She held her hand up.

"Then don't drink it." I was annoyed.

"Abe," she let out a breath, "Mr. O'Donnell, we've gotten off on the wrong foot."

"Have we?" I drank down my breakfast and turned to rinse the cup before putting it in the dishwasher.

"Look, I didn't intend on seeing you again," she said in a voice just above a whisper. "But we should make the best out of the situation right?"

"Are you going to drink that?" I pointed to the glass I had poured for her.

Her nose curled up as she reached for it.

"Don't smell it," I warned.

"That bad?" she dipped her tongue in the glass tasting it and I kid you not, shit jumped in my pants. I should have let her suck my damn dick in Ft. Lauderdale.

"No, it's good." I turned away and grabbed a key out of the drawer.

When I turned back around, she was plugging her nose and drinking it. I had to hide my amusement, but it wasn't all that easy.

She set the half-full glass back on the counter and gagged and covered her mouth. I tried not to, but I laughed. I stopped when she did it again.

"Sink, Miss Bassett," I pointed and she nodded and ran to the sink.

After dry heaving a couple times, she stopped and tried to regain her stiff composure.

"I apologize for that display," she took the paper towel I offered.

I picked up the glass, slammed down what was left in it, took it to the sink, rinsed it, and put it in the dishwasher right next to mine.

"Not a fan of shakes?" I asked as I wiped the counter where the cups had set.

"Not a fan of slimy raw eggs going down my throat." As soon as she let the words out, she looked up at me wide-eyed and blushing furiously.

"Interesting."

"That's not–"

"Shall we head out?" I interrupted not wanting to enter into a discussion about swallowing cum while alone with Miss Bassett.

"I need to ask you something first," she said after clearing her throat.

"Go on."

"What are you going to say?"

Oh, now I got it. She was nervous I might tell the police why I jumped out of my vehicle. I wanted her to sweat it. She deserved to.

"I'll think about it on my way. Use the same door you came in. I will meet you outside."

She nodded eagerly and forced a smile, "Of course."

After this, all ties would be severed because I wasn't sure from one moment till the next if I wanted to fuck Miss Bassett or kick her ass, and that was not me, not at all.

I stood by my car waiting for Abe when the garage door opened. I heard an engine rev and out pulled Abe on a motorcycle. It was black and chrome and shiny as hell. He pulled up close to me and flipped the shield on his helmet.

"You riding or following?"

I watched his eyes travel down, assessing my attire. I had a skirt on, same thing as last night. I didn't change. Hell, I didn't even sleep. I needed to know if he intended on telling the police it was my fault. When he looked back up he smirked a cocky smile that I am sure women everywhere would find alluring, however, I didn't. The man was an ass.

"I'll follow."

"Try to keep up," his smile faded as he snapped his shield shut and revved his engine while he waited for me to get in my car.

It was an interesting ride to the police station. My eyes were glued to Mr. O'Donnell's backside the entire time. I tried to look away, but it was impossible, it was right there and the only other thing to look at was his trim waist and very broad shoulders.

I had to figure out a way to let him see I would be very professional in the way I wrote his story. A way to make him give me some information that was a little more personal, something not everyone knew about him. And then I wouldn't bother him any more.

When we pulled into the police station, he hopped off his bike and pulled his helmet off. When he lifted his arms, his shirt raised bearing just a few hairs that lead right down to his manhood.

I got out and he stood holding the door open as I entered the police station.

He was greeted right away with one of those man handshakes by a uniformed police officer at the desk before we were buzzed in with a "Detective DeAngelo should be in his office."

We walked into the office and sat down. Abe O'Donnell took over the conversation. He explained that he saw me at the traffic light and jumped out to tell me I had a turn signal out and winked at the detective who smirked and nodded.

I wasn't sure what that was about, but it made me uncomfortable.

The detective said the perp, a thirty-year-old man whose name was Joey Stomboli, had a record, and had just been released from a six-month stay in County. He was sure with the evidence they had they would be locking him up for even longer this time. With other eyewitness statements, the whole thing only took twenty minutes. We signed our statements and that was it.

When we walked out, I had to muster up the nerve to plead my case.

"First, thank you for that. I know you could have made me look foolish in there."

"You're welcome." He started walking away.

"Wait!" I took a deep breath, "I promise," I stopped when he looked down and shook his head. "Mr. O'Donnell, I promise to be professional. I will--"

"Not interested. Do whatever it is you need to do. All I ask is that you let me see it before it goes to print so that I know what shit storm I'm up against."

"What makes you think you can't trust me?"

His eyebrow slowly raised and he put his helmet on, "Make sure you get your landlord to have that electrical problem checked out. Have a good day, Miss Bassett."

Before I could say anymore, he was on his bike and revving his engine again.

And when he rode off, he didn't look back.

***

Thomas was standing outside smoking a cigarette when I pulled up to my apartment.

"I called the landlord," he said as he blew a cloud of smoke in the air, "Says it'll be fixed tonight."

"I wonder what the problem is."

"Old house, old fuses I assume. But, hun, I got you covered. If you get scared you just walk next door."

"Thank you."

I walked up the stairs and decided I would stay the extra night at the hotel. I packed some clothes and grabbed my wallet. I would not allow Abe O'Donnell to pay for my room.

"You headed out again, hun?" Thomas startled me as I walked out the door. "Did I scare you?"

"Just surprised me, that's all," I smiled politely.

"Hun, as much as I like surprising my women around here, I'm gonna have to try not to do that to you again. You're a jumpy little bunny aren't you?"

I laughed a little as I walked away. He was kind of a creepy guy. I'm sure he meant nothing by it and I am also sure that I was just on edge about last night.

***

I spent the weekend trying to devise a plan on what to do about the O'Donnell issue. I sent an email to my editor and he granted me permission to work on the story from home the following week and told me that he would not be happy if I didn't pull this off.

On Monday, I went to Steel again and tried to gather as much information as I could, even trivial things such as when he went to work. I parked in the adjacent parking lot so that he wouldn't see me. And when I pulled in at six forty-five in the morning, his Land Rover was already there.

While I sat there, I decided I would post on our blog page. My friends and I had started it in high school and continued posting random things weekly. Things such as books we were reading, music we were into, movies we loved, things of that nature. It was a great way to keep in contact when our schedules were as messed up as they were now.

I jumped when someone banged on the window. I didn't even have to look to know it was him.

I rolled the window down and smiled, "Good morning, Mr. O'Donnell."

"You're a pain in the ass, you know."

I don't know why, but it made me smile even bigger and then he huffed and straightened. I opened the door and stepped out.

"Is your electricity problem solved?"

"It is. I also paid for my room, so make sure they don't charge you."

He looked up at the sky and shook his head back and forth.

"I get the final okay, OK? And so help me God, if you make me out to be something I'm not. I will put an end to the article and make sure you--"

"I am just going to do the basic interview and a photo shoot. I think you surfing would be a great place to start. All the female readers would love that."

"No photo shoot. I can have the article written for you."

"I will be writing the article."

"You really shouldn't be telling me how this will go, Miss Bassett. As a matter a fact, I will have legal draw up an agreement between you and I about what will and will not be allowed to be put into print."

"Abe?" I looked around him and at a very pregnant woman walking our way.

He turned and looked at her, "Is everything okay?"

"Yes, I just saw you storm out of your office," she pointed up to what was probably his windows, "And wanted to make sure you were alright."

"Everything's fine, Carly."

She smiled at me and stuck out her hand, "Hi, I'm Carly Steel."

I shook her hand, "Nice to meet you, I'm Nikolette Bassett."

"Oh," her dazzling white smile spread across her face, she turned and giggled as she looked at Abe.

"Carly I can handle this," there was a bit of a warning in his voice.

"I know you can," she patted his chest and for some reason that made me a bit jealous. *Why?* "But if you can't — Nikolette you feel free to call me —and I will give you some inside information on Jersey's most eligible bachelor."

She threw her arms around Abe, gave him a big hug, and an obnoxious loud kiss on his cheek, "I love you."

"You too, Carly," and he nodded to the building.

When she was out of earshot, I finally allowed myself to look back at him.

I couldn't say anything for fear that whatever ground I had gained would be lost due to this feeling inside that I knew was jealousy.

He must have sensed it because the corner of his lip turned up. "She's beautiful, isn't she?

I nodded and he laughed.

"What's so amusing?"

"You should see the pictures of her and I, we used to look almost identical."

He looked pleased with himself and I wanted to leave. I hadn't pegged him as a mean person. A man with very sexually deviant ways and an unnaturally strong sex drive, but not a cruel man. Apparently, I was wrong.

"You shouldn't be jealous of Carly, Miss Bassett."

"Jealous?" I tried to act like I wasn't.

"Yes, jealous." He laughed and started to turn away. "Tomorrow night at six thirty. My home. You can come in and wait. If I am not available, I will be soon after. Use the code," he paused and smirked, "Four, four, four, four. That will be yours exclusively; it will keep record of when you come and when you go. Only use it when I ask you to. If I'm going to trust you with personal information, you'll earn it. Don't prove me wrong."

I watched him walk away and tried to come up with something to say, but I chose not to. Partially because I think I just got my way and partially because I was watching a beautiful vision walking towards the sun. Dear God, please help me keep my wits about me.

I went home and showered. A cool shower, although the electricity was working just fine, the air conditioner was not. It was hotter than Hades and I certainly couldn't afford to stay another night in a hotel.

As I was toweling my hair, there was a knock on the door. I threw on a tank top and a pair of shorts and went to answer it.

"Your place hot, Nikolette?"

It was Thomas and he looked like he had just run a marathon. His face was red and perspiration was evident on his face and hair.

"Are you okay, Thomas? You look nearly overheated."

"Me, no I'm fine, Hun, just wanted to offer you a cooler climate," he winked. "I just got a portable air conditioner since the central air here seems to be on the fritz."

"No I'm fine; I have fans running, but thank you."

I was about to shut the door when he reached out and stopped it.

"Nikolette, don't be so hardheaded, you look incredibly … " his eyes traveled up my body, "hot."

"I actually have some work to do, but I appreciate the offer," I quickly closed the door.

Thomas always seemed to be around and it was getting worse by the day. I looked out the peephole to make sure he was gone and he wasn't. He stood there for another full minute before he turned and walked next door to his apartment.

I had only slept nude once and it was for reasons other than the heat, but tonight I really had no other choice. I went to bed that night with the fan blasting over my body. I woke feeling extremely hot and noticed the fan wasn't running. I sat up to flip on my bedside table lamp and it wasn't working. The electricity was out, again.

I reached for my phone and decided instead of calling Mr. Smith, the owner of the house, I would text him. I was a little more than annoyed at this point and if I spoke to him, I would more than likely be rude. This place was where I had to be for the next six to eight months. Hopefully, after that, I would be gainfully employed and able to find a home of my own.

In the morning, I sat up completely unrested to a stifling hot apartment. I headed to the shower hoping that a cool shower would help me be a bit less cranky. When I had finished I decided I would go to get breakfast at a place that had working air conditioning and maybe simply being off the third floor would help.

When I walked out the side door, the landlord was coming up from the basement.

"Miss Bassett, thank you for the text. I really apologize. I can't believe that three times in less than two weeks this has happened."

I smiled politely. I was sure he was just saying that. I was even surer that it would happen again in a day or two.

"My in-laws live in the apartment downstairs, Miss Bassett, they have for years. I can assure you this is abnormal and the interesting thing is, it's always just a tripped breaker. I went through and better labeled the panel on the breaker box."

"That's all it is?"

"Yes, I could show you if you'd like." He motioned to the stairway and I followed him down. After pointing out the box, he showed me how to check for loose breaker switches that may indicate that it would be the culprit.

"Nikolette," he said as he walked up the basement stairs, "I really appreciate you not being angry about this."

"It's upsetting."

"I understand and I will get a new electrician as soon as I can find one. It shouldn't take too long. In the meantime, call if you need anything." He started walking to his big white Dodge, "Oh and take a week's rent off next month. I truly am sorry."

"Thank you."

I turned, walked into the building, past Thomas, who said nothing, absolutely nothing to me. Odd.

***

I punched the code on Mr. O'Donnell's security system and the gate opened. I pulled in, parked my car, and grabbed my briefcase, a gift from my parents. They were upset I was coming to New Jersey a week early, but I needed a change. They mailed it to me and when I called to thank them, my mother explained that had I kept to my original plan she would have been able to give it to me in person.

I entered through the garage per the instructions Mr. O'Donnell had sent me in an email. Bouncing off the concrete walls, "*Back in Black*," played loudly. I opened the industrial door leading to a home gym that was no less impressive than a commercial gym, and I saw him.

He was running on a treadmill. Shirtless. Dear God, help me remain professional. With each stride, his back muscles and calves flexed. His backside was so toned, that I could see his muscles contract while he ran. Sweat dripped down his golden tan body and I decided I needed to turn away, so I did.

The song stopped and I heard the beep, beep, beep, of the machine being turned down to a lower speed and then I heard him panting, trying to catch his breath.

"Miss Bassett, you're early," his said through labored breath.

I was ten minutes early, "It's a habit I apologize."

I still didn't dare turn around.

"Go on upstairs," he panted, "I'll meet you in a few minutes."

I walked up the concrete stairs and into the spacious living-kitchen-dining room. I sat on the sofa and pulled out my notebook, pen, and recording device. He walked past me and up another flight of stairs.

I heard water running as I sat and pictured him showering off his spectacular body. How on God's green earth would I remain professional? How would I not want to ask him why he said all the things he did in Florida when he already had me in bed. How would I not wonder if he had said those things to the two women I had seen here just days ago.

I looked down at the paper I was doodling on and realized I had drawn what appeared to be waves. I quickly pulled the paper free from its bindings and tore it up. If he saw it, he would know that I thought of him often.

I got up and walked into the kitchen area trying to find a trashcan. I opened a few doors thinking it may be inside one of them. Everything was perfectly placed in each cupboard I opened.

I heard him clear his throat and looked up. He was leaning against the brick wall wearing loose fitting jeans and a navy tee shirt that fit perfectly with his arms crossed, "Did you find what you were looking for?"

He thought I was snooping, damn, "I was looking for your trashcan."

He took three long strides to me and held out his hand for the waded paper I held tightly balled in my fist. Begrudgingly, I gave it to him and he opened the cupboard next to the one I had just closed and tossed it in.

"Thank you." The words had a double meaning, thank you for throwing it away and thank you for not looking at it.

"You're welcome," he motioned to the stairs, "My office is up here."

I followed him up the stairs to another open area. He pointed to the left where a large wooden desk sat, but my eyes looked right to his bedroom area. Against the far wall, an enormous bed covered in a dark gray comforter was made up neatly with white pillows and a white bed skirt. Directly opposite was a wall of windows that overlooked the city and the shore.

"Miss Bassett?"

I looked up and he was already seated behind his desk while I stood at the top of the stairs.

"Have a seat."

My face was in flames when I looked at the amusement dancing in his eyes. I couldn't even be angry, but I certainly was mortified.

"You like my bedroom?" he asked smugly.

"Very utilitarian," I answered as I sat across from him.

He looked down and his jaw tightened as if he were trying not to respond to me. He opened a file and pulled out a paper and pushed it, along with a pen, toward me.

"This is our agreement. Before we begin, I ask that you sign it and understand that what you are signing is a legal document. It will hold up in court."

I was immediately irritated, "You do understand that I don't really need to interview you to write a story, Mr. O'Donnell," I said as I pushed the paper back toward him.

He pushed it back to me, "You do understand that when I spoke to your editor this morning he agreed to me having you sign this don't you, Miss Bassett?"

"What did you say to him?" I snapped.

"I don't understand the question, could you be more specific?" He leaned back in his chair and steepled his fingers.

"Did you tell him about ... about–" I stopped, too embarrassed to ask the question.

"Miss Bassett, what happened between you and I in Florida–"

"Don't, please just don't bring it up," I could feel the flames burning my face under my skin.

"To be fair, you brought it up. I would love to forget about it completely," he chuckled.

"What's that supposed to mean?"

He cocked his head to the side and scowled. "Why don't you decide whether or not you want to discuss it or forget about it after you sign the paper?"

"I'm not signing anything," I mumbled like a little kid.

He was beside me in a split second. He pulled my chair back and I grabbed ahold of the desk to stop from moving under his stronghold.

He leaned over my shoulder and very quietly said, "Miss Bassett, without this agreement being signed we have nothing further to discuss. That means it's time for you to leave."

He smelled wonderful, which made me angry. What had come over me? I was acting like a fool, a complete and total fool. I needed this, I couldn't mess it up, "Fine, I'll read it."

He stood and walked around his desk and sat again.

"The paper simply states if I say something off the record, it's off the record, and that this story is completely on my terms. I will allow you to use your creative voice as long as you do not paint me out to be something I am not. I also get to read everything and approve it before it goes to edit. Your editor doesn't get a copy of your interview until I say it's okay. Do you understand, Miss Bassett?"

"Yes," I looked at the paper. What he said was accurate, but I wouldn't sign it until after I read it.

When I finished, I pushed it over to him and he let out an exaggerated deep breath and pushed another paper over to me.

"This is how I see this interview. I want you to keep it and understand that you have my permission at any time to turn this in and call it yours."

"Why would I do that?"

"Because we are going to have one hell of a discussion off the record before we move forward."

I looked at his stone cold expression and felt slightly chilled myself.

"Shall I begin?" he asked.

"Do as you please, Mr. O'Donnell," I huffed. *You will anyways.*

Off the Record

"**P**erfect. I ask that you hear me out before you get all pissed off and storm out."

She nodded. She was already pissed off, which was fine by me.

"I don't trust you at all."

"That's not fair," she began.

"Don't interrupt, Miss Bassett," I warned and her jaw clamped shut. "Trust not given is trust not earned, do you understand what that means in our situation?"

"No, but I assume you're going to tell me."

"It means you left Ft. Lauderdale not because you had something at home to deal with. Deception number one. You probably told yourself that you were afraid of what I may have done to you, but right there was deception number two. You enjoyed every moment of the pleasure my body and mouth gave you, pleasure, Miss Bassett, beyond your wildest imagination. You are as sexually inexperienced as they come, Miss Bassett, but you portray a sensual and sexy-as-hell confidence that led me to believe otherwise. Deception number three. When you saw me at Steel the first day, you're gonna tell me you weren't completely turned on by just the thought of me having a bit of control over this situation, just as I had in Florida, and that, Miss Bassett, would be deception number four. I think we should stop right there at four, don't you?"

"Why's that? Because it's easier to keep track of your conquests that way, Mr. O'Donnell? Who was it leaving here the other day, one and two?" She huffed.

"Deception, number five, is what you're doing to yourself right now," I stared into her eyes.

"I don't want to do this." She stood up and I got up and grabbed her elbow stopping her.

"You want this very badly, Miss Bassett. So badly you can think of nothing else."

She shuttered a bit and then closed her eyes. When she opened them she stepped into me and looked up, I knew what she was asking for, but I wasn't even close to being there yet.

"Have a seat, Miss Bassett," I said no more than an inch from her lips.

Her eyes widened and she stepped back.

"You're playing a game with me?" I didn't answer; part of me wanted her to figure it out for herself. "I'm not one of your whores."

I walked around and sat, "Never said you were, Miss Bassett. But while we are on the subject, let's discuss shall we?"

I pointed to the chair and she sat down.

"Off the record," I waited for her to nod and she did, tossed in with a bit of an eye roll. "What did you see the other day?"

"You know what I saw."

"I'm not sure you truly understand, so before going into detail I want to know what you saw, Miss Bassett." When she didn't answer, I continued, "Miss Bassett, the sooner we get through this the sooner we move to the interview."

"You slept with two different women in a day?" she gasped.

"I have before. Not a normal thing, no."

"You pay them?"

"Off the record, yes. I have to be very careful with who I choose to bed. Like you for instance, we didn't exchange names, you knew nothing about me, I knew nothing about you so it was a safe hook up."

"Hook up." She whispered and quickly looked away.

"That only offends you for two reasons. One, you are not the type of girl who does casual hook ups, and two, because you're comparing your sexual experience with me against that of mine with them."

"I'm not a hooker!"

"That's right; I never treated you like one."

She shifted uncomfortably and crossed her legs.

"Miss Bassett."

"My name is Nikolette. You've been inside of me, Abe, you didn't act like this there," her eyes filled with tears, which I didn't expect, "You are making me feel like one. You! Not me."

My heart beat faster and I had to grab hold of the arms of the chair to stop myself from standing. She left Ft Lauderdale, I didn't.

"How so?" I tried not to hide the anger.

"You're going to own my body, you're going to … you said a lot of very crude things."

"Which made you come even harder."

"You son of a bitch," she stood up and grabbed her things and walked to the stairs.

"Off the record, Miss *fucking* Bassett, you left a goddamned note and ran."

One tear fell from her face and she wiped it away, "And I did so in the wrong direction."

I listened as her heels clinked down the stairs and the door shut.

"FUCK!"

***

The next day I sat at my desk waiting for a reply. Miss Bassett had left the interview I had written for her to submit on my desk when she walked out. I emailed her a copy. When I received an email from her editor, I nearly spit my coffee on the computer.

Subject: Interview

Body: I wanted to thank you for agreeing to do this exclusive interview with The Shore. Miss Bassett said she had a chance to meet with you yesterday and that even though you had a very tight schedule; you were gracious enough to give a bit of your time.

To be honest, I was going to send a male. But now, I'm glad Miss Bassett showed up a bit early.

Bogart Humph, Editor

The Shore

I didn't reply.

Jase walked into my office and smiled that "I got laid last night" smile.

"Bro, please turn it down a bit, your wife is my cousin."

"I know," he sat across from me and kept smiling.

"I don't wanna hear about it, Jase."

"Yeah you do," he chuckled.

I looked up at him, "No really I don't."

"Let's just say pregnant women are fucking hot in their third trimester."

"For fuck's sake, Jase I–"

I stopped when Carly walked in with the female version of Jase's smile plastered on her face, "Good morning, Abe," she looked at Jase and smiled. "Good morning, Jase Steel."

"Certainly was, Carly Steel." He winked at her, "Come here, baby."

I stood up and walked out of my office, I don't even think they noticed.

I sat in Jase's office, because apparently, when I left for vacation, my office became Fuck Central. Carly walked in just a few minutes later.

"Hey," she looked concerned.

"Hey," I looked away.

"You wanna talk about it?" She sat on the edge of Jase's desk and looked at me.

"About what?"

"The beautiful girl that you met on vacation who happens to be doing this interview and is apparently stalking you."

"Does your husband tell you everything?"

"No," she smiled and rubbed her round belly. "I love you, Abe. You keep a lot inside. That doesn't always work out well for people, you know."

"I'm not like them, Carly," I assured her.

She smiled and shook her head, "More alike than you care to admit."

"What's that supposed to mean?"

"Well for starters, you bury your hurt and forbid anyone to acknowledge it."

"Carly, don't."

"Okay," she leaned forward and kissed my head before standing. "And because when you fell, it pissed you off, so you'll fight it. Which is more Cyrus than the others, but you're doing it now."

"Not at all the same as he and Tara."

"Maybe not the same exactly."

"Not even close, Carly."

"Fine, but you're scared to let her know how you feel and I think you need to tell her."

Holy shit, Jase could keep some shit to himself. She didn't know Four took off on me.

"How is she?"

"Carly," I warned.

"No, Abe, how is your Mom?"

"Fine," I stood to walk away and she hugged me so goddamn tight. "I love you Carly, but that's --"

"Off limits?"

"Way off limits."

"If you ever want to talk, let me know."

"Yeah." I gave her another squeeze and a kiss on the head.

When I let go and looked up, Jase was walking in with a grin on his face and Miss Bassett was standing in the doorway with a shocked expression on her face.

Carly nudged me and I rolled my eyes.

"Come on in, Nikolette. We were just talking about you."

"Carly," I snapped at her.

"You be nice to our sexy little pregnant woman, O'Donnell, or I will have to take her away again. Come on in, Nikolette." Jase opened the door wider.

"I have to use the bathroom," she said before running away.

"What the hell was that all about?"

"No idea, but she looked like she was going to get sick," Carly started walking out the door after her.

"Leave it alone."

"Baby, Abe wants to do this his way."

"What if she's pregnant?" Carly whispered.

"What?" I gasped.

"Bro she thinks everyone is knocked up around here. Says it's in the water." I must have looked panicked because he appeared amused, "Jersey Shore water, not south Florida, bro."

EMAIL

I walked into the bathroom and tried to take a few deep breaths to calm myself. Somehow I had gotten myself involved in a very twisted situation. If my instincts were right, that Carly woman who was married to Jase Steel had something going on with Abe O'Donnell, too.

I pretended to wash my hands as a petite brunette walked in and smiled a shy, sweet smile. She pulled up her shirt, looked at her belly in the mirror, and smiled at it adoringly. Just then, a tall curvy blonde came out of the bathroom and she bent down and kissed the brunette's belly.

"I cannot wait to hold that baby," the blonde gushed.

"You should get pregnant."

"Oh hell no, there are gonna be enough little Steels running around here, so many in fact that I'm afraid we'll get them mixed up. We'll have to ask "who's your Daddy" to figure it out and then they won't even know because this family is so twisted up in each other."

I had to tune her out. I didn't want to know anymore. I felt nauseated for a moment and then even worse when Carly entered the bathroom.

"Is it a party in here?" She smiled and hugged the two women.

"Party in the potty," the little brunette laughed as she rubbed her very small bump.

"Nikolette, are you alright?"

I nodded, "Yes just, this is all a little much."

"You're telling me," the blonde laughed, "You'll get used to it though, and love each of them the same."

Oh God, "I'm not into that sort of thing."

Carly looked at me as if she was confused, yeah right, she just didn't want it getting out that this family, Abe O'Donnell included, may as well be polygamists.

"I signed a contract. I can't write about anything unless Mr. O'Donnell okays it and I'm sure he wouldn't want this story to get out."

"What story is that?" Carly still looked like she was being nice, but I am sure it was fake.

"Well, from what I see you and Abe have something," Oh dear god how do I say this without sounding like I am judging, because I'm not, or at least I'm trying not to. "Special? And if your husband is okay with it—"

Carly started to giggle and so did the others. I was mortified.

"I'm sorry, Nikolette. Abe and I do have something special. We shared a grandmother. He's my cousin."

My jaw must have dropped.

"Stick around girl, I can promise you these boys don't share. All of them are like 'Me Tarzan you Jane' and stuff. I know it sounds kind of nineteen fifties, but it's not. Zandor, my husband, and I will never get sick of one another."

"And Cyrus, my husband, saved me, in every way possible. No man on this planet could ever compare to him."

Carly laughed and pointed to her belly, "You sure about that?"

"Ninety-nine point nine percent, yes," she smiled as she rubbed her belly again.

"And my Jase would, okay has, flipped out when I was given sex toys as a bridal shower gift. They don't share and they would never stray. Abe, when he finds the right one, will be the same."

I huffed and didn't even realize it until they all looked at me.

"It was wonderful to meet you all," I washed my hands and then walked towards the door.

"Don't be a stranger," Carly yelled.

I like her.

When I walked out of the bathroom, four men were leaning against the wall, all in suits and all unbelievably attractive. *Men of Steel*.

"Did you need something, Miss Bassett?" Abe asked.

"Oh for god's sake, Abe, her name is Nikolette," Carly walked out and hip checked me, "Jase Steel, I'm hungry."

He gave her a naughty little grin as he took her hand and they walked away. The other women walked out of the bathroom and left with their husbands, leaving Abe and I standing silently looking at each other.

"Will you be turning in the report I wrote up?"

I shook my head.

"Cat got your tongue?"

"No, I just need to warn you about something and it's very embarrassing."

"You're not pregnant are you?" He whispered.

"What? Oh my goodness, no. What?"

"Shh, Jesus, come into my office." Abe was a little less in control at that moment and it made me laugh, silently of course.

He held the door open for me and when I walked in he closed it, but didn't shut it completely.

"While we are on that subject … " I began.

"No, I apologize; we really don't have to go there." He sat in his chair.

"Fine. You may hear it through the grapevine that I may have just –"

"Just what?" He asked as he shuffled some papers in a pile.

"I thought maybe you all shared."

"Shared what, Miss Bassett?" He looked up waiting for an answer.

"You tried to get me to think you and Carly had something going in the parking lot," I stopped when his lip started to curl up. "It's not funny."

"No, it's quite funny, Miss Bassett. She's my cousin and my best friend's wife."

He leaned back and did that steeple thing with his hands on his lap again.

"You did try to get me to think that."

"You were jealous. I was annoyed, but never did I imply–"

"Yes you did," I laughed.

He bit his lower lip and then smiled and shook his head back and forth.

"What?"

"Nothing, Miss Bassett, you just have me all wrong, that's all."

"I don't think I have you all wrong, maybe that, but clearly, the reality would lead me to believe--" I stopped when he got up and shut his door.

"Off the record, Miss Bassett?"

"No."

"No?"

"No, if you want something off the record you can call me Nikolette or Nikki."

"Fine, Nikki," he looked up when he said my name. "I am probably a better man for paying for certain favors."

I laughed, "And why's that?"

"Feelings are never entered into that equation."

"So you don't think you could fall in love with one of them?"

"Hell no." He sat back. "It's an even exchange."

"I don't believe that for one minute," I giggled. I instantly regretted it, the way he looked at me softened and intensified.

"Off the record, Nikki, what went on between you and I was not what normally goes on in my bed."

I felt my checks flush and I tried to swallow down the lump rising in my throat, but I couldn't because my mouth had suddenly become dry.

He handed me a glass of water, "Take a drink, it'll help."

After taking a drink, I had to ask, "Help what?"

"The dryness in your throat caused by a desire deep inside of you that had you so damn afraid that you ran."

"Right into hell," I whispered before taking another drink.

He laughed and I looked up and rolled my eyes.

"Tell me why."

"Why I ran?"

"Yes Nikki, and why you couldn't face me the next day."

"Off the record?" I asked. He smiled and nodded. "I had just gotten over a heart break and thought maybe I could just have a fling and bounce right back to the way I was before."

"It didn't happen."

"Not yet." I took another drink and he stared at me, just stared at me, through me, dear God, he was beautiful.

"It wasn't a question, more a comment. It didn't happen because of the pleasure I gave you, you'd never felt like that before."

I looked down.

"I'm not trying to make you uncomfortable, just trying to make you understand."

"Can we talk about something else?" *Please, please, please.*

"Like what?"

"Hookers?"

"Companions?"

"Uh huh."

"I don't want you to think that I'm ashamed of it."

"Do your friends know?"

"They may assume, but honestly my sex life is very detached from my personal relationships and business life. It's more of a stress release."

"Oh."

His phone rang and he held up a finger. "Dom … yes I sent the financials over this morning to the bank in Italy … Perfect … I will send you a copy as well … Alright … Talk to you then."

He hung up the phone and looked at me. "Where were we?"

"Umm, why don't we do the basics? Name?"

He smiled, "Abe O'Donnell."

"Middle name?"

"Really?"

"For God's sake yes, could you let me have some information?"

"Patrick," he smiled.

"Age?"

"Twenty-six." His answer shocked me. "Did you think I was older?"

"Not the *you* from Florida, but the you behind the desk I would have pegged at thirty."

"Ouch," he held his hand to his heart.

"How did you get to this position at such a young age?"

"I traded Carly for it."

I didn't look up, I just kept writing.

"Miss Bassett?"

"Um, yes?" I looked up.

"That was a joke."

I scratched out what I had just written and he laughed. "Jase and I met freshman year at NYU, his grandmother who was worth a mint passed away. He asked me to come on board and it was minutes after I received my Master's so I said hell yes."

"Hell yes?" I teased.

"Hell yes," he smiled.

"Can I quote that?"

"Absolutely, Miss Bassett."

It took only an hour to get to know the personal side of Abe O'Donnell, but between the amount of calls he took and the people in and out of his office, I was there for three hours. When we finished, I stood.

"I think I have enough for the day," I stuck out my hand to shake his and he chuckled as he stuck his out. "Tomorrow, Mr. O'Donnell?"

"Can we do it at my place?" His wry smile seemed to imply a different meaning, or maybe it was just me and my desire hoping it did.

"Sure," I pulled my hand back.

"Good, because I have back-to-back meetings tomorrow."

He walked me out to the elevator and shoved his hands in his sexy suit pockets, "Goodnight, Nikki."

"Goodnight, Abe."

***

When I got home, a large truck sat in my spot, the side read *Falcon Contracting*. I parked on the road and walked in the side door as a man was coming up the stairs on his cell phone.

He nodded and continued his conversation, "I don't know what to tell you Abe. Everything looks fine."

When I stopped and looked back, I could swear I'd heard him say "Abe." Maybe I was simply losing my mind, or maybe it was wishful thinking?

I laid in bed that night unable to stop thinking about Abe Patrick O'Donnell and knowing how wrong it was. He didn't think hiring hookers, or "companions," as he prefers to call them, was immoral. He manhandled me in Florida, and he was still handling me in a way. After overthinking every last detail, I finally fell asleep.

I woke to a muggy room and of course, no electricity. I grabbed my phone and looked at the time, it was three in the morning. I rolled my very tired self off the bed, grabbed a pair of shorts, and pulled them on.

I grabbed my phone off the charger, turned on the flashlight app, and made my way through the dark to head down the stairs to see if my newly learned skill set could be put to good use.

I was in the basement jiggling breaker thingies when I found a loose one. I flipped it off, turned it back on, and crossed my fingers that it would work. I walked up the basement stairs and flipped the switch and would have celebrated if I weren't freaked out by Thomas's sudden appearance.

"You fixed it?" he smiled.

"I did. Pretty impressive, huh?"

"It certainly is."

I walked past him and took the stairs two at a time to get back into my apartment. I didn't like being in my pajamas in front of strangers, especially braless.

***

When I woke it was very late morning and I stared at the ceiling. I had no idea when I was supposed to meet the very sexy Mr. O'Donnell who had, in fact, interrupted my dreams again last night. I grabbed my phone when it chimed alerting me of an email.

Subject: I need to reschedule tonight's meeting

Body: I apologize but some things have come up. Would tomorrow evening say seven o'clock work for you?

Abe O'Donnell, CFO

Steel Incorporated

Subject: Reschedule

Body: I am a very busy woman Mr. O'Donnell. I will have to check and see. May I get back to you at a later time?

Warm Regards,

Miss Bassett

<u>Subject:</u> *Reschedule*

<u>Body:</u> *May I ask what is on your schedule aside from stalking, I mean interviewing the Jersey Shore's most eligible bachelor?*

Abe O'Donnell, CFO

Steel Incorporated

<u>Subject:</u> *Reschedule*

<u>Body:</u> *Well if you must know, the story seems to be heading in a different direction than I had anticipated when I accepted the assignment. Apparently the subject matter desires his story to read much like a boring old interview when his reality is much more interesting.*

But the real answer to your question is that I have taken on the task as resident electrician here on Park Street and the hours are grueling.

Warm Regards,

Miss Bassett

<u>Subject:</u> *Reschedule*

<u>Body:</u> *You don't give yourself enough credit, Miss Bassett. I am quite sure you could make even the simplest task of conducting an interview into a scorching story, and still allow for the subjects personal life to remain as such.*

How many times has your electricity gone out since you have lived there?

Abe O'Donnell, CFO

Steel Incorporated

Subject: Reschedule

Body: I am glad you have faith in me. I hope to do the story justice.

The electricity has gone out four times. But I know how to fix it now. If this journalist career doesn't pan out I am sure I can fall back on electrician.

Warm Regards,

Miss Bassett

Subject: Reschedule

Body: Four?

Abe O'Donnell, CFO

Steel Incorporated

I gasped when I read his response and then I smiled. A big goofy smile, too. I lay back in my comfy bed and looked at it again. I was trying my best not to read into this, but I was, I so was.

I was typing in my response when he sent another email.

Subject: Reschedule

Body: Did we lose our connection?

Abe O'Donnell, CFO

Steel Incorporated

Subject: Reschedule

Body: No, of course not. Yes, four times in two weeks.

Warm Regards,

Miss Bassett

Subject: Reschedule

Body: *Change of plans. I will come to you tonight. Is nine pm to late?*

Abe O'Donnell, CFO

Steel Incorporated

Subject: Reschedule

Body: *Sounds good.*

Warm Regards,

Miss Bassett

FUCK TO FUCKED

I grabbed my phone and called Falcon, the electrician I had sent to her apartment house. He'd done a shit load of work for us here at the office; he was good and I trusted him.

"Doesn't make sense, Abe. It's a newer installation by a company called Jolt, they're good. Sounds like some kid prank to me."

I thought about what he had said for exactly two point two seconds, "Yeah, now that you mention it, that's exactly what I think it is."

I sat through meeting after meeting and then spent a few hours in my office jotting down notes that I obviously felt were more important than my secretary did. I looked up at the clock and it was seven thirty.

"Fuck," I wasn't ready to stop working, but I needed to go home and beat the shit out of the bag and run before showering, picking up dinner, and going over to Miss Bassett's.

***

I walked up the stairs to her apartment and looked down the hall. That Thomas character peeked out his door. Creepy fucker.

I knocked on the door at 8:58pm and heard the television shut off. When she opened the door, she smiled a gorgeous bright smile that made me want to pick her up and kiss those full, sexy lips.

Instead, I held out the take out bag, "Hope you like pasta and salad."

She took it and smiled, "You didn't have to."

I stood looking at her waiting for her to invite me in and she just stood smiling at me. "Miss Bassett?"

"Oh, right, right I'm sorry, come on in," she stepped back and opened the door wider.

"Thank you," I walked in and looked around.

I had only seen her place in the dark with a flashlight and it was even nicer than I thought it was then.

"This is much nicer than the place I lived in when I was a senior in college."

"Right, at NYU," she grabbed her pen and notepad.

Right down to business. I would have liked to enjoy dinner first, but it was getting late and it wasn't a date, not yet anyways. We needed to clear some things up first.

"Yes, four years and then my Master's, which led me to this job," I sat at the table opposite her.

"And the most eligible bachelor on the Jersey Shore."

"Not really all that eligible." I pulled the containers out of the bag and sat one in front of her and the other in front of me.

She sat looking at me, her sandy eyes looked beautiful, and the wonder in them was abundant.

"Do you have any forks, Miss—"

"Nikolette, and yes."

"Nikolette could you get us some forks, please?"

She stood and walked around the small island, grabbed some silverware from a drawer, returned and sat.

She grabbed her notebook.

"Okay, but you don't want to discuss that part of your life. You've made that perfectly clear."

"Off the record?"

She smiled and shook her head, "I suppose, but if we don't get a few things on record, I may miss a deadline."

"Off the record," I took a bite of my salad and sat back. "I need to be sure that the people I am sexual with don't have cruel intentions, Nikolette. I don't want an attraction to be based on status or money. I don't want someone to get pregnant in hopes of collecting child support or landing a man who has money so that whatever attraction I had to them to begin with, fades. So dating is a nightmare because work keeps me very busy. I also don't want my dick on the internet or my sexual desires and ways to be sold to the highest bidder. So I hire companions."

She was busy writing when she looked up, "These companions, what do you enjoy doing together? Dinner, watch movies, go to charity events? Give me something to work with, please."

She seemed annoyed and I knew her aggravation would get even worse the further we went along, but it was something that needed to happen. "No, Nikolette. No movies. No dinner. This is not a romance novel. A few times I have had women accompany me to an event, but not often. These women come to my house, strip down, shower, then they go into my room and wait until I am ready."

"To have," she swallowed hard, "sex."

"Off the record?" she nodded. "Not sex, we fuck."

She blinked rapidly a few times before shifting in her seat. I really hoped she could have contained her composure a little longer, but apparently not. I knew her little panties were getting moist and it was gonna kill me to hold back, but I had to.

"It's not love making, seldom kissing. I don't give them oral pleasure, but they give it to me."

Her head snapped up and her jaw nearly hit the table. I continued.

"Sex isn't always about needing to or wanting to be near someone, to touch them. Sex can be purely physical."

She cleared her throat, "A power trip."

I laughed and she scowled. "Not always. But yes, sometimes."

"Go on," her tone was clipped.

"I enjoy being in control when I have sex. I like being in control in most every part of my life."

"So you're looking for a woman who will just give it to you? Like a June Cleaver type?"

It was almost comical watching her body language. Desire fighting contempt, interesting sparring partners.

"No. I want someone who wants to give it to me when I want it. Who takes pleasure in knowing that them giving up control in the bedroom brings me an extreme amount of pleasure when the mood calls for it."

"Your mood, not hers?" she asked with her eyes not leaving the note pad.

"I am very capable of giving pleasure, Nikolette," she shifted again. "Don't you think?"

Her eyes were still fixed on the paper before her as they widened.

"Dating," she nodded. "What's your idea of the perfect date?"

"It's been awhile since I have been on a date," I strummed my fingers on her table and pretended to think about it. "Why don't you tell me what yours is?"

"Because I am conducting the interview." She looked up smugly and then back down.

"Alright, then let me think hard about this." I sat for a few minutes knowing full well what it is I was going to say, but I also knew that building anticipation always made the delivery that much sweeter. "I love to surf. I never have time to do that anymore. So my perfect date would be to take a woman, who I found attractive and she felt a mutual attraction to me, to the beach. Maybe have a picnic that included wine. Then we would surf. If she didn't know how to, I would teach her. I am a damn good teacher, patient, gentle, but stern when the situation calls for it. Then, Nikolette, if things went well, we would more than likely end up back at my place. Off the record, and I won't go into specifics, but I could assure you she would come at least *four* times. The perfect end to that date for me would be to wake up in the morning and she would still be there so we could do it again. Because, Nikolette, if I had a date that great, it wouldn't be just a thing for me. It would be because I was interested in knowing her."

She didn't look up and her face began to flush.

"A date would always be my preferred method of hooking up. It's far less expensive and much more satisfying than calling for a companion. But you know there are a bunch of crazies out there and who knows, maybe even with a date I would wake up in the morning and feel as if I had been used."

Her head shot up, "I didn't use you."

"Miss Bassett, now you'd like to discuss our brief yet satisfying night together?"

"No, yes." She looked up, "You didn't use protection."

Wow, never addressed that before. "You said you were on the pill."

"Did you, do you," she stopped and covered her face with her hands, "Use protection with all those, those hookers?"

She looked up at me and I rolled my eyes, "I'm usually well prepared."

"Usually."

"I'm clean, are you?"

"What's that supposed to mean?"

"Clean meaning, you don't have any--"

"I know what that means. Of course I'm clean," she whispered and looked around as if someone might hear her.

"So you've been tested?" I took another bite of my pasta and pointed at hers with my fork, "It's going to get cold."

"I have."

"How many people have you slept with?" I took the bottle of wine out of the bag avoiding the horrified look on her face. I stood up and opened the drawer in her kitchen that she had gotten the forks out of, "No corkscrew?"

"No," her voice squeaked.

"Do you have any tools?"

"What's that supposed to mean?"

I had to stop myself from laughing. She was hot as hell and wrecked by sex talk, "Drill or a screwdriver, preferably."

She stood and walked to the closet, pulled out a tiny little pink toolbox, took out a pink power screwdriver, and handed it to me.

"Screw?"

"Excuse me?" she gasped.

"Do you have a screw?"

"Of course."

"Let me show you a trick."

I took the wine bottle and shoved the screw in the cork and used the screwdriver to open it. "Magic."

She grabbed two glasses out of the cupboard.

"Will you answer my question? Off the record?"

"Two."

"Two?" Holy shit, I fucking knew it, "And four orgasms?"

"Don't flatter yourself." She picked up her glass and tossed it back, the whole damn glass.

"Nikki ... "

"Please, I don't want to talk about this. I want to do the interview." She poured herself another glass.

"Fine, just answer one question and then I will answer five of yours."

"How many?"

"I already answered that," she finished the glass.

"No, you didn't," I took the glass from her and set it down. I bent down so that we were eye level. "Four?"

She closed her eyes and nodded.

I am not kidding I swear I had to turn and walk away. *All mine, every fucking one of them. Hell yes!*

I sat and closed up the containers and she picked them up, set them in the fridge, grabbed the bottle of wine, and sat down.

"Before you get all fucked up, I wanna ask you to do me a favor. Next time the electricity goes out call me. Don't go messing with it."

"I can do it."

"No. Just please don't. I will send someone."

"Why?"

I closed my eyes trying to figure out a way to keep my suspicions to myself. I didn't want to burden her if I was wrong.

"Because I am doing you a favor, so I am asking you to do one for me."

I walked over and sat on her sofa.

She stood, grabbed the bottle of wine, and walked over and sat next to me.

She offered it to me, and I held up my hand declining.

"Your parents? Tell me about them."

"Don't you need your little pad of paper and pen?"

She took a drink right from the bottle and it made me laugh.

"Sorry," she set it on the coffee table and sat back.

"My parents are both Irish."

"Interesting."

"You didn't know that?"

"No, I thought you were Italian."

I looked at her for a minute wondering if I had been wrong about her intelligence.

She smirked, "Abe O'Donnell, very Italian."

"They own a pub, O'Donnell's."

"Italian pub?"

"Very Italian."

"Do you have siblings?"

"No, do you?"

"I'm the interviewer, you're the interviewee, Mr. O'Donnell."

"

"We're back to that, are we," I reached over and pushed her hand. It was not a good idea. She looked at me with those big sandy brown eyes.

She looked down and shook her head. "How many long term relationships have you been in?"

"Depends on your definition of a long term relationship."

"Avoiding?"

"No, clarifying."

"I don't know, like a month."

"One."

"One?"

"One."

"Okay, two weeks?"

"About twenty."

"Twenty?" She gasped.

She looked like she was in shock and it was funny as hell, so I laughed.

"You're joking right?"

"No," I grabbed the bottle of wine, took a drink, and handed it to her.

"Is this off the record?" she asked and took a drink.

"It all is."

"Care to explain?"

"I don't do random hook ups."

"Oh really?"

She looked at me like she didn't believe me.

"Okay, look. I know guys who fuck to fuck. I'm not like that."

LOST CONTROL

He sat on the coffee table, knees nearly touching mine. "I'm not a bad guy, Nikolette."

"Okay," his being so close made my head spin, that and the wine.

"When I was younger, I didn't sleep with a girl unless I was interested in more. If I did randomly hook up, I always gave it a chance, but if there was nothing there, if the proverbial honeymoon period wasn't going well or if there wasn't a deeper connection, I saw no point in continuing."

"So you broke hearts?"

"I was never mean about it, and honestly it was discussed and I am sure by the end of each of those very uncomfortable conversations the girl agreed that it just wasn't working."

"Two weeks isn't a long time though."

"Exactly," he leaned forward and looked intensely into my eyes, "If there isn't an insane connection still after two weeks then I couldn't imagine twenty years. You know what I mean?"

"I suppose."

"Let me ask you something, Nikolette," my name leaving his lips was arousing. "How many boyfriends have you had?"

"A few."

"But you only slept with one?"

"Yes."

"Why?"

I sat and thought about it for a while, "Partially because of how I was raised and partially because I didn't feel that way about them."

"So you broke a few hearts, huh?"

"No, not really. It was like sixth grade through tenth."

He smiled, "I bet you did break hearts."

"I would hope not."

"The only difference between your dating and mine is that sex was involved. You dated to find out if they fit with you just like I did. What were they missing, Nikolette? What were you looking for?"

"My interview, remember?" he took a drink, nodded, and sat back.

"What does Abe O'Donnell, CFO of Steel Incorporated, want in a girlfriend?"

"To own her."

"Own her?"

"Body," he looked me up and down, "Mind, heart and soul. I want a woman who wants to please me, who steps outside of her comfort zone and takes on whatever challenge I put before her. I want to be her main focus, the reason she gets up in the morning, and the reason she smiles throughout the day, anticipating what the night will bring. I want someone who craves intimacy and desires a connection deeper than she has ever felt. So yes, Miss Bassett, I want to own her."

"And what do you have to offer a woman who would give up everything to--"

"She would give up nothing."

"Except her freedom."

"That depends on your definition of freedom, Miss Bassett."

"Freedom to choose to do what she wants. Not be your property." He laughed. I got up and retrieved the wine bottle and a glass, filled it and drank it down.

"This conversation shouldn't be had while drunk, Nikolette. I'm sure you'll want to remember everything I have to say, for your," he paused and looked up at me, "interview."

"Is that so?"

"Yes, of course."

"But I can't write half of the stuff you're telling me, so what does it matter?"

"I think you should answer that question for yourself."

The way he looked at me made me realize how badly I craved him. His intense gaze caused even more desire to build inside of me. A man like Abe O'Donnell, one of power, incredible looks, and a self-confidence that didn't come off as arrogance could do me in. Knowing that what he portrayed wasn't a front had already done me in.

My heart had been broken by a man who didn't make me feel one tenth the desire Abe had in Florida. Abe would shatter me and I knew it like I knew myself. But it didn't matter right now. I wanted more, craved more, and I couldn't possibly be so inexperienced that I couldn't tell that he wanted it, too.

We heard a loud crash and both looked toward the wall.

"What was that?"

He held his hand up to stop me from standing and then stood himself and walked in the direction the noise had come from.

I started to walk toward him and he took my hand and held his finger to my lips, hushing me. My body trembled from his touch and his jaw flexed tightly. He stood as still as a statue and slowly pulled his hand away from my mouth, but he didn't release my hand.

He moved toward me, his mouth now inches from my ear; I took in and held a breath.

"Does your neighbor give you bad vibes?"

"What?" Came out louder than intended and he covered my mouth. I wasn't expecting that, I was expecting a kiss, a touch, not that question.

He huffed and looked agitated when he stepped back and uncovered my mouth.

"Take me to your bedroom." He whispered.

I nodded up and down; I wanted him so bad. I didn't care about all the other stuff, the call girls, the way he felt he needed possession of someone, or that he could shatter me. All I knew was that I wanted him again. I wanted what he had promised before I made the mistake of leaving Florida with nothing but a note and the false sense that I was saving my dignity and self-respect.

As soon as we walked into the bedroom, I turned and took his face in my hands. "I shouldn't have left. I'm sorry."

"Nikolette not--"

I stood on my toes and pulled his face towards mine. I pressed my lips to his and he let out a slow and steady breath against my face. His hands found my hips and his fingers gripped them tightly.

"This happens and there is no turning back. If this happens, Nikolette, you'll give me everything I want and I will give you pleasures you didn't even know existed." He whispered against my lips.

"I know."

He turned and walked to my bed and sat on the edge; his gaze darkened.

"Remove your clothes, all of them."

"You don't want to?"

"I want to know that you can follow instructions."

"Why?"

He stood and looked at me as if he was annoyed.

"Just answer why?"

"Say please, Nikolette."

"Excuse me?"

"What did you say as a child when you wanted something, Nikolette? What's the magic word?"

"I'm not a child."

"As a child when you said please it's because you wanted something. The concept is the same, only what you want has changed."

"But--"

"You're also not ready for this if you can't follow one simple command."

"But--"

"Did you get spanked as a child, Nikolette?" He asked looking past me and at the wall as if he was inspecting it.

"Once."

"I assume it wasn't something you liked. That changes too as we get older."

"Something else that changes when we get older, Abe, is that we can control what we want to give up and not give up."

"Sometimes giving up control is beautiful, Nikolette. Like your sexy hot little body is, which brings us full circle. One more time, remove your clothes Nikolette, all of them." He finally turned and looked at me.

"I think I've changed my mind."

"Interesting."

"What's interesting?"

"I think I read you wrong that's all."

I started walking toward the door, "Don't. Just don't walk away. Let me ask you some questions, Nikolette. Let me interview you."

"For what?"

He cocked his head to the side as if I had confused him, "To be mine, of course. It's what you want."

"What makes you think that?"

He stood, "We've covered a lot of ground already. I'll be going now."

"No."

"No?"

"Can't we just." I stopped. "Fine."

I pulled my shirt over my head, reached around, and unclipped my bra allowing it to fall to the ground.

He turned and walked to the bed and sat again.

"Please don't watch me."

"What would be the point in asking you to remove your own clothes if I couldn't watch?" His eyes never left my body. "Continue, please."

I was doing as he asked even if it went against what I felt was right.

I stood before him in black lace panties.

"Those too."

I stared back at him and his jaw tensed again, "If you weren't so fucking beautiful I'd have left by now, Nikolette. Remove the panties now."

"Say please," I whispered.

He smirked and then sucked his cheeks in and shook his head "no."

"Tic-toc. Nikolette, turn your back to me while you remove them." There was an amused tone in his voice, but his dark gaze still held my eyes, commanding and captivating me.

I turned, bending in front of him as I pulled them down.

"You are impossibly beautiful Nikolette Bassett." I heard him stand and walk toward me. "How dare you wonder why it is I want to own you."

His hand took mine and he walked towards the mirror and I followed.

"Art collectors lineup to see visions half as beautiful as you, desiring nothing more than to keep the piece of art that has them enamored all to themselves."

He turned me toward the mirror.

"Tell me what you see when you look in the mirror." He motioned to my reflection.

"A naked body," I answered knowing he would demand I did and not give up until he had his way.

"A piece more beautiful than any other." He stood behind me, pulled my hips back against him, and kissed my neck unbelievably softly and I whimpered. "Here, what do you see here?" He pointed to my eye.

"Brown eyes."

"Sand before the ocean. You know how much I like the sand don't you?"

I nodded.

He cupped my breast.

"A perfect handful," his thumb rubbed over my erect nipple forcing it to pebble even more. "Fucking beautiful. And you dare ask why I would want to own this body?"

He was waiting for a reply and I didn't know what else to say except, "Sorry."

"I can't let you think that a sorry is all you'll have to say next time you misbehave. I'll have to perform some sort of punishment. Consider yourself lucky we aren't at my place or I would paddle you, which hurts more than a hand. You'll get off easy tonight. Now say thank you."

"For what?"

"For the spanking you might receive tonight."

I know the look of shock crossed my face, which made him groan softly against my shoulder blade.

"No." Down deep I knew I would regret it.

"Since we're just starting out I will give you a learning curve. But for future reference, no isn't a word you'll ever say to me in the bedroom." He stepped away from me and I immediately missed the closeness. "Go lie on your bed and spread as wide as you can."

I lay on the bed and looked up as he approached. It was uncomfortable laying spread before him.

He grabbed my ankles and widened them as he knelt on the bed before me allowing no movement and no means to escape the completely vulnerable position I was now in.

"You are doubting yourself again." He bent and nipped at my inner thigh. My hips thrust forward on their own accord, which furthered my embarrassment. "Your body is more confident than your mind." He nipped my other thigh and again my now wet sex tilted upwards toward him, begging for his mouth. "How bad do you want me to eat your sweet, sweet pussy, Four?"

"Nikolette."

"Four for now, she was much more confident."

"Nikolette," I said insistently.

"Arguing now? Interesting. Let me tell you what is going to happen now. We haven't worked up to the spanking, so that's off the table," His finger connected and sent a feather light touch up my seam and then he stepped back. "On your knees."

"What?"

"You're going to suck my cock. I'm going to cum in your mouth and then when I am done I will be leaving."

I was pissed, beyond pissed actually, "We could just skip the part about me on my knees and you could leave now."

"That's not what you want." He pushed his finger harshly inside of me and curled up so that I swear his fingertip was hitting the back of my clit.

"Oh, God!"

"So wet." His finger curled again, but this time he pushed harder on that spot and my back arched, thrusting my sex against him seeking more.

"Yes, oh god yes." If the pleasure weren't so intense, I would be embarrassed.

"Take what you can for now, I'm feeling generous. Fuck my hand Four. See if you can get there by yourself."

Unashamed, I did just that. I held his wrist as I thrust my hips back and forth, taking pleasure from his touch. "Yes, oh yes."

"Ride it harder, faster, come on take what you want because it'll all be gone in five, four... "

He continued his countdown as I continued riding his hand, and then he pulled away leaving me empty and unfulfilled. I looked up at him ready to scream just as he was undoing his pants.

"My turn, Four. Suck my cock until I cum."

I could not believe I was about to do this. The thought had always turned my stomach, but as Abe stood at the foot of the bed and began stroking his glorious, long, broad cock up and down slowly, my mouth began to water and I wanted nothing more than to give him what he had asked for.

No Mr. F'ing Rogers

I watched as she fought a battle within. She was questioning why she so badly wanted to do as I asked. I was hoping for the outcome I so badly desired. When she sat up, she looked angry and a bit confused. Inside I was pleading for her not to hurt my dick.

I didn't look away, defeat wasn't an option. I had laid it all on the line and there was no turning back. In my life, there was room for a tremendous amount of love and compassion, but true to what the books all say about who I had become in the last two years, I needed control. I needed to dominate women sexually. It was a control I couldn't give up. And after dabbling in this lifestyle that consumed my thoughts, I refused to turn back. I knew exactly what I was looking for in a partner and I wouldn't settle for anything less.

My heart was beating like a motherfucker as I waited to see what she would do next. It was sink or swim time right here and right now. The girl before me was exactly what I wanted in my life before I was awakened sexually. I swear to fuck, she better be what I needed now, too. Nothing less will do, nothing.

"Now or never," I hissed as I pumped myself.

She rose to her knees and crawled to the edge of the bed. She looked up at me, anger had disappeared and desire remained. She was nervous.

I cupped her jaw and rubbed my thumb over her sexy as hell plump lower lip. "Show me what you're gonna give me."

I pushed my thumb into her mouth and she sucked gently on it. "Perfect. Absolutely fucking perfect."

I rubbed the tip of my cock across her lip, and I swear, looking at her naked body, on her knees in a submissive position sucking harder on my thumb as desire's heat shown in her eyes, was more fucking beautiful than a sunset on the shore on the clearest day.

I pulled my thumb out and gripped the back of her head, fisting her hair, pulling her head gently back, and pushing into her mouth. Her eyes widened as I tried to restrain myself from thrusting too hard.

I was half in when her tongue swirled around my head and then she sucked. Gone was the look of wonder, she looked hungry.

"Perfect, Nikolette." I thrust in until I felt my tip rub the back of her throat and held her head still, "Breathe through your nose and don't you dare move for any reason other than to suck."

I pulled back and she gasped, tears had formed in her eyes and she wiped the saliva from her chin.

"Open," she didn't hesitate and this time she had more confidence in what she was doing and her tongue actively participated.

I groaned as she licked up the underside of my cock laying her tongue flat and applying the perfect amount of pressure. She reached up and laid one of her hands on my stomach and then pulled her head back and took me in her hand. She licked the pre-cum from my tip and then licked it again. I pulled my hand away and she looked up seeking approval as she slowly stroked me back and forth. I pushed into her hand and she began pumping faster, now with confidence. Her lips wrapped around me as she took me in her mouth sucking, and licking, hollowing her cheeks and then pulling her mouth away. She flicked her tongue across my head and looked up as she swirled it around the rim causing me to just about lose it.

Fuck she was beautiful. She continued greedily lapping at my now throbbing cock and I pulled back and looked down at her. The light from the hall shone on her just enough so that I could see how badly she wanted more. I looked up to the wall trying to distract myself. I saw something that I never expected to see. Something that immediately infuriated me.

I pulled back and looked down at her. "Hey beautiful, stop for just a minute?"

"Did I do something wrong?" Her voice was thick and sexy as hell.

"Not a damn thing. "

I looked back at the wall and I swear to fuck I wasn't seeing shit. A tiny bit of light was coming through the wall.

Not wanting to alarm her based on my suspicion, I bent down and kissed her, "I need you to lay back down and give me a few minutes okay?"

"But—"

"No buts. Nikolette, that was amazing." I kissed her again as I pulled the covers up from her sides and wrapped her in them.

I buttoned my pants as I walked next door ready to rip that motherfucker's head off.

I walked out of her apartment, shut the door, and walked next door. Rage was what I felt. A rage I had never in my life felt. I had suspected her creepy neighbor had something to do with the electrical problem, but not this shit.

I reached down and turned the nob. Luckily it was unlocked. I walked through the apartment that was identical to Nikolette's, but cluttered as fuck, and toward the open bedroom door.

When I saw that sick son of a bitch jerking off staring at a computer screen, I flipped.

"You motherfucker!"

"What the hell--"

He stopped when I grabbed ahold of his neck and pulled him away from the bedroom into the living room.

"Get out or I'll call the police!" He screamed.

My grip tightened around his neck and my other hand fisted and collided with his face, he screamed out and I did it repeatedly.

"Abe!" Nikolette ran toward me and grabbed my elbow stopping the next blow.

"Call the cops Nikolette," I yelled.

"But you'll get—"

"Now!"

She jumped when I yelled this time and fear flooded her face.

"Nikolette, do as I say right now," I said trying to keep calm.

She ran from the apartment and I looked down at the motherfucker who had been tormenting my sweet Nikolette for weeks now.

"You sick son of a bitch," I couldn't hold back I hit him again and again.

"Abe, stop!" she cried out and began sobbing.

I let go of him and my hands began to shake.

"Why? What is wrong with you?" She was a fucking mess.

I walked toward her and she stepped back as if she was afraid of me. "No, don't you dare." She ran around me and knelt beside Thomas, "Are you--"

"Fuck that," I grabbed her and yanked her up. I held her forearms in my hands and shook her, "He's a sick son of a bitch, Nikolette, go back to your place and--"

"What the hell is going on in here?" Another man appeared at the door.

"He broke in here and attacked--"

"You better shut your fucking mouth you fucking scum--"

"Abe, stop! Mr. Smith, I am so sorry--"

"Get. Your. Ass. Back. To. Your. Place. Now. Nikolette!"

"I don't know who the hell you are, but you need to leave." Smith pointed at me and Nikolette tried to pull away.

The landlord helped the sick son of a bitch up and I dragged Nikolette to the hall.

"He's a bad man--"

"You! Your–"

"You fucking know better. Goddamn it, Nikolette–"

"Do I know better? Do you really think?"

She stopped when I pulled her against me and hugged her tightly, almost against her will, almost. "You sure as hell do."

"He broke into my apartment and attacked me." I heard that bastard say.

"I'm calling the cops Mr. Thomas, your nose is busted up pretty bad," The landlord said.

"No, no I don't want any trouble; just get him out of here."

"Nikolette, go in and pack a bag, you're not staying here until that son of a bitch is in jail."

"Why? What--"

"Please," I pleaded, "Just do it. We'll talk in a few minutes."

She nodded and started to pull away.

"I won't let anything happen to you. I take care of what's mine."

I knew she was confused, but I also knew that there was a trust building between us, one that I needed so badly, especially now.

After she was in her place and had shut the door, I turned and walked back to the neighbor's.

"I don't know why the hell he doesn't want to press charges, but I can assure you I will. You get the hell off of my property--"

I pushed past the landlord and walked into the bedroom as he followed threatening me.

I stopped at pointed to the wall, "I am going to assume this wasn't here when you rented him this place."

"What are you--"

"This is my personal property!"

"She is NOT your property! You sick son of a bitch!" I stormed toward him ready to end his fucking life when two officers walked in.

Nicholas DeAngelo was not one of them, *fuck!*

I grabbed my phone out of my pocket and dialed it, "Jase, I need you over at 1273 Park Street. Bring Carly if she's awake. Nikolette needs a lift to my place. Don't ask questions, just do it. Don't leave her alone and keep your damn phone handy, I may need some help. Thanks, bro."

Nikolette walked in as the officers were asking questions, she looked mortified when I told them about the light I saw on her bedroom wall and even more so when she heard what I had caught him doing. But when they said the computer would be confiscated and an investigation would be conducted before arresting him, she looked scared. The worst part was when they told me that I was being arrested for assault. Apparently, there was no disputing the evidence in a man whose face was already black and blue and whose nose hadn't stopped bleeding since my fist had made contact with it. It was enough to lock me up for a while.

Jase and Carly arrived just as I was telling one of the uniformed officers that they could give me a few fucking minutes to make sure Nikolette had a safe place to go, emphasized *safe* while glaring at the piece of shit landlord who allowed scum like him to live here.

Nikolette had that same expression on her face as she did the other night when I got scratched with a knife. I knew she felt like this was her fault, but it wasn't; she was the victim here. I saw her battling inside and knew there wasn't a fucking thing I could do about it right now.

"Nikolette, look at me, beautiful. This isn't your fault." She looked toward Carly and Jase, scowled, looked down, and shook her head. "Hey."

"We've waited long enough," one of the uniforms said and held out the cuffs.

"You have got to be kidding," Jase huffed. "Call Nicholas DeAngelo, you fucking reta--"

"Jase," Carly gasped.

"Baby you need to take Nikolette and go. We'll meet you at our--"

"My place," I said as the officer tightened the cuffs, "Easy, there buddy, I'm not Harry fucking Houdini."

"Hey, it's all gonna be fine. Carly, get her to my place." She looked up at me fighting tears and I winked.

"You gonna take mug shots?" Jase asked the officer, "That would make one hell of an employee of the month photo."

"Fuck you, Jase."

"Damn, haven't even been to the pen yet and you're already asking for the sausage."

"Jase, the only sausage I want is the shit I put in my mouth for breakfast."

"Well, pretty boy, you might just get that tomorrow morning from your cellmate. Keys?"

"Front pocket, take your time in there when you're looking for them. It's been awhile, you know."

CLEAN SLATE

I sat in the back of the Town car next to a very pregnant Carly. "When are you due?"

"Any day now."

"I'm so sorry."

"Don't be sorry. That's what family is for."

"Family? I'm not family."

She smiled, "Abe is. He is my favorite cousin, you know, and so much different than the Steel men. He's kind, gentle, and sensitive, and he doesn't act like some overly alpha romance novel type thinking he needs to get his own way all the time."

I huffed and she looked at me.

"Oh dear," she whispered and rubbed her belly. "Do you wanna talk about it?"

I shook my head as a tear fell, "I just wanna go home."

"He doesn't think it's safe for you there."

"No, my home. I want to go back to Georgia."

She reached over, grabbed my hand, and held it. She didn't say another word; she just sat there holding my hand. God, I missed my girls, too. More tears fell as we drove up to the gate at Abe's.

Inside, I set my bag on the ground and looked around. I never really thought I would be back here, not like this anyway.

"Are you tired?"

"Exhausted," I admitted to Carly.

"Me too, so unless you want to talk, we should go rest," she pointed to the stairs.

"Will he be okay?" I asked as I followed Carly up the stairs.

"He didn't do anything wrong did he?"

I didn't want to talk about it. I didn't want people to know what I assumed was on that computer and I knew eventually they would.

"I think he broke his nose."

"So unlike him." She said as she walked into the loft bedroom. "You don't mind sleeping with me in here do you?"

"No, I think I can trust you."

"Yeah, I think you can, too." Carly smiled as she pulled the duvet down and climbed onto his enormous bed. "I need to see if my girl is alright." She pulled out her phone and made a call. "Hey, Momma Joe, I just wanted to be sure Bella was still asleep. She's been doing this thing where she comes into our room at night just to make sure we're still there … No, I think she's more worried she'll miss her brother's birth … Well, Abe kind of got arrested tonight," she held the phone out away from her ear while a woman was going on and on in what I assumed was Italian and Carly smiled and waited. "Jase is with him … No, Jase didn't get arrested … No, I don't think he will, he's a grown man now … I think Jase was going to call Nicholas DeAngelo … I know it's not like Abe," she smiled. "I think you are pretty close to right … I will … If she wakes up tell her to call me … Tell her I'm at Abe's with his … " she paused, looked at me, and raised her shoulders. But I just shook my head. I was hardly Abe's girlfriend. "Abe's friend. Love you too."

She lay back down and smiled at me, "You should sleep, everything will look better in the morning. There is nothing you can do now anyway."

"Thank you."

I rolled to my side hugging the massive pillow that smelled just like him. The cool cotton on my skin was soothing and allowed me to relax a bit, but not enough to allow me to fall asleep. In tomorrow's light, I would find out if the man who lived next to me had videotaped Abe and me, and how long he had been taping me. I always changed in my room. I'd slept naked.

It made me sick to my stomach and the thought of pressing charges and possibly having to testify in court was almost as bad as knowing that I would have to tell my parents.

I hugged his pillow a little tighter because for some strange reason, I did trust him. I yearned for his touch and the escape it gave. At first, my attraction to him was purely physical, but ever since the day I walked into Steel, the effect he had on me was unfathomable and undeniable.

I didn't know where things would lead, but I had a feeling that after walking out on him in Florida, a carjacking and an arrest, Abe would think twice about protecting what was his. I had done so much damage that I had no clue why I was here in his bed. Why he would even want me here? And I wondered when he would decide I wasn't worth the hassle.

***

I woke to whispers.

"Wait, don't wake them up. Remember back at NYU when I said we should dabble in some shit like this and you Mr. Fuckin' straight and narrow thought it was ridiculous that I would even think about something like that. Check them out. Tell me that's not hot."

"Jase you're fucking sick, man."

"You better be joking, Jase Steel," Carly whispered harshly.

"Hey Baby, I thought you were sleeping," Jase chuckled. "Of course I was joking, trying to get preppy boy to loosen up, laugh a little, life's too fuckin short to let shit like this bring you down."

I kept my eyes closed not wanting to interrupt their conversation and so I wouldn't have to talk about anything that went on earlier.

"Whatever, take me home," the bed rose when she got up.

"Do you know how sexy you look carrying my baby, Baby?"

"Do you think that's gonna help, Jase? You're on the shit list with me and if we don't get home soon you'll be on little Bell's, too. Hey, Abe, I like her a lot."

"I'm glad, Carly."

"Tomorrow we meet with the lawyers. Get this shit fixed." It was Jase.

"Of course. Thank you both."

"Goodnight, Abe."

When they left, I felt his eyes boring into me and a few moments later I heard him walk away. I opened my eyes and saw him walk into the bathroom, and then I heard the water running.

I sat up and looked toward the wall of windows. I had imagined what his room would look like in the morning. I walked over to the windows and watched in the distance the moons reflection off the ocean. It was beautiful and calming.

"Son of a Bitch! Goddamn it, Four." I turned to see Abe's naked body streaking across the room toward a closet and then hop out, putting his leg through his shorts and pulling them up as he rushed to the stairs.

His voice wasn't curt or harsh, it was more like a soft plea.

"I couldn't sleep." I said, stopping him from running down the stairs. I turned back to the window wishing that I hadn't gotten up, wishing that I had just laid there pretending.

"I thought you left."

I saw his reflection in the window as he walked toward me. He didn't touch me, he just stood beside me with his arms crossed over his chest. I didn't understand why.

"Did they find anything?"

"Yes. And not just of you, they went back a year and found out he's been taking videos of his neighbors before you as well."

"Will I have to testify in court?"

"I don't think it'll get that far. I think he'll end up fucking dead in a ditch-somewhere."

"You can't say things like that."

"The neighbor before you had a teenage daughter. That son of a bitch deserves whatever he gets."

"Will the media be told? I mean, when they release the news will my name be involved?"

"There's something called victim's rights, hopefully, that applies in your situation."

"Good. I don't want my parents to know. It would crush them."

He turned and looked at me, "Can I hold your hand?"

"What?" The question shocked me. He was asking me if he could hold my hand.

"I want to take your hand, walk you back over to my bed, and lie you down so you can get some sleep. I would also very much like it if I could sleep next to you. If not, I'll take the couch. But more than anything, I am going to ask that you do not take off in the middle of the night. I want you to stay. I want to go over some things tomorrow and I want you, Nikolette Bassett, to be able to sleep tonight in my arms knowing that I am going to take care of everything."

"Why aren't you telling me I have to?"

He closed his eyes and then when he opened them he appeared hurt, vulnerable. "Nikolette, there's a time and a place for all things. Right now, I just want to take care of you."

He held out his hand and I reached out to take it.

I lay in bed that night with my head on his chest and his arms around me.

***

I woke in Abe's arms, but I must have moved because I was on my side with my back to him. He hadn't let go, in fact, if it were possible, he was holding me even tighter. His breathing was deep and rhythmic; he was still asleep.

Needing to use the bathroom, I attempted to slide out of bed and his grip tightened even more.

"Don't leave," he whispered.

I looked over my shoulder and his eyes were still closed, he was still asleep. I rolled towards him hoping to loosen his grip and his eyes began fluttering until they opened.

"Good morning." His brilliant blue eyes were a bit dazed.

"Good morning."

I expected his grip to loosen, and when it didn't, I closed my eyes and he pulled me closer and kissed my cheek softly. I wrapped my arms around him and he exhaled a slow groan. I leaned in further and kissed his chest once, and then again. I felt his excitement growing and his distance as well.

I leaned in and kissed his neck. When I looked up, he was scowling a bit, which made me incredibly insecure about what I was non-verbally initiating. "I'm sorry. I--"

"No, I just don't know if it's a good idea right now."

"I understand," I smiled and nodded as I rolled away from him. "The bathroom is there, right?"

"Nikolette—"

"Pfftt no big deal," I waved my hand dismissively and walked as quickly as I could to the bathroom.

Once I closed the door, the tears began to flow down my cheek. It had been an insanely emotional week. I didn't trust myself, and now I didn't trust that Abe wanted anything more than for me to be his toy. He wasn't the man Carly thought him to be, or the one I'd heard whispering last night as I pretended to be asleep. He was moody, demanding, and overbearing. And the side of him Carly saw, the side he shared with others, apparently was not for me.

I sat on the floor and hugged my knees. I looked up as the door opened and wiped my face.

Abe peeked in and held out his hand. "Come on, let's talk."

"I don't want to," I must have sounded like a child.

"You do, and I need you to hear me out."

"No. I wanna go home."

"You can't yet, he hasn't been arrested," he held up his phone. "I just talked to the detective."

I stood up, "I'm not a toy. I'm going home."

"I'm not a goddamn toy either, Nikolette."

"You're kidding right?"

"Tell me how I know that this," he motioned between us, "isn't all part of the story. I don't trust you a hundred percent either you know. When you left Florida you--"

He stopped talking and shook his head and looked down at the ground.

"That again, huh?"

His head snapped up, "It was pretty damn fucked up."

"What would you have done if you were me, huh?" I batted away some more tears. "Stay next door to a guy who says he wants to own me without my friends in a scream's earshot?"

His jaw dropped and then snapped shut, "Scream from what besides an orgasm, Miss Bassett?"

"You—How did I know you weren't some, I don't know, some sicko?"

"Do I look like a sicko to you?"

Arrogant ass. "Because you're a preppy All-American boy?"

"Stand up, Miss Bassett."

"Nikolette. My goddamn name is Nikolette."

He turned around and walked out the door and returned in seconds with some of my clothes in his hand.

"Take a bath, you'll feel better."

"What's my name?"

"Nikolette Bassett, your friends call you Nikki, and you were Four a few weeks ago." He walked over and grabbed my hand and pulled me up. "You have been through some shit and I truly want to help you sort it all out with minimum damage. But I have no fucking clue what you want from me from one second to the next, and quite frankly you scare the shit out of me."

I stood as he started the bath water in the enormous bathroom, one that I just now allowed myself to see.

He turned to me and tugged the hem of my shirt, "Lift your arms, please."

And I did. He undressed me quickly. He redirected his eyes away from my naked body, like he did when I was clothed.

He held my hand as I stepped into the tub. Then he turned his back and walked to the other side of the room.

"I wanted to know you when I first saw you. After the beach and then having you in my bed, I didn't want to settle for Four anymore. When I woke up, you were gone. Then you show up at Steel and completely catch me off guard."

"I didn't know."

"I know you didn't. In the past week, you have pursued your story and discovered things that I'm not ashamed of, but they're private things. I have watched the way you look at me and I know you want what I can give you, you crave it. I want it, too. I stepped over the line last night. I knew I would. But what do I have to lose, hell, you know everything about me, you could be in this to ruin me."

"You demand trust yet you don't give it."

"Tell me why I should trust you. Tell me what you want from me."

"It's all very overwhelming, all of this."

"I agree."

"Last night I laid in your bed thinking about what could happen, ready to give you what you asked of me, and this morning you reject me. I understand that I have brought a lot of drama and unwanted attention. I want you to understand that I won't hold you responsible for anything you said last night. I can take care of myself. I'll finish the article without exposing anything you don't want uncovered. I'll do the little--"

"Stop."

Exposed

She looked at me with sadness and shame in her eyes. Two emotions I had brought on that I hadn't meant to. When she was naked in front of me, I never wanted her to feel ashamed.

I pulled off the shorts I had slept in, stepped into the opposite side of the tub and sunk down. I leaned my head back and closed my eyes thinking about what I wanted to tell her.

"My parents have been married for thirty years. My sophomore year in college we found out Mom, Margret, had multiple sclerosis. A woman who had worked side-by-side with her husband every day was now tired all the time. Then she started dropping things, and even fell a few times at the pub. The doctors ran tests and diagnosed her right away. She had numbness, blurred vision, and extreme pain in her legs, hands, and face for years. Things moved so fast."

"One weekend I came home and found her crying. Urinary incontinence is common in the more advanced stages. She was pleading with my father to let her go live in a home. She didn't want her family taking care of her. But my father wouldn't hear of it. Mom became very depressed. The next time I was home, she fell trying to get from her wheelchair to the toilet. Pops and I fought about him ignoring her wishes, subjecting her to the shame and embarrassment of losing her dignity. Long story short, she now lives in a rehab facility, but now she also has Dementia. Can you believe that? A double fucking whammy."

"I'm so sorry."

"Thank you. I'm sure you mean that. I'm not telling you this so you can have something for that story of yours, but because, I want to get to know each other. I want you to know that I'm not just some prick eligible bachelor playboy who meets girls on Spring Break, beds them and then goes back to fucking hookers when vacation's over. But here you are, angry, hurt, naked, fully exposed, and vulnerable. I need you to see that I can be that, too. I don't talk to anyone about her. Not even Jase or Carly. They know it's off limits."

"How often do you see her?"

"I used to see her weekly. Now I go every couple weeks. I prefer to go when she's asleep.. She's peaceful then, and it's less like a hospital, you know people are sleeping, less staff to interrupt, things like that."

"Why don't you move her home and have around the clock care?"

"Great question. Um, my father refuses to let me help financially. She's his wife. I wanted to move her home, but it's a fucked up situation in which I have no control over."

"I see."

"You see what?"

"Nothing. The water is getting cold would you mind if I got out?"

"I think you better sit still and let me grab a towel for you."

"I can--"

"No. Because if I see you naked again, I won't be able to control myself."

I got out and grabbed two towels, quickly dried off then left her to her privacy.

I returned a call from Nicholas DeAngelo.

Nikolette was standing in front of me in shorts and a tank top, pulling her hair into a ponytail, watching me.

"Thanks … I understand. It doesn't mean I'm fucking happy though … Two days … Yes I know. Keep in touch."

I wanted to break something when I hung up the phone, but she was here, and this was about her and … *FUCK*!

I shot my assistant a text to message me Dominick Segrettis file and to let him know I'd plan to call him no earlier than Thursday.

When I looked up at her, she rubbed her forehead. "The media know?"

"They do."

"My name will be used?"

"No, but when his information goes out, it won't take too much for the media to figure out who his neighbor is."

"Right."

"Do you think you should talk to your parents before that happens? Let them know?"

"Will we, I mean our video, be broadcast."

"No."

"You sound confident about that."

"A trial won't happen overnight. There are ways to delay things. That may or may not be used as evidence."

"Oh god."

"Nikolette, it could be a year or two."

"This will ruin my career. I will be that girl. The victim"

"I understand but--"

"Yours too, Abe. Oh my God, what have I done?"

"What have *you* done? Honest to God, Nikolette, you need to stop blaming yourself for things way beyond your control. I think you and I should take a trip to Georgia."

"What?" she was shocked.

"You can talk to your folks and I can let them know I won't allow anything to happen to you ... "

"What am I supposed to say to them, this is Abe O'Donnell the guy that got me off in Florida and now on film?"

"Well, that wouldn't be accurate. It was four times in Florida and I didn't actually let you get off last night. I was in a mood, remember?"

"Oh my god," she covered her face and then started to laugh. "This is awful."

"But you're laughing."

"What else can I do?"

"See, that's one of the four reasons I like you."

"Four, huh? That's it?" She looked up as she shook her head.

"So is it a yes or no?"

"I have no idea."

"Because you don't know how to introduce me?"

"Because of all of it."

"You can tell them that we met in Florida and chance brought us back together here in New Jersey."

"Is that what I should tell them?" Her cheeks turned pink.

"First thing's first, Nikki."

"Nikki?"

"Is that alright?"

"Yes."

"Because that's what your friends call you?"

She nodded.

"Are we friends, Nikki?"

"I hope so."

"Good, me too. Now let's talk about furthering that friendship and taking it to the next level. I need something from you."

"To let you have control."

"In the bedroom."

"Right."

"It bothers you?"

"To give up my freedom, yes of course."

"It's so much more than that. It's trust in the truest form. It's allowing me to be the man I am. It's accepting that I will make decisions based on what I know you need."

"How do you know what I need?" It wasn't an argument. She wanted badly to give herself to me, I just had to convince her that it would be the best decision she could make.

"I know you very well already, Nikki. I know you're legally of age, I know that you're single, which gives me the opportunity to have you when I want. I know there was an immediate attraction on both our parts. You live close, so I won't have to miss seeing you as often as I am going to want to see you. I know what you dream of being and I will do everything I can to help you achieve that goal. I know you're on the pill and you are STD-free and you know I get tested and don't make it a habit to have unprotected sex. I know some of your limits and you know I want to test them. When you trust me more, I know you'll without a doubt trust that whatever I choose to do to your body will not just be for my benefit. I know you value family, which if you didn't, would be a deal breaker for me. I'll never do anything to you that will hurt you and I know you trust that. I know I was with you when you experienced your best sexual experience, and I can promise it'll only get better. I assume you've never been spanked in a sexual way, but I promise you, you'd understand why it's necessary and you'd do what I need to avoid it. I know you're more turned on by anticipation than of what comes after a session, or experience. I also promise I'll make sure you crave that, too. I know you're not completely comfortable naked, and I can assure you, I will want you that way all the damn time. I know you were turned on when I was stroking myself in front of you, which gives me high hopes that someday soon you'll show me how you get yourself off."

"I don't."

"You will when I ask you to." I continued, not wanting to deviate from my expectations, or what her's should be. "I know you're intelligent enough to communicate your needs when you accept that what you want may not be vanilla. Until then, I will expect outbursts like the one in the bathroom."

"Outburst?" She snapped.

"Based on not trusting me to know what you need."

She held her own, still stubborn and defiant, even if underneath all that bravado, she knew I was right.

"The bath did make me feel better," she conceded.

"I also know your support system is pretty far away, so I'll make sure punishment is given at a minimum because I will be the one to supporting you. The one you talk it through with after if you're confused."

"So you think I am sexually twisted?"

"I think you're afraid I am, and that I will make you become something you aren't. But I see it in you. You have a very naturally submissive personality."

"You think I'm weak?"

"On the contrary, I think you are strong enough to be what I want. What I desire. Erotic sex isn't twisted, Nikki. It's unreserved and more intimate than you can even imagine. It builds a closeness that cannot easily be broken. And it's what I want with you."

"I don't know." Her body language said otherwise, and I had to smile.

"All I ask is that you give it a chance."

"And then what? If I don't like it, then what?"

"You will. You already do."

She stood quietly for a while. "So that's what I tell my parents? I'm your sub?"

My smiled widened. "Pack a bag."

***

"I don't know if this is a good idea," she said, stopping on the staircase.

"I know, let's see if we can change your mind." I grabbed her hand and walked down the two flights of stairs to the garage and grabbed two helmets off the shelf.

"Oh, I don't think *that's* a good idea."

"Again, let's see if we can change your mind."

I pulled the ponytail out of her sexy black hair and she rolled her eyes playfully.

"See, I got you." I grabbed my leather jacket and held it out, "Arms in."

I stood back and looked her up and down. After I took my time checking out her fine figure, I grabbed the helmet and pulled it over her head and buckled her up.

"Lookin' fine, Miss Bassett."

She gave me a thumbs up and I pointed to the muffler, "This is hot. Don't let your leg touch it."

"Anything else?" her muffled voice came through the shield.

I lifted it and kissed her nose. "Just hang on tight."

She nodded and gave me a big fake-as-fuck grin.

I hopped on and she hopped on behind me. "Hold tighter and don't let go."

We were headed to the shore. I hadn't been to my favorite spot since Jase and Carly got married.

The faster I went, the tighter she held on, so I went faster.

We parked behind Forever Steel, the tattoo shop Jase and his family owned and operated.

Nikki got off the bike and I followed. I took off my helmet and watched as she fumbled with her buckle. It was cute as hell watching her fight that buckle and funny when she put her hands on her hips and tapped her foot.

I unbuckled it for her, thoroughly amused.

"It's really not that funny."

"It was cute as hell, Four. Just like your hair that's sticking up all over the place."

She immediately combed her fingers through it, pulled the hair tie off her wrist, and threw her hair in a ponytail. I must have stared a little too long because she looked at me and asked, "Is it a mess?"

"No." It was sexy as hell.

"Then what?"

"You sure you wanna know?"

"Yes."

"I'm picturing you bent over with my hand wrapped around your ponytail and--"

"Okay, maybe I don't want to know." She looked down.

"Like hell you don't, your cheeks just flushed."

"That's called embarrassed."

"That's only because it's intriguing to you and you're embarrassed because you want to know what it would be like." I grabbed her hand and walked toward the Snack Shack across the road.

I knocked on the back door and Ruthy opened it, "Abe, where have you been?"

"Busy taking over the world. You have any of those breakfast wraps ready? I'd love a few of them."

"You never could wait, had to grab and go so you could be the first in the water." She laughed as she walked back in.

I grabbed some cash out of my pocket and Ruthy stepped out and handed me a bag. I gave her a kiss on the cheek and shoved some bills in her hand. "Thanks, you're a doll."

"Don't be a stranger," she yelled from behind me.

"She seems nice."

"She's great. Wait until you taste these burritos, best breakfast ever." I pointed to a picnic table, "Have a seat."

I handed her one of the foil-wrapped burritos and leaned back against the table looking out over the Atlantic.

"We're having a sort of picnic on the beach, Nikki."

"That we are." She offered a weak smile.

"I don't have time to teach you to surf, but I would love the chance. So what do you say? Knowing everything you do, would you trust me enough to allow me to teach you to surf?"

She smiled, "You brought me here to ask me if you could teach me to surf?"

"Yeah, something like that."

I reached over and rubbed her cheek with the back of my hand and she pushed gently against it.

"Come on, I'm waiting. And very impatiently, I might add."

"Yes, you can teach me to surf when we get back."

"When we get back, huh?"

"Yeah."

"So, how will you introduce me?"

"My surf instructor."

I laughed, "Oh yeah?"

"Yes. One who wants to pull my hair and spank me."

I looked over at her and she laughed.

"What are we doing here?"

"You're giving in."

"I think I am."

I reached over and pulled her to me.

"So aside from no surf board or lesson being given, do you remember how my perfect date ends?"

"I do."

"Good. We have two hours before the plane takes off."

"The plane?" she asked as I pulled her up.

"Yes, the one to Georgia." I pulled her up tight against me and ran my hand right down to that ass.

"We're in public."

"We fucked on a beach."

"A private beach."

"Semi-private."

She closed her eyes and laid her forehead against my chest.

"You okay?"

"Yeah. I just." She stopped and looked up. "I don't want to be spanked."

I tried not to laugh, but failed, "Now that I'm your—surf instructor. There will be times when it's just plain old sex."

"I'd love to see what your idea of plain old sex is."

"I may bore you."

"I highly doubt that."

"If you don't stop talking I'm going to end up either coming right here or bending you over the table."

"Take me to bed."

"Fuck."

My Instructor

I sat on the back of his bike holding tightly around his waist. He was driving faster than he had driven on the way to the shore. It was interesting that someone who was all about control seemed not to have any right now.

He pulled up to the gate and punched in four fours. I took a deep breath and climbed off the back of the bike when he had killed the engine. I tried to unbuckle again and had the same exact results as I did at the beach. He didn't wait this time though, he unbuckled and removed the helmet and then pushed his jacket off my shoulders so it hung low. I tried to shrug it off, he shook his head no, and then his lips collided with mine.

The warmth of his mouth and the possessive way he kissed me made my head spin. Lips over mine, tongue rubbing slowly across my lower lip until I opened my mouth to him. His tongue slid into my mouth. Bravely, I gave him my tongue hoping it wouldn't upset him to be so assertive. He began sucking it, drawing it into his mouth. My nipples hardened immediately.

I moaned and he groaned and our pleasure's noises did an erotic slow dance. I squirmed out of his jacket and reached up for his hair and tangled my fingers in the silky softness of it. I may have pulled a little too hard and he groaned again.

His hand rose up under the hem of my tank top and then ran slowly up my back. Goosebumps trailed behind his fingertips and then settled just under the back of my bra. I wondered why he stopped, and then he sucked hard on my lip as he pulled away.

"Nikki, I don't want to be just your surf instructor or the subject of an interview."

"No?" I all but panted.

"I want to be your teacher in everything you'll experience from here on out and I want you to be my girl."

"Yes," I pushed my painfully erect nipples against him.

"Right now I want you naked," he unclasped my bra with one hand. "And after that I want to be so fucking deep inside you that you can't think of anything else but trying to catch your breath."

"You're a naughty man, Abe O'Donnell," I tried to sound as sexy as he made me feel, and I'm sure I failed miserably, but he kissed me hard, pulled my shirt over my head before pulling my bra and shorts off.

Abe ran a finger over my lace panties, "And you are so fucking wet. Why is that?"

I bit my lip, not wanting to answer, "If I tell you, that'll make me just as bad."

I looked down as he knelt before me, "You are going to love being a bad girl, Nikki. You're going to love what I will give you."

His mouth covered my panties and he sucked. "I love your taste, but not now. We'll save that for later. I want you to come all over my cock. Would you like that, Nikki?"

His kisses trailed up my body until he came to my breast. He licked my nipple lightly and I arched my back wanting more, "Yes. Yes."

"I won't make it up the stairs to my bed. I need inside now."

"Please."

"All I get is one word? Tell me what you want."

"You."

"Only me."

"Only you."

He sucked hard on my breast and then moved to the other. "Your tits are beautiful. I can't wait to fuck them."

I didn't say anything. I didn't know what to say.

He dropped his pants and I reached down to touch him.

"Damn, Nikki, not ... " he stopped when I stroked him. "Fuck. I need you."

He lifted me up, squeezing my butt hard. "Legs around me. Good girl. I can't go easy right now, it's gonna feel good though, I promise."

Before I had a chance to speak he rubbed his beautiful cock against my opening and then pulled me down hard onto him.

"Ouch, ouch, ouch." He didn't stop. He hammered into me and my back hit the brick wall of the garage.

He was right; it quickly began to feel amazing. He thrust deeper, then he stilled, and rolled his hips stretching me to a limit I only knew possible because he had been here before. I gripped him, holding on tightly as his sculpted body pinned me to the wall.

"You feel so fucking good. Better than I remember." He kissed my neck hard, and I was sure he'd bruised the skin.

He lowered one of my legs to the ground, held the other around his waist forcing him to thrust more downward and hitting my burning clit pushing me faster to the point of no return.

"Come for me, girl." He thrust deeper.

His rough, sexy, commanding voice sent sparks throughout my body. "Oh God!"

"That's right," he hit the spot deeper inside and another orgasm swallowed the first.

My leg gave out and he pulled me up again forcing himself even deeper.

"Oh, yes."

He growled into my neck as he held me and carried me up the stairs.

"You're little pussy is choking my cock, Nikki. It's begging to swallow my cum. I don't wanna stop yet."

"I don't want you to."

He smiled as he sat down hard on his couch. "Feet flat on each side of me. Don't disconnect us or there will be hell to pay."

My eyes widened.

"It was a joke, Ni--"

I lifted up and then allowed my body to fall onto his.

"Fuck!"

The way he looked at me made me feel like this one time I had pleased him.

"You liked that."

"Hell yes, I liked that."

I did it again, but this time I rolled my hips and his head fell back slightly.

"Nikki, you ever drive stick?" He hissed.

"Yes."

"Then drive it, baby, no more stalling out. You wanna drive, you fucking drive."

"I can?"

"Let's find out. Fuck me, Nikki, take what you want."

I rocked forward and he groaned, "Like that?"

"Just like that," his jaw clenched as he looked down at where we connected. "F-u-c-k."

He reached between us and rubbed my clit.

"Oh god," I moaned. I rested my head against his shoulder and continued rotating my hips.

I was lost in sensation and desire, I continued grinding into and against him. I felt his hand wrap around my ponytail and he yanked it back so that I looked up at him again.

I moaned and his eyes bore into mine. "You still with me, Four?"

"Yes, oh yes."

"Good fucking thing," he hissed. "Eyes stay on me so I know where you are."

"Here, I am so here."

He released my hair and gripped my hips firmly, "Hang on, girl."

He pushed into me hard as his hands took charge of my hip movements. His hot gaze entrapped my eyes.

"I'm gonna come so fucking hard inside you."

"I'm there, oh god."

He twitched inside me and his hot liquid filled me so full that it seeped out as I came down from my orgasm.

"Damn," he was trying to catch his breath.

"Damn," I sat up and looked at him. "Am I a good driver?"

"You're a damn good driver."

"Even though you brought it home?" I asked as I played with his hair.

"It was a relay race. We did it together."

"I think we're leaking oil."

He laughed out loud and so did I.

He stood up with me in his arms, "Shower, plane, meet the parents, and then baseball."

"Baseball?" I asked as he took the stairs to the bathroom.

"Thursday night, bar league. Fuck, look at your tits bounce."

"Abe," I gasped.

"They're fucking beautiful."

"You're beautiful."

He stopped dead in his tracks and looked at me with a very alluring smile. "That was very nice."

"I'm a very nice girl."

"Except that one time."

"What?" I laughed.

"That one time when you took off."

"Yeah, you scared me."

"I know I'm a scary looking dude."

"Ha ha."

"What?"

"Do you know most serial killers are charming?"

His jaw dropped, then he walked over, set me in an empty tub, and walked into the shower.

I got out and followed him in.

"Are you pouting?"

"Me? No, not me." He turned his back to me.

"You have a great bottom."

"I know."

"You know?"

He turned around, grabbed my boobs, and pushed them up. "Your man is very smart."

"And modest."

He smiled, "Of course. Now as great as my bottom is and as much as I can't wait until my dick is between these tits." He bent down and rubbed both thumbs across my nipples, "We have to be at the airfield in an hour."

"We could go one more time."

"I like the way you think, Four."

"Seven."

"Seven and all mine?"

"Make it eight?"

"Later."

***

By the time the plane touched down, we had hit ten and I was exhausted.

"You ready for this?"

"I'm good, are you?" He rubbed my back as we walked down the tarmac to the waiting rental car.

He opened the door for me and then got in the driver's seat. After we got onto the highway, he reached for my hand. He held it as he rubbed his thumb in soft slow strokes over my knuckle.

"Tell me what you're thinking?"

"Nothing, really."

"Nikki, talk to me. This works better if we're open and honest with each other."

"It's going to be very difficult to tell them about that, that--"

"I know," he kissed my hand.

"And I really hope they like you."

"Yeah?"

"Yes."

"Good."

I decided not to tell my parents I was coming home; I didn't want to worry them. They would find it odd if I just dropped in mid-week and of course they would be suspicious of why their normally predictable daughter was being not so predictable.

I was always pushed to step outside of my comfort zone as a child and continuously as a young adult. I was the girl who didn't complain about my parents because there was nothing to complain about. They were great, constantly supportive, and encouraging. I rarely spent nights at friend's homes as everyone always wanted to come to mine. There was always laughter, music, an adult with a tender heart and caring words when anyone was going through rough times and needed to get good advice or just needed an ear.

As we neared my home, I looked over at Abe who was tapping his thumb nervously on the steering wheel and looking over at me every so often.

"You're making me more anxious," I sort of joked.

"I apologize."

"You're nervous?"

"A bit, yes."

"Why?"

"I hope they like me."

"Do parents normally like you?"

"I haven't met very many."

"How many is very many?"

"Well my best friend's mother loves me, but she has to, she's kind of been a surrogate. My parents like me," he winked.

"That's always a good thing."

"It is." He smiled as we passed the *Welcome to Thomasville* sign.

"How about girls you've dated?"

"One girl's parents, and they liked me enough I guess."

We remained quiet for a while.

"Abe?"

"Nikki?"

"Thank you."

"For?"

"You've been wonderful."

We pulled into the driveway and Abe smiled, "This is it?"

"Yep."

"Are they home?"

"I see Mom's car. Dad's isn't here."

He drove up the driveway smiling. "Holy shit, Nikki, this is beautiful."

"What did you expect?"

"Not this. Something nice, but this is insane."

"It's home."

He looked at me expressionless for a moment, then leaned towards me and kissed me, "You ready to do this?"

"I suppose."

RHETT'S PLACE

What a beautiful property. The long driveway was lined with trees and Spanish moss was hanging down like a canopy over the driveway. A spectacular vision. After parking, I stepped out of the rental and looked at the Southern plantation home. It had been beautifully cared for, so I wouldn't even dare guess the home's age. I felt like I stepped into a scene from *Gone with the Wind*. I walked around to the front of the car to get the door for my girl.

When she stepped out, she inhaled the fragrant air. I looked around and noticed all the trees that were covered in flowers.

"The Dogwood trees. I love the smell."

I inhaled and smiled, "Smells a lot like you."

"You think?"

"I do."

"Sugarplum, is that you?" I looked up at a woman on the porch smiling from ear to ear and waving.

"Who else would it be, Gran?" Nikki was just about jumping out of her skin, so I let go of her. She ran up the driveway, onto the porch and hugged her Grandmother.

I was relieved that she seemed happy and not stressed like she was from the moment we got off the plane. The plane. Hot as fuck. I am officially a member of the mile high club. She is fucking perfect, and I am officially pussy whipped.

I grabbed our bags from the back of the rental and we started for the porch.

She stopped hugging her Grandma, looked at me and smiled.

"Gran, this is Abe O'Donnell. Abe, this is my Gran, Ivy."

I walked up the stairs and set the bags down, "I see where Nikki gets her stunning looks."

Ivy looked me over with a smile, but her eyes said something else. "Abe, you are very kind." She turned her attention back to her granddaughter. "What brings you home, and with a friend, Nikki?"

"Maybe I just missed y'all."

That was the first time I had heard her say y'all, and I liked it. Sweet, beautiful, southern accent was hot on Nikki, almost as hot as I was on her.

"Mmm hmm," her Grandmother shook her head back and forth. "I'll get the truth out of you with sweet tea and corn bread."

"Can we wait until Dad's home?"

"He's here, sugar. Car's in the shop."

I couldn't tell if Nikki was relieved, disappointed, or terrified. There was no stopping the truth now. I took her hand in mine and offered her the most supportive smile I could.

"Boyfriend, huh?"

"Guilty," I smiled and nodded.

"You ready for the inquisition?" Ivy sighed as she opened the screen door, not waiting for my response.

"Sure thing." I pulled Nikki in under my arm and kissed the top of her head. "I got you."

Nikki tensed up. "Gonna be an interesting night, sugar plum." Ivy disappeared into the expansive home.

We followed her inside where it was just as traditional as it was on the outside. She and Nikki removed their shoes and I followed suit. I heard laughter from beyond the wall to the left. I hope it helped ease her angst knowing that they are in a good mood.

Despite it, I felt myself tense. I don't know the players, haven't even read their bios like I would have before meeting potential business associates or employees. Nope. Meeting the parents was a little out of my comfort zone.

We entered the family room where her parents sat watching old family videos of a birthday party. Nikki must have been about ten. Her hair was in little poufy pom pom pigtails on the side, and she wore a *birthday girl* tiara. She was absolutely beautiful, even then, as she sang with her friends. I was almost certain three of the five of them were the same girls I'd met in Ft. Lauderdale.

"Mom, Dad, I'm home."

Both her parents jumped up when they heard her. They came around the sofa to embrace her. It seemed as if they didn't even notice me. It was damn cool. You could feel and see the love these people shared for one another. I remember when things were like that in my family. Nothing better.

"What are you doing home?" her mother asked, looking in my direction.

Her mother was drop-dead gorgeous. Her skin was darker than Nikki's and she wasn't quite as tall, but she had the same round deep-set eyes. Her cheeks too, high cheek bones with round cheeks. And her lips were full, the lower one a bit more full, just like Nikki's.

"Mom, Dad this is Abe O'Donnell, my boyfriend." She said it quietly as if she was asking permission, which didn't feel all that good to me.

Her father was tall and lean. Not thin, but not big either. He looked like a bicyclist. He had blond thinning hair and pale blue eyes.

"Oh?" her mom seemed shocked.

I stepped forward, extended my hand, and smiled, "Very nice to meet you, Mrs. Bassett."

She stared at me and shook my hand.

"Hello, Mr. Bassett, you have a truly beautiful home." I extended my hand to him as well.

"Thank you, Abe?"

"Yes, sir."

I glanced quickly over at Nikki, who looked amused.

"What?" I asked.

"Nothing at all," she giggled.

"Did you drive all the way here without letting us know you were on the road?"

Okay, that didn't feel good either. "We flew and I can assure you she was in good hands."

Her grandmother giggled and everyone looked at her. "Lord knows they look capable."

"How? Did you have enough money?"

"Mom, Dad, we need to talk."

They both immediately looked at me, and what comes out of me, Abe O'Donnell CFO of a billion dollar company's mouth? "She's not pregnant."

Nikki gasped, her parents' mouths dropped open, and her grandmother started laughing.

"Fuck," came out of my mouth instead of staying in my head. I sounded like Carly. I shit you not, I have no idea what had come over me, but I was fucking this up hardcore. I looked at a mortified Nikki, "Sorry."

"Nikolette, we need to talk," her father glared at her.

"I apologize."

"Abe, it's okay. Mom, Dad, please just sit down."

Her parents sure as fuck didn't wanna sit, but when they did, I sat with my head down avoiding eye contact at all costs. Nikki sat on the sofa next to me and I took her hand. She was turning pink. I wasn't gonna ride bitch here and I wasn't gonna have her keep thinking she did something wrong.

"I got this," I whispered and kissed her hand.

I looked up at two sets of extremely annoyed eyes and one slightly amused set. "Nikki has been through a pretty rough couple of days. She wanted to let you know because it may come out, and we wouldn't want you to be caught off guard."

"Nikolette, you can tell us anything, you know that," her father was peacocking, and I knew how he felt. He had been her protector at one point, but there was a new kid in town, me.

"For a few weeks," I interrupted, "The electricity in her apartment would randomly go out. I had someone look into it because her landlord wasn't handling the problem, and--"

"You did?" Nikki asked.

"I told you I take care of what is mine."

"Nikolette, a minute please." Her mother stood.

"As I was saying. I had someone look into it, and we suspected it was being tampered with. Nikki's landlord had taught her how to flip the switch on the breaker box, thinking something was shorting it out. Last night while I was at her place ... " I stopped and looked into her eyes, "You good?"

And she just blurted out, "There may be a sex tape that will surface that stars me."

Holy fuck! She did not just say that.

"What she means--" I began.

"Nikolette! As your mother and I have both said, we would like a minute alone with you."

"We do this together," I insisted.

"This is none of your--" Her father interupted.

"She is *my* concern."

"Abe, you don't--" Nikki began.

"How long have you known this man, Nikolette? This isn't like you, not at all."

"I met him in Florida."

Her mom's jaw dropped, "The creepy neighbor?"

Now I was shocked. I looked at her trying to get a read on whether or not they were talking about me. Sure as fuck they were. *Redirect, O'Donnell, you can table that shit for when you're alone with her.*

"Her neighbor, in Jersey," I felt I needed to clarify, "Drilled a fucking hole in her goddamned wall. She didn't do a damn thing wrong."

"I think it's time for you to leave," her father stepped towards me.

"That's fine, when you calm down and realize your daughter was a victim here, then you give us a call." I stood and pulled her hand to help her up, but she didn't move. "Nikki?"

"Just let me talk to them for a minute, alone."

"I told you I would take care of this."

"Nikolette, now," her parents exited the room and she let go of my hand. It was like a punch to the gut.

"Nikki, we just leapt a mile you're about to set us right back to square one."

"They're my parents, Abe," she closed her eyes.

"That's fine. I'm out."

I didn't look back. I just walked out past her parents and then out the door.

Fuck! Fuck! Fuck!

I walked to the rental and realized I'd left my bag in the house. I turned and her grandmother was standing there with it in her hand.

"You seem like a nice man."

"Not sure if I would agree with you. I think as far as first impressions go, I just royally –messed up."

"Nikolette is very close to her family." She reached out and handed me the bag.

"I respect that, admire it actually."

"So you should understand that she needs them right now and they need to make sure she's alright too."

"I made sure she was alright. I made damn sure she was alright." I looked up into disapproving eyes, "I'm sorry, I meant no disrespect."

"I'm sure you didn't. Nikolette is a very special young lady."

"I am well aware of that."

"I know you are. You need to give her time, they were here first."

Even though she was right, it didn't change how I felt.

"Two days, Abe." Her smile was gentler now. "Give her two days."

I looked past her hoping to see Nikki coming out the door with her bag, ready to go back to the shore. But when she didn't, I turned and walked away because if I didn't, I was gonna go fucking crazy.

I sat in the rental and sent her a text.

Abe: I'll get a room in town, message me when you're ready, I'll pick you up.

Less than a minute later, I got a response:

Nikki: I need a couple days. Go back. We'll talk later.

"Fuck!" I yelled and looked up to the porch where her grandma was standing shaking her head back and forth.

***

Two days I sat at my desk pissed that I had still heard nothing from her. It was noon, I was done returning emails and going over Dom's proposals for the takeover. I decided to head over and see Mom, it had been awhile, then hop over to Pop's and toss back a few before the big game.

I sent a message telling Jase to make sure everyone was at the field by five so we could toss around a few balls. Seemed fitting since I felt like my balls had been tossed, beaten with a Louisville slugger, and driven over by a fucking Mack truck. I'd taken Nikki home to face her parents and she basically told me to go fuck myself.

I hopped on my bike, threw on my helmet, and headed to my place to change clothes and rides.

I pulled up in front of the rehab center feeling the same way as I always did, sick to my stomach and like I was walking into her funeral. She had stopped recognizing me a year after the diagnosis, she had stopped looking at me like she knew she loved me six months later.

She was propped up in her chair when I arrived to put fresh flowers in the vase on her bedside table.

"Hey, Mom," I bent down and kissed her cheek. "You look beautiful. It's Abe, your son."

I sat in the chair next to her and took her hand. It was balled into a fist and harder to open than it had been before. A sick part of me always wondered if one day I would end up breaking a damn finger when I pried her hands open. And then I wondered if she'd even feel it if I did.

Her hair was completely white now and she looked hollow. Her eyes didn't sparkle anymore, hell, they weren't even blue.

They were grey and black. I hated seeing her like this. Every time I left, I swore it would be the last time I would do this to me or to her. I wondered if she was trapped inside, down deep inside trying to fight her way back. I wondered if when I was saying goodbye to my Mom, not this shell of a woman whose hand I held now, was crying inside and if it hurt her like it did me.

"It's a beautiful sunny day outside. I wish I could take you to the boardwalk to feed those damn birds you love so much. We wouldn't tell Dad. He'd of course be annoyed, tell us someday they were gonna shit on our heads, and we'd never feed them again." I pulled my chair in front of her so that she was staring at me and not the wall. "So I met a girl, her name is Nikki. I like her, but she's trouble. Not trouble like Jase and the boys, but trouble as in she'd break my heart if I gave it to her. She's a knockout, Mom. I would have loved you to meet her, but well, I'm not even sure I'll see her again. I've changed a lot, Mom. I need things to go just so, you know what I mean? My house, which I would love you to see but of course you won't because I'm not even sure you're in there anymore, is beautiful. An old warehouse that I help refurbish. I really wish I could get some advice here. Mom, would you just wake up for a few minutes? I need you to tell me what the hell I'm doing wrong. Please just wake up. Wake up, Mom. No? You know, it's your fault I'm the way I am. You made everything perfect, right down to ironing my damn boxers. You did everything he asked and acted like it was what you wanted."

I don't know what I expected her to say or do. Squeeze my fucking hand or anything to let me know she'd heard me, that she was still there. But why the fuck would she? I was being a fucking prick. I sat forward and rubbed her hand on my cheek then kissed it.

"Sorry, Mom. I really am. I just miss you, that's all."

I grabbed a book off her nightstand, the one I had given her a month ago. I suppose I should read some more, because if she was still in there, she'd want me to read to her like she read to me every night for ten fucking years.

"*The Four Loves*," I laughed when I read the title, four, "by C.S Lewis. Chapter three."

After reading four chapters, I set the book down and gave her a kiss, "Love you, Mom. I promise I'll be back soon."

I drove out of the rehab parking lot feeling even shittier than I did when I first got there. I had an hour before I needed to meet the guys. I drove over to the Pub and parked. I grabbed my phone and saw a new email from The Shore.

Subject: *Interview*

On behalf of The Shore, I would like to personally thank you for taking time out of your busy schedule to allow Miss Bassett to conduct this interview. We have just received it, and per our agreement, I will personally review it before sending it for your approval.

Bogart Humph, Editor, The Shore

I read it three times after thumbing through my email trying to see where she had sent it to me first like we had agreed upon. She hadn't.

Only one of three things would calm me, actually a combination of any of the three. Number one, drink whiskey. Jamison's Irish whiskey to be exact. Three shots and a chaser. Number two, fucking someone hard with every tool in my arsenal. Number three, spanking the ass of the one who got the anger brewing inside in the first place.

Instead, I headed into the pub.

"There's my boy," Pop's voice boomed through the air.

"You back where you should be, Abe? Ready to take over and let your old man retire?"

"Sal, you look like shit," I said before walking behind the bar.

"Abe," my pops gasped.

"You trying to shut me up, boy?" He hacked.

"Yep." Un-fucking real. Every time I walked in here it was the same thing.

I grabbed the bottle of whiskey and lined up three shots.

"Big spender gonna share the wealth instead of letting your Pops bust his ass?"

"Go fuck yourself, Sal."

"Abe!"

"Let him go, Shawn, at least he's not blowing smoke today." Sal chuckled.

"Uniforms in, Pops?"

"In the back. They came a few hours ago."

"Gone are the good old days where you just wore shorts and a tee shirt, huh, boy?"

"Yeah sure." I was not in the mood for his shit. I grabbed a beer and popped it open.

"You should stick to what works son. O'Donnell's Pub is a landmark and so were those ball shirts. This place has been here for seventy-five years. Never had fancy uniforms."

Not listening to this shit. I grabbed another beer and walked out back.

Fuck him.

Once Again

I deboarded the plane nervous, about the choice I had made. But I promised my parents I would be strong, like I was raised to be. I finished the article on Abe O'Donnell yesterday. I hoped it wouldn't give away everything about him, but I had decided to write the truth of what I saw Abe wanting in a relationship.

My parents also made me promise to reconsider looking for another internship and they wanted me to finish my senior year back in school. The truth was, I didn't want to go back and face seeing Sally and Steve. I guess I should be thanking them both for betraying me. If they hadn't I wouldn't be here now.

I got a cab and went straight to The Shore to make sure everything was going well with my article. I also wanted to see what they would give me as my next assignment.

"Look who's here, the girl who got the inside scoop on the ever so elusive Abe O'Donnell, and to my surprise you threw in some of the Steel men, too. Do you think they'll go for it?"

"I hope so. Which, brings me to why I am here. My next story, what is it?"

"Patience, young one." God, that man made my skin crawl. "I will email back the edits and any suggestions I have and then we'll send it back to O'Donnell. If things go smoothly I will see what strings I can pull at the Meadowlands."

"Giants or Jets?"

"Whatever we can get a wannabe female sports reporter in on. Beggars can't be choosers. We do need some exclusive photos, though. I know what a controlling prick he can be, so even just a few cell pics would work."

"He's really not all that bad."

"Then it should be a piece of cake."

I walked out of The Shore and looked at my watch. It was Thursday at 5:00.

The cab pulled up to take me home.

***

I parked in front of the community baseball field at six. There were four different fields and eight different teams. One team stood out, I mean really stood out. White baseball pants, green baseball jerseys, and white hats. If there had been an award for best-dressed team, they would have won it.

I liked the way Abe dressed, really liked it. Suits on some men were sexy in their own right. It just gave an air of confidence. Men who wore suits to me had always been hot. But in Abe's case, the suit wore him. The sleeves were a perfect length allowing the shirts cuffs and his cuff links to be seen. The few times I had seen him in a suit it was either black or dark gray. Without a doubt tailored and cut to fit across his broad shoulders with gentle lines around his trim waist giving the appearance of a perfect V. Which reminded me of how amazing his body was under that suit. Dear God, I was getting a bit moist.

Abe in jeans was just as hot. They always rested on his hips. Not too baggy, but not those awful skinny jeans that some men wore. To me, skinny jeans should be reserved for rock stars and my gay male friends who were a bit showy. I'm sure Abe O'Donnell didn't even own a pair.

Abe in board shorts, dear merciful God above, that was the sexiest sight to ever behold. The ink on his side and hip. The V that led to what I am sure is the most beautiful, pleasure- giving piece of male parts on the planet.

What I loved most about Abe O'Donnell, was his arms. They were strong and very well formed. They had carried me to the beach house in Florida, held me up against the wall, carried me up the stairs of his home, held me all night when I was scared and needed to feel safe. Arms that for two days I missed just as much as I missed my family when I was away from them, maybe even more. This revelation both scared and excited me at the same time. I loved Abe's arms.

It had only been three weeks, an insane three weeks might I add, since I saw Abe walk out of the ocean and turn my life upside down. Falling for him at that moment was a first for me. It scared the shit out of me, completely irrational, even as I explained it to my parents for the past two days it seemed unreal. And for the first time, we argued, distance growing between us over a man I hardly knew.

I decided to take some photos. Watching Abe wind up and throw a pitch was a whole new level of sexy. Cyrus Steel was catching, Jase was playing first, Zandor playing third, Xavier was shortstop, the man who looked very much like the electrician at my apartment house was playing second, and the outfield was made up of men who were heavily tattooed.

I sat on the hood of my car taking pictures. Abe struck out the first two men before the third batter hit one to center. The outfielders scrambled and my heart began pumping. Have I mentioned how much I loved watching sports? It was exhilarating. I will be the first to admit that I wasn't gifted athletically, I was more a thinker, a reader, and a writer. I ran track in school, didn't break any records, but enjoyed it. I loved watching though, and right now, I can honestly say baseball was my favorite.

When the inning was over, I watched Abe stretch, bat in hand above his head, and then behind his back. He turned, and let me just tell you, the ass was god-like, but the package in the front was just as glorious. I took more pictures. Holy hell.

He took his sunglasses off and stared in my direction. I watched his eyes narrow and his jaw muscles twitch, he was pissed and even that was sexy so I took a picture of that, too.

I set the camera on my lap and waved.

He started walking toward me and Jase grabbed his arm and held up five fingers. I was pretty sure he mouthed, *No shit,* and then resumed his long, angry strides towards me. I have no idea why, but it made me smile, which seemed to piss him off even more.

He stopped dead in his tracks about two feet from me, and his hands fisted into balls at his sides. He didn't say a word.

"Hi," I slid down the hood of my car and sat my bag on it. I turned and took a step toward him.

"What the hell are you doing?"

"I missed you." I reached out and took his fisted hand.

"You can't fucking call, return a text, and you turned in the goddamn story without consulting me first?" he hissed.

"Besides all that what have you been up to?"

"What the fuck do you think I've been up to?"

"Brooding."

"Brooding?"

"It means acting all angry and dark. Being intimidating and—"

"I know what it means, Miss Bassett." He hissed.

I took a step closer so that I was standing against him, "Nikki."

He tensed up even more. I put my hands on his hips and held onto him. "I missed you," I repeated.

"You should leave," he looked up and away from me.

"Abe," I reached up and held both hands behind his neck.

"I've been drinking." He still wouldn't look at me. "And I am beyond pissed at you. That means you should leave."

"Is that what you really want?"

"I want to blister your ass right now. That's what I really fucking want."

I heard a familiar laugh from behind me, "Well, look at you two."

I turned to see Carly, the other three wives, and a little dark haired beauty.

"Uncle Abe has a girlfriend?" She smiled.

I let go and stepped back waiting to see how he'd answer.

"Little Bell," he smiled and his entire demeanor changed. He picked her up and threw her on his back. "Let's go play some ball. We need a water girl. Nikki was just leaving."

He glanced at me and glared.

"No, she's actually gonna sit with us, aren't you, Nikki?" Carly took my hand.

He started jogging away and left me standing with the women.

"I should get going."

"Like hell you should, my cousin likes you." Carly tugged my hand.

"He's mad and I understand."

"Why is he mad?" She asked.

I didn't know how to answer.

Tara chimed in, "It's how they all get. When they feel an interruption or loss of a control they act like asses."

I looked up and Cyrus was behind her.

"Is that so?" He asked in the same pissy tone Abe had used with me.

She turned around. "It is and you know it."

Seeing her poke him in the chest was almost comical. He was a very big man, as were his brothers, but he was much broader.

"Gotta tame that ass," she giggled.

"Since when have you wanted my ass tamed, Birdie?" He asked, trying not to smile.

"About the same time I realized I knew I wanted you to tame mine."

"You're confusing two words," he winked at her.

"Oh yeah, and what are they?"

"Claim is not the same as tame."

He grabbed her by the hips and lifted her up so she was eye level to him. "Did you have a good day, Mrs. Steel?" He kissed her.

"Good day, yes. But this is what makes it a great day."

Oh my God, could they get any more adorable? I grabbed my camera and took a picture.

"Hey now," he set her down. "Personal use only."

"I'll make sure you get a copy, Mr. Steel." I shouldn't have done that.

Xavier was now at Taelyn's side, "Any fucked up cravings I missed?"

The way she smiled at him and the way his eyebrow shot up, there was no doubt there was double meaning behind their exchange. She laughed. "It's passed though."

"It better come back real fucking soon," he grabbed her ass, pulled her into his side, and they walked toward the field.

"You win the game, we'll talk," I heard her say as she smacked his butt.

"Here, kitty kitty," I looked left and saw Zandor Steel walking towards Bekah.

She laughed and ran up to him. He lifted her and went right for her neck. I swear he bit her and I swear she liked it. It immediately made me think about Abe and his sexual desires, which immediately made me want him even more. I saw Carly making a *shoo* motion to her husband as he was walking over. He stopped and shook his head back and forth crossing his arms over his chest. She shooed him again. Then turned to me and linked her arm in mine.

"Come on, let's go watch some baseball."

We sat on the bleachers as Carly's daughter handed out baseball caps that said *O'Donnell's Pub*.

She smiled when she handed me one. "Is your Momma dead?"

"Bell, not everyone's mom is dead." Carly laughed and pulled her onto her lap.

Carly read the look of confusion on my face. "I'm her new Momma."

"Momma Carly," Bella smiled a big toothless smile.

"Momma Carly, that's right. My mother passed away--" Carly began.

"And so did Tara's, double whammy there huh, Tara? Mom and Dad." Bella interrupted.

"Sure was." Tara wrapped her arm around her and kissed her cheek.

"That's why she needed Uncle Cyrus, he's like two people." Bella smirked.

Tara and Bella laughed. I looked at Carly.

She whispered, "It's her way of dealing and honestly it's helped both Tara and I. Odd I know."

Carly reached in her bag and retrieved two bottles of water, then handed Bella one before drinking about half of the other. "You want one? Help yourself. Bending over has become a chore."

Zandor was up to bat. Jase and Xavier were on first and second. He hit a fly ball to right field and it dropped right behind the outfielder.

Bases were loaded and I decided I was going to enjoy watching the game even when I knew there were two angry, yet beautiful blue eyes boring holes into the side of my head.

"He's staring at you." Carly giggled and nudged me.

"Glowering."

"Ooo ooo ooo," Bell pointed, "Go, Uncle Cyrus! He bats fourth do you know why?"

"Clean-up hitter," I smiled at her.

"You like baseball?" she asked.

"I love baseball."

Cyrus nailed the ball, but the other team was quick and only Jase made it home. Bases were loaded again. The next two batters popped out and then Abe was up to bat. I whistled very loudly and he looked back at the bleachers.

"Let's go, O'Donnell!" Bella and I yelled.

"Strike one!" The umpire called and Abe shook his head.

He swung on the next pitch, but missed.

"What the fuck, O'Donnell? Don't leave us out here all alone. Hit that bitch." Zandor yelled.

The next pitch was a beautiful backdoor slider and he nailed it. Zandor, Xavier, and Cyrus all made it in as Abe was looking to come home. It was tight, a bit of a run-down began until Abe made it safely back to third.

I stood up, stuck two fingers in my mouth to whistle, and clapped. "Nice hit, O'Donnell!"

He looked up, then down at the bag and kicked some dirt around.

"He's ignoring you?" Jase laughed as he walked up to us.

"I like to think he's just really focused."

***

The game ended with O'Donnell winning by four, which apparently meant both teams had to go to the winning team's sponsoring bar. I watched as Abe talked to the other team, shook hands, and laughed. I also watched as the women on the other bleachers checked him out. I wasn't really the jealous type before, but after Steve, I had a few trust issues *and* Abe was angry at me. Still, I decided to let it be known that he was *mine* and to let *him* know he better be getting over two days of no phone calls or texts. I came back even knowing all of his secrets and what his intentions were with me.

I stood beside him, he glanced over, and then away. One of the other team members asked if I was with him. He didn't answer until the man continued with, "God, please tell me she's single."

"She's not single and she's a pain in the ass. Walk away while you can."

I shook my head as I looked down and grabbed my phone.

Abe took my hand and continued chatting with everyone around us. He seemed to know everyone and he was very friendly. Interestingly enough, they all liked him too. This side of Abe took some getting used to.

Played

I was fucking pissed. She had a lot of explaining to do, even if I was glad she'd come back. A. Lot. But now wasn't the time or place. I helped clean up the equipment and carried it to Jase's car.

The night had gone as planned. Thirty people were at the pub and Pops was gonna make a lot of money tonight. About damn time.

She was waiting for me at her car and I still wasn't in the mood.

"You played well." She smiled that sweet sexy smile, and I almost lost my fucking mind.

"Thanks."

"So everyone heads to the Pub now?"

"That's how it works."

She blew out a breath and looked at the ground. No doubt waiting for me to say something.

"You wanna give me a lift?"

"Yes, I would like that."

I sat in the passenger side of her car and slid the seat back. "When did you pick this up?"

"Two hours ago."

"Who went with you?"

"No one."

"What do you mean 'no one?' "

"I had my keys. I just got out of the cab, into my car, and came straight here. See? I'm fine."

"No Nikki, you're fucking lucky. Do you get that? What do you think he was gonna do to you next time? That sick fuck watched you, videotaped you. Who the fuck do you think was tampering with the electricity, Nikolette! Huh? What do you think he was gonna do when he finally got you alone in that GODDAMMED basement! He was gonna fucking hurt you. So fuck, no it's not okay that you went there." I slammed my fist into the dashboard. "I would fucking kill someone if they hurt you. You wanna see me back in jail? Keep this shit up."

She didn't say a damn word. She fucking knew better. Shit. The mere thought of that son-of-a-bitch hurting her made me want to blow.

"Two more blocks, take a left and it's on the right. O'Donnell's."

"Italian?" she tried to joke, but I wasn't in the mood for her shit.

"Yeah."

We pulled up and I got out. I looked back and she was like a little lost puppy dog. "You wanna come have a drink?"

"Yes." She got out, slammed the door, and hurried to my side.

We walked into a packed bar. It was fucking awesome.

Pops was smiling from ear-to-ear. "You won!"

"We sure did."

There was one stool left and I pulled it out for Nikki.

"Pops this is Nikki. Nikki, this is my Pops."

"What's your flavor?" he asked her.

She looked up at me and seemed to want me to answer. "We gotta go easy on her Pops, she's driving. Guinness?" I asked and she nodded. "And then tea. Two Guinness."

The bar was slammed. Dad needed help.

"I'm gonna give him a hand."

"Okay."

Two hours later and after having to empty the till three times, things finally quieted. Only about fifteen people were left.

"You ought to open up the kitchen next Thursday, Pops. You could make a killing."

"We made two weeks in one night. I don't wanna hire anyone, son. This is perfect."

"I'd help," I looked up at Nikki sipping tea and smiling.

"You cook?"

"No, but I could pour a beer and a shot. Looks like that's what they all wanted."

"Abe, who is this beautiful young woman?"

"Nikki Bassett."

"And what brings Nikki Bassett to O'Donnell's pub?"

"Well a guy, of course," she flashed him that billion dollar smile, the one that I knew was gonna do me in.

"A guy, huh?"

"Yes, but he's pretty grumpy."

"And why's that?" Pops asked.

"Control freak."

Pops laughed and looked at me, "Is she yours?"

I looked over at Nikki who was grinning. I don't know what the hell happened from the time I left Georgia until now, but she was different, something had changed.

"She is and will remain that if she learns to abide by a few simple rules."

"On that note, I will say Nikki, welcome to O'Donnell's. I will leave you both to hash this out."

I grabbed a bar mop and wiped off the bar.

"Should we start hashing?"

"Hashing?"

"It out, like your pops said."

"Hashing wouldn't be appropriate here, Nikki."

"At your place then?"

"Hashing at my place? No, I don't think so."

"Why not?"

"I don't think you deserve any hashing."

"What do I deserve?"

"Nothing until I read what you submitted without my consent. Then, Nikki, you and I might just be a thing that almost happened. I don't take kindly to some of the things you've pulled on me in the past."

"Three weeks. It's been three weeks today that you and I met."

"Three weeks isn't all that long of a time to have broken my trust at least five times."

"But three weeks is a week longer than more than twenty previous relationships, and a week longer than you normally keep someone around that you don't want around for a longer amount of time. You said so Abe, remember?"

"That may be true, Nikki, but when there isn't trust there is nothing."

I was over this conversation and needed to walk away before I got even angrier.

I was serving a couple draughts when my phone vibrated in my pocket.

Nikki: Trust me. I trust you. If there will be no hashing later maybe, we can do a little #thumpanassthursday.

I looked down at her, she looked up, held up her phone, and mouthed '*waiting*'.

Abe: Drink and anger don't mesh well with #thumpanassthursday Nikki. I need to #controlyounotbruiseyou.

She smiled and shook her head, but I would be damned if she could change my mind. She would learn her place.

Pops was looking tired and those fifteen people weren't leaving anytime soon.

"Take off, Pops, I can close up."

"No, you have that big fancy job to go to in the morning."

"I'm good. Go make your deposit and take off."

"You sure?"

"Positive."

It had been two years since I had closed up the pub. I had only done it a handful of times, but it was pretty cool to be the last one here. Just like those few times I had closed in the past, I had company. But this was a much different kind of company. It was Nikki, not the guys who would hang out with me and shoot some pool.

A few guys were talking to Nikki, and it was pissing me off. I didn't know them and they didn't know me. Another hour and

I'd be kicking them all out. Pops always said nothing good came in the door after that, not since Lipton shut down. Their second shift used to frequent the place, and he kept it opened for them. Back then Pops, had a couple people working for him. Now he didn't need it. "If a man can't work twelve hours for his family he should retire," was what he always said.

When they were getting a bit too close, I walked over, "Nikki, you wanna come back here and help me out?"

"Doesn't look that busy," one of the guys laughed.

I looked at him and Nikki stood up, "Sure thing, babe."

"Oh, you tapping that?"

"Motherfucker, you may want--"

She squeezed between me and the bar, facing them, "He is."

"Is that so?"

"You see that door, punk?"

"Punk?" He looked at his friends and laughed, "Says the bartender."

"He's not just a bartender, his name is on the damn bar."

"Nikki, my battle." I turned her around, "You all badass now?"

"If I have to be."

"That's the thing, when you're with me you don't carry that burden. That's my job and my privilege."

I heard the guys laugh and I looked up.

"Closing time."

"What, no last call?"

"You should just be happy that you're walking out of here intact."

"Oh yeah?"

"Come on, man, this guy's a douche."

I looked down at Nikki as the bar quickly emptied. She was looking up at me, her hands holding onto the bar behind her with that look in her eyes. The same damn look they always had when we were this close.

"You want me all the time. Doesn't even matter if I'm pissed or threatening you with punishment."

"Yes," her voice quivered.

"It wasn't a question, Nikki. I see it. I feel it and I swear I can smell it." She looked embarrassed for a moment. "That scent does shit to me."

"Shit?"

I took her hand and placed it on my erection. "Shit like this."

Her mouth formed an "O," but the word didn't come out. Her hand started moving up and down slowly. I had to stop her, so I took her hand in mine.

"No."

Her "Why?" was a whisper.

"Just like you are my privilege, I am yours. You are a greedy little girl, Nikki. If that's what you want, that's what I will withhold."

"I'd rather you spank me."

I sucked in my cheeks trying not to smile. "Yeah I know. That's why you won't get that either. Not until it's for pleasure and you, my beautiful little budding nymphomaniac, are on punishment."

"Pleasure from spanking?"

"You'll see. Well maybe, if you could ever behave for more than the length of time I'm inside you."

"Maybe that means you should spend more time inside me."

I turned around because I couldn't hide how badly she was turning me on.

I felt something hit my back and turned to find she'd removed her shirt. Then came the shorts.

Nikki stood there in a thong and bra. I was hard as stone. I couldn't move. She started walking toward the door. She locked it and pulled the strings turning off the florescent window signs. Then she dropped the shades.

She walked back around the bar, climbed on the stool Pops always sat on, and then onto the bar. She sat facing me as she unclasped her bra and let it drop. She caught it with her foot and then kicked it at me.

"Are you just gonna stand there or are you gonna help me out?"

"Looks like you're doing one hell of a job all by yourself, do continue."

She leaned back on the bar and spread her legs wide. Something I always encouraged and she always fought. I walked away, grabbed a rocks glass, filled it with ice, and then some Jack. I sat on my pop's stool and took a drink.

"You just gonna sit there, or you gonna show me something?"

She reached between her legs and pulled the smallest strip of fabric known to man to the side. "I shaved."

"I see that."

She ran her finger down her slit with a little less confidence than before. Confidence was sexy as hell, but a little bit of helplessness turned me on even more. That's why Nikki still sat there. That's why she was different than any other, and that was why I was sure I was falling for her.

"How wet are you?"

"Why don't you come and find out."

"Uh, uh, uh, you've got a lot of explaining to do before you get my cock again."

She raised her finger to her mouth and ran it across her lower lip. "Do I at least get a kiss?"

"As much as I would like to kiss your lips right now, I think we both know where that would lead."

"I'm counting on it."

"I'm a strong man, Nikki. Stronger than you think."

"What if I told you that I fought for us when I was gone?"

"I would hope so."

"What if I told you I told them I'm falling for you? That I'd fallen for you in Florida, but was afraid of it then. But now, I have fallen for your possessive ways, how safe yet vulnerable you make me feel, how you make me speechless. The way you say my name, whatever variation you choose, they all sound the same and I have fallen for all *four* of them. What I didn't tell them was that I had fallen for your thoughts and I burn inside when I think of what it will be like to explore them with you, all of them. How when you caress me — and not just the parts that use to be considered private that I now consider yours — I want more, I need more. I ache to have you touch my face. I want all your kisses, not just the soft ones, but the hard ones, the ones that I am sure will bruise my lips, but I don't care, I want them just the same. I didn't tell them that when I am in your arms, I feel safe, beautiful, and adored. I also didn't tell them that distance, any distance, even this two feet between us, makes me wonder if I was wrong about your feelings for me. I don't like it, not one bit."

Her eyes started tearing up and I felt like the biggest ass in Jersey.

"I told them something else, too. But if I tell you, you better promise not to say it back, it would cheapen it, so don't you dare." She looked down and blew out a breath. "What if I told my parents, and my granny, that I was sure I was in love with you?"

"Nikki," I started and she stopped me.

"Please don't say anything. Please just come over here, pick me up in those big old arms, and hold me."

So I did. *Son. Of. A. Bitch*!

I sat on the stool with her legs wrapped around me as I kissed her cheek and her lips.

"I promise the article is good. I wanted to surprise you with it, that's all. I promise."

"Okay, shh," I rubbed her back as I rocked back and forth.

"I need you now. I need you."

I stood up and pulled my pants down far enough to release my cock. I reached between us and snapped her panties. She leaned forward grabbing my face and kissed me.

Her tongue plunged into my mouth, lapping, tasting, worshiping, and tormenting my mouth. My hand captured, cupped, and spread her juices around her sweet fucking pussy. I pushed in one finger, then pinched her clit, and she screamed out. I reached down and rubbed the crown of my cock against her slippery lips, then pushed inside her, rotating my hips, stretching her. When I just couldn't take it anymore I rammed my cock inside of her.

"Abe, oh god, Abe." She screamed out, I sat on the stool holding her hips tightly in my hands, pinning her, not allowing her to move, forcing her to take everything I had as I rotated my hips into hers.

"Oh god! Oh god!"

"Is that what you wanted, Nikki? My cock? You wanted my big cock shoved so far inside of you that you understood the line between pleasure and pain?"

"Yes, teach me. God, please Abe, teach me."

"You sure you can handle more than this?" I shoved into her more forcefully.

"I'm gonna come. Oh God, Abe."

And I pulled out.

"No, no damn it." She hit my shoulder with her tiny little fists.

"Go stand by the pool table, Nikolette," she looked at me, "Do it now and wait."

I wasn't gonna let her love me, the Abe she fantasized about for two days. She didn't know me yet. Not the Abe that demanded. She needed to love that too before I could trust what she said was true.

I walked into the office and grabbed a few Zip Ties. Pops had them to hang banners and shit, but they would come in handy tonight.

I walked out and she stood naked next to the table. "Lay down under the light, Nikki." She did as I asked. I grabbed a pool stick and her eyes widened. I stood at the end so she was looking up at me. I laid the stick on the table.

"Rest the back of your wrists on here." She did. "Have you ever heard of a spreader bar Nikki?"

"No."

"No, what?"

"No, I haven't."

Shit, I wasn't sure I could make her call me sir. I would table that for another time.

"This will act as one for now. I am going to tie your hands to the bar so that you can't move them."

"Why?"

"Because I said so."

I zip tied her hands to the pool cue tight enough that she couldn't free herself from them and loose enough that she wouldn't bruise.

I walked to the other end. "Same thing with your ankles, understand?"

"Yes."

"Good girl."

I walked around the bar, grabbed a bottle, a dish of cherries, and some ice cubes.

I sat at a bar stool, took a drink, and enjoyed the whisky's burn. I stared at Nikki all bound and spread on the pool table.

"You look beautiful."

"What? Where are you?"

"Do I need to blindfold you as well? Don't worry about where I am. Just mentally prepare yourself for your punishment."

"How do I do that?"

"Just listen and do exactly what I say."

PLEASURE V. PAIN

"**Y**ou look beautiful."

"I feel like a fool."

I heard him walk toward me and then saw him standing between my legs with a bar mop over his shoulder.

"I did this to you. Do you think I'm foolish?"

"No." I felt my face heating up.

"When you sat on the bar with your legs spread, touching yourself, do you know how incredibly sexy you looked?"

"Better than I do right now, I bet."

"That's one." He lifted the stick that my legs were attached to, threw the bar mop under me, and straightened it before lowering me back down.

"One what?"

He reached between my legs, cupped my sex, rubbing his palm up and down until I arched my hips into his hand. He shook his head "no" and let go. And then, without warning, he brought his hand down on my moist lips in a dull thud.

"Ahh!" I cried out and instinctively tried to close my legs.

"Do you know how many I owe you?"

I shook my head "no."

"Two starting from when I bound you up." He ran his finger up my slit but didn't push inside of me. "You're wet, Nikki. I think I was too easy on you. What do you think?"

"I don't know."

"Of course you don't." His hand came down on me again, but this time he didn't stop, he gave fast gentle spanks against me that caused me to moan out of pleasure. He pulled his hand away. "I'm being gentle with you, Nikki, you should thank me."

He shoved a finger inside me without warning. I cried out and arched my back pushing into his hand, but he pulled it away immediately.

"Do you understand what I am doing to you, Nikki?"

"No."

"Pain," his hand came down harder on my pussy. His finger shoved into me and curling up, hit that spot that only Abe could find. "Pleasure."

I nodded.

His other hand came down on me as he fingered me. "This is nothing Nikki. Just a taste of what I can do to you. "Pain," smack, "Pleasure."

"Oh God!"

"No, Nikki. Abe." He pushed another finger inside me. "I am going to fuck you hard with my fingers and you'll come for me."

"Pain," smack, "Pleasure"

His fingers fondled, gripped, pushed into me with twists and spirals.

"Pain," smack, "Pleasure." Was repeated, and what was at first torment, turned into a ritual calling deep inside of me until I felt my pussy clench, capturing his fingers.

"I'm gonna come. Stop, oh God, stop," I pleaded.

I couldn't roll away, or close my knees, or stop the teasing. I couldn't lay back and absorb the orgasm like I had before. I was pushed harder and harder until I screamed out. I felt myself release and wanted to float down from the high of my climax, but he continued.

"Pain," smack, "Pleasure."

Orgasm after orgasm, I screamed out. Each scream softer than the last due to exhaustion, even as the intensity remained the same.

He stopped only when I lay limp.

I heard a snip and I pulled my legs together. I whimpered at the relief I felt. My arms were next and then he was gone. I curled into a ball and waited until he came back.

He was gentle as he sat me up and pulled a shirt over my head. I opened my eyes and saw the green baseball jersey covering me. He wasn't looking at me, but he smiled gently.

He lifted me, holding me for a moment as he kissed my head over and over again.

He sat me on the bar stool and returned to cleaning up. I leaned back into the soft leather and must have drifted off.

When I woke up, he was lifting me again.

"Hi." I nuzzled into his warmth and hung onto his neck.

"Did you rest well?"

"I did, but I want to sleep."

"Do you think I'm done with you yet?"

I looked up at him and his lip curled up in the corner.

"Yes, I do," I gasped.

"Do you think you'll remember that next time you think about taking off, or not calling, or not texting or."

"Okay I get the point." I whispered, kissed his neck, and nuzzled closer. "I'm not going anywhere."

"That's for me to decide."

"Oh, Abe," I yawned.

"Oh what?"

"I really have fallen in love with a beautiful and multi-talented man."

"Tell me his name. I'll kill him." He joked.

I laughed and looked up at him, "Neptune."

"Lucky bastard."

"I hope he feels that way."

"If he doesn't, I'll kill him."

***

Abe had had a lot to drink, so I drove him home.

As soon as I pulled in the driveway, he told me I was staying with him until we figured out my living arrangement.

I didn't tell him that was my plan all along. I slept, really slept, in his arms, and right now that's all I wanted to do.

"Shower," he dropped my keys in the dish on the entry table and kissed my head before taking my hand and leading me up the stairs.

"Shower sounds good."

We walked in and he began stripping. Then looked at me. "Shirt, Nikki."

I looked down at his erection standing very tall and proud. "Maybe we should take them separately."

He laughed, "Hell no, I'm not done with you yet."

"Oh God."

"Remember pain and pleasure."

"How could I forget?" I asked still looking at his dick. "How about I, you know, go down?"

"Not an option, and if you want to keep arguing I could grab the toys." He lifted the shirt over my head and dropped it on the ground. "Have I told you just how much I love your tits?" He asked as he cupped them and pushed them together. He bent and sucked one harshly, then the next.

"I think they like you too."

He walked into the large shower and turned on the water, "Get in here, Miss Bassett, or I can start counting punishments and take them out on your ass next time. You wouldn't believe what I do to pleasure it."

I walked in and he smiled.

"Not gonna happen, big guy," I reached down and grabbed ahold of him.

"Mmm, I like that."

"I'm all about pleasure," I smiled up at him, he leaned in, bit my lip, and then sucked it.

"I'm all about sensation." I stroked him faster and he smiled, "I'm getting in tonight, don't think a hand job is gonna cut it."

I huffed as he reached up and cupped my breast again.

"You could do them."

"Pussy," he whispered against my neck before licking his way down to my boobs.

He sucked each nipple, then kissed up to my neck again and whispered, "I can't wait to fuck you, Nikki."

His hand reached around me, cupped my ass and spread me wide. He kissed me again as his erection rubbed against my belly.

He licked the shell of my ear and then whispered, "I love being inside of you, Nikki."

He squatted down a bit so his dick went between my legs.

"I love being inside of you almost as much as I love making you come, over and over and over again."

He kissed me. His tongue stroked mine in hard slow movements up and down.

"I love being inside of you as much as I love eating your pussy."

He turned me around, "Now bend and hold onto the wall so I can see if I love fucking you from behind as much as from the front."

I did as he asked. When I bent he groaned in approval. "Your ass is a fucking masterpiece and as much as you think you wouldn't like it, I promise when I fuck it you'll beg for it again."

"That's repulsive."

"But it makes your pussy wet Nikki."

He spread me wide, bent over, and kissed down my back. His teeth grazed my ass cheek right before his tongue licked me from front to back. All the way back.

"Nikki I want to try something stay right there and don't move, not an inch."

He left, and I stood trying to figure out what it is he was up to. When I heard him return, I quickly resumed the position.

"Remember when I said no is not an option? That I want you to trust me and even if you think you won't like something you'll at least try?"

"You're making me nervous."

"No, baby." He rubbed my ass, then I felt him rubbing his dick up and down my slit. "I need in."

He pushed in, stilled, and held one of my hips. "God you're tight."

"You're huge," I whispered.

"One would think you were trying to butter me up for something, but I know what I got here," he pushed in a bit farther, "And it's well above average."

"Abe!" I cried out. He slammed into me and stilled.

"I will never get over how fucking good you feel wrapped around me. I'm gonna go easy, nice and slow."

He pulled almost all the way out and then in.

I whimpered.

"I think we're a perfect fit, beautiful," he spread my cheeks and groaned as he pushed in and pulled out slowly. "I need to know just how perfect."

"Yes," I moaned.

He stopped and leaned over me forcing himself further in. "I'm not happy that you turned in that article without me seeing it first."

"I promise you'll like it." I moaned as he pulled back.

"I trust you or I wouldn't be fucking you right now, Nikki. Do you trust me?"

"Yes," he slammed into me several times and stilled.

"Good, now relax and trust me."

I felt something cool and then he was massaging my puckered hole.

"Abe?"

"Trust." He rotated his hips and I moaned. "My pinky is all we're playing with for now. When I ask you to take a deep breath do it and relax beautiful, I got you."

He rubbed my back as he moved slowly in and out of me. I felt liquid being spread around my rim. "Fuck, please don't make me wait too long. Deep breath, beautiful."

I didn't move as I felt him pushing in.

"Deep breath, beautiful, I swear you'll love my cock in your pussy and this too, trust me."

I took in a deep breath as he pushed into me and stilled when I exhaled.

"Don't fight it." He rotated his hips and applied downward pressure—there. "Good girl."

His voice was low and raspy as he continued his assault on my body. I was surprised when my clit began to throb, to burn, and even more surprised when I felt the knowing feeling of an orgasm building in my belly.

"Oh fuck, yes," he groaned as he moved in and out of both places, "Fuck, baby, I am gonna come so hard I fear for your safety."

"What?" I gasped.

"Hang on, Nikki," he placed a hand on the wall over my head as he thrust in and out of me grunting and hissing.

He sounded like a beast and he was certainly fucking me like one. "Come now, beautiful, I won't last much longer. Now, goddamn it, Nikki!"

We both yelled out our releases together and he pulled his pinky from inside me.

"Fuck," he gasped as he held himself up against the wall above of me.

He pushed himself up, grabbed my ass in his hands, and squeezed. Then I felt him scattering soft little kisses all over my butt.

"Until we meet again," he whispered.

I laughed and he swatted my butt. "This is between me and your ass, you stay out of it."

"Did you get spanked as a child?"

"You already asked me that."

He pulled out of me, and I stood facing him.

"Does it bother you?" He asked as he grabbed body wash and dumped it into his hand.

He stepped towards me and rubbed his hands together.

"You spanking me, or the finger thing?"

"Any of it," he reached out and grabbed me, "Come over here."

I stood as he rubbed soap all over my body, taking his time with the parts he liked the most.

"That feels good."

"And earlier, did that feel good?"

I looked up at him. "I never thought it would."

"Doesn't make you a bad person."

"I swear I would've thought it would."

"Our tastes change, our desires deepen and God willing, we meet someone who wants the same things and experiences in life. Turn around let me have a go at your back."

"You already had a go back there."

"And I will again."

"What makes you so sure about that?"

He turned me, pulled me against him, and whispered from behind me in my ear, "Because you love me."

He kissed my cheek and then head. "Lean forward, hands on the wall again, please."

"Abe, I am so tired."

"I know, but please, and remember I'm all about sensation."

He started drawing on my back.

"Are you writing on me?"

"Sensation, pay attention, Miss Bassett."

"I?"

"Yep, next," he ran his hand back and forth as if he was erasing it.

I felt him spell out "love" and my heartbeat faster, until I felt him draw a D.

He waited for me to speak and I didn't want to. It hurt a little to think he loved someone before me.

He did the erase thing again and drew a "U." He erased and did it again. I nodded still not wanting to speak.

I loved you? Until what, what did I do?

He drew a line and a smaller "S" and "T." I shrugged. I felt tears building and I wanted out.

"Abe, I'm really tired." I fake yawned and the whole works.

"One word left."

"Can we do it tomorrow? I really wanna go to sleep."

"No," he laughed.

"Abe," I tried to walk away.

"Nikki, hold up," he forced me to turn around and I lost it. "Baby, what the hell is wrong?"

He held me against him as I cried.

"Okay, let's get you to bed."

He got out, grabbed a towel, and wrapped it around me. "You go climb into bed let me shower off, okay?"

I nodded and wiped my face as he lifted my chin so I was looking up at him.

"We're good right?"

"Yep."

PUT THAT THING AWAY

I was scrubbing up as I thought about the fact the first girl who I said "I love you" to broke down crying. How fucked up is that? Pretty damn fucked up. I knew I pushed her hard tonight, but she was begging for it, and I needed to know if she was what I knew she would be, which is perfect for me. Not only did she make my heart do that thing, but she made my cock do it, too.

Yes, I was in love with her, probably from the minute I saw her on the beach, but I didn't allow myself to realize it then. That was not the mission of my getaway. Not until I was inside her then I aborted mission one and concocted mission two. I was gonna do a long distance thing with her just to test the waters. Yeah right, just to fuck her hard and good enough that she didn't wanna get it anywhere else. Then she bailed and I was sure I was gonna live the life of a perpetual bachelor, which wasn't all that bad. Then she shows up again and fuck if she didn't have "I wanna get fucked by you again" written all over her face. A face that I will admit I beat off to until I saw her again. I had no intention of getting her off again, she didn't deserve it. But that was out the window when I caught her stalking me. And right now, I was damn glad she did.

I toweled off and headed off to the bedroom.

She was all covered up, and I swear she was fully dressed.

"That's a lot of clothes for bed, you know," I said as I got in and pulled her against me.

She sniffed and shook. "You're a mess, Nikki, come on, talk to me."

"No, I want to sleep."

"How is that going to work when you obviously have something going on in your head? Remember how this works. Trust, complete trust." She didn't answer me and shit started going bad in my head. "Let me ask you something. You worried about what's in that article because I swear to God I would like to hear it from you if you are."

She sprung up and snapped at me, "Are you serious right now? I gave you rave reviews, wrote all about how focused you were. How you held yourself up to very high standards of honesty. Yes, I said honest, what I didn't say is that you were mean and cruel and hurtful."

I sat up now, "Excuse me? You could have very easily stopped anything that went on tonight. If, for one second, you didn't act like you were enjoying yourself, I would have stopped. What the fuck?"

"Sure, I liked it. Hell, I loved it, I even went so far as believing I loved you, but then you pull that shit in the shower."

"What, the pinky in the ass? I went easy on you, I could've - -"

"No! I loved you, you son of a bitch. After everything, I trusted you with, you write 'I loved you' on my back." she jumped off the bed. "That was cruel! You know what? I'm out. Screw you." I started laughing, stood up, and hell yes, I was hard again. The dick wants what the dick wants. Feisty Nikki was hot.

"Put that thing away!" She pointed at my dick.

Now I was rolling.

"Bastard!"

She started for the stairs and I grabbed her, "Say you're sorry."

"Fuck you."

"That's one."

"Oh really, one what?"

"Spanking."

"You are sick, aren't you?" She started getting really squirmy, and I hoisted her up over my shoulder. I smacked her ass hard right before tossing her onto the bed.

I straddled her, held her arms above her head with one hand, and pulled her shirt up.

"Really, Abe?"

"Sensation, calm down and feel." I drew a line on her stomach as she squirmed some more. "What did I just draw?"

"I really don't care. Get off me or so help me God I will bite that, that, very offensive penis."

"A line represents a number one, Nikki. And what's this?" I drew an S and a T.

She scowled, "I don't get it! I just want you to--"

"First. I loved you first. Do you get it now, Nikolette? I. Loved. You. First."

I got off the bed and fixed the blankets her little outburst caused to get all dicked up. Then I got into bed, lay on my back, and stared up at the ceiling.

I looked over as she glanced at me.

"Trust, Nikki. This doesn't work without it. Now roll over here kiss me goodnight and get some sleep."

"You didn't love me first," she pouted as she rolled over and rested her head on my chest.

"Now you want to argue?"

"Maybe," she yawned.

"What do you say we table it until tomorrow?"

"Fine."

"Fine," I mimicked her and she gave me a little push.

"Hey, Nikki?"

"Yes, Abe?"

"I love you."

I felt her shake again and then tears falling on my chest. "I love you, too."

"Good. Now go to sleep so I can and dream about what it is I wanna do to you for punishment."

I kissed her head and she wrapped her arms around me tighter.

***

I woke up to the girl I professed my love to blanketing me. I wished I had waited, you know, not done it the way I did. Well maybe I just wished she hadn't reacted the way she had. I pushed her hard last night, real hard, and for the most part, she took it like a champ. I loved making her come, fuck she looked amazing when she did. She looked amazing when she did anything. I still wished I had waited. I really wished I wasn't getting wood right now because she's gonna wake up sore and want to run for the hills.

I looked up at the ceiling trying to will it away and it wasn't happening.

She was starting to stir. *I wondered if I woke her, I hadn't meant to. Damn. She'll never want to sleep over again. Not that it mattered I was pretty damn sure I would tie her up if she wanted to leave and I'm also damn sure that thought didn't help make my dick any softer.*

What do men think about when they want to lose a hard on? Seriously, I had no clue, when I woke up like this I would normally just beat off.

Mom, that's what guys think about, their mothers; that would certainly help bring the evergreen down. Alright, Mom, help me out. Timber.

"What are you thinking about?"

I looked down as she was lifting her head and rubbing her eyes.

"About my mom."

She glanced down, and sure as shit, I was pitching a tent.

"Okay, let me explain."

"No, that's alright I knew you were into some messed up stuff, but--"

"What!"

She started laughing. I flipped her on her back and pinned her, "I was trying to get this to go away."

"Now why would you do that?" She giggled.

"Trying to let you rest. I can be a gentleman."

"Yeah right."

"You think I can't be?"

"I think you really want to be, bud, but I already know what you're all about, so I say wave that flag, just let your inner freak fly."

She was laughing, and damn if she didn't look even more beautiful today than she did yesterday.

"I'm totally fucked, you know that?"

"I was trying to say it nicely."

"No, smart ass," I pushed my hands under her and squeezed her ass, "You are gonna have me wrapped around you little finger and there isn't a damn thing I am gonna be able to do about it. I like the upper hand and for some reason I don't need it as much when I'm with you."

I slid my hands down, grabbed the back of her thighs, and spread her legs.

"I've smashed panties in my day, but this is ridiculous." I slid down under the covers and pulled off her pajama bottoms and underwear.

Oh man, Houston we have a problem. Son of a bitch!

I kissed her belly and came out from under the covers.

"Is everything alright?"

"How freaky are you gonna let me be?"

"What do you mean?"

"Are you against sex during menstruation?"

"What?" She sat up and looked under the covers. "Oh my God. I'm so sorry. I can't believe it."

"It's gonna happen right? I really have no reservations about it."

"You're not going down on me when I'm bleeding."

"Like never?"

"Abe!"

"Just clarifying."

"Yes, like never," she scooted off the bed and ran to the bathroom.

As soon as I heard the shower running, I stripped the bed. Blood stained sheets and as much as I loved the girl, there better not be any shit on my mattress.

Son of a bitch. Okay, I know it's no big deal to most people, but I have some quirks. A clean house and unstained shit were two of them.

I could flip the mattress, but it was pillow top. How the fuck is it that I have whores here and they don't stain my shit, but this hot little almost virgin who I have fallen in love with comes in and messes shit up. I'm not a douche or uptight okay? I just have a system.

I grabbed my phone, Googled "how to remove blood stains", and then ran down into the kitchen to see if I had any salt or hydrogen peroxide.

I did and I hauled ass up the stairs because I wanted to make sure she didn't think I was pissed.

By the time she returned I had conquered the stain removal and all that was visible was a faint stain that I was certain would go away after the mattress dried.

By the time she was out of the shower I had successfully removed a stain, changed the sheets, and made the bed.

I was standing back admiring my work when she said, "I'm sorry."

I held my hand out behind me and she took it, "It's not a big deal. See, its all better."

I looked down and she sighed.

"Look, if we're gonna be living together, I am going to have to expect things like this and you're going to have to get over any embarrassment that comes along with it."

"Abe?"

"What's up?"

"We aren't living together, I just stayed the night."

"Fine, but tonight when we go load up your belongings and bring them here, then we'll be living together."

"I can't do that," she let go of my hand and started walking towards her bag.

I felt my blood start to boil as I watched her pull her panties on and then drop the wet towel on my hard wood floor. Okay, that discussion would have to wait, right now I needed to get her to agree that yes, she was in fact living with me.

"Explain why."

I sat on the bed as she pulled a bra out of her bag and turned her back to me again so I couldn't see her. She still hadn't answered me.

"Nikki, turn around and explain."

She shook her head, grabbed a tank top out of her bag, pulled it over her head, and turned around.

"I promised them I would still be me."

She looked completely miserable and as pissed as I was I didn't wanna make it worse for her.

"I don't want you to be anything else."

"I'm independent, self-sufficient, strong and--"

"Kind, caring, so much that you don't want to disappoint them."

She nodded.

"I won't push, I have you here now and until you find a place, right?"

She nodded again.

"Good. Now I want you to think about something else, too, okay? I want you to consider telling them how we truly feel about one another. Maybe then us wanting to live together wouldn't be as hard for them to come to terms with. I'm sure they want you to be happy. If this makes you happy they would eventually embrace the idea."

She looked down at the ground.

"Just so you know, you make me happy."

I stood, kissed her head, and walked down the stairs, leaving her to her thoughts.

I went down to the gym to get in at least two miles. A late start to my day was gonna cut my work out time down. I was alright with that when I thought I'd be getting some extra cardio in this morning. That is until fucking Shark Week went live on my bed.

I turned on Fox news, go ahead and judge, I'm a conservative guy, not a democrat or republican, I don't play a side, I play what feels right. Which is why after fifteen minutes, I turn it to CNN. I catch both sides.

When I was done, I ran upstairs and decided to boil some eggs while I showered. I knew how much she hated my shakes, which still had me concerned that I may possibly be going without a blow job for—maybe ever. But I was willing, that's how much I liked this girl. Fucked up, huh?

I ran upstairs and she was doing her hair. I kind of chubbed up a little as I stood and watched her in the mirror primping.

Out to Sea

"You're upset with me."

"No. I understand the thought process."

"What's that mean?"

He walked over, stood next to me, and took his toothbrush out of what I am sure was a sterilizer that cost way too much.

"I'm an only child, too. We want to please our parents, that's all."

I turned and watched him brush his teeth. "So you think I'm being childish?"

He put both hands on my hips, moved me to the left, then spit in the sink, and rinsed it. "You're not being childish, you're doing what any twenty-two-year-old *only* child would do. And don't try to argue, I was twenty-two and an only child, so I get it."

"That's when your mom got sick."

"Yeah," he continued brushing his teeth.

"And that's when you fought with your Dad."

He leaned over, spit again, and rinsed the sink again.

"That's when I voiced my opinion, and he didn't like it."

"So you're telling me I should fight with my parents so that I can live here with you. Do you know I fought with them just to come back here so that I could be with you?"

"Thank you for that."

He grabbed a Dixie cup, filled it, and rinsed again. Then he grabbed the mouthwash and filled it.

"That's it? Thank you, but in your head you're thinking what? That I'm a child?"

He finished gargling, spit in the sink, and rinsed it out.

"You do know that you'll have the same effect if you just wait until you're finished to rinse out the sink and you'll save water, too."

I didn't like him treating me like I was a baby almost as much as I didn't like him not answering me.

"You hungry? When I get done showering, I'll make you breakfast."

I turned around and walked out of the bathroom. I heard the shower start and I grabbed my phone. *Jerk.*

I flopped back on the bed and stared at the ceiling. I looked at my phone and it was only 6:39 A.M. Living with him would not be a good idea.

He walked out butt naked and into his closet, for a minute I doubted the whole living with him thing. That alone would make it worth it. He was F.I.N.E fine.

When he reappeared, he was in suit pants and an off-white button down with a tie slung over his shoulder.

"You should go back to sleep for a while. You might feel better."

"I'm not sick I'm--"

"Emotional, which is worse because of your period. I get it."

"Wow, and the zings just keep coming."

"Nikolette," It occurred to me that I was Nikolette when he was frustrated with me, Miss Bassett when he was pissed, Nikki when things were cool, and Four when he was, well you know. "I don't want to argue with you. Like I said, I want you to be you, too. You're battling yourself, not me. Let's grab some breakfast; maybe you'll feel better."

I sat on the bar stool as he cracked and shelled hard-boiled eggs, then he buttered toast. He set it in front of me with a large glass of orange juice.

"Make a list of things you like to eat and I will have Nancy, our housekeeper, pick them up." He retrieved a pen and paper from a drawer and set it in front of me.

"I can go to the store."

"I want you to just relax for a few days, you have a lot to consider."

"Like what?"

"Nikolette."

"Nikki."

"Okay, Nikki, you talked about finding a place, wondering what your next assignment will be, wondering about your next internship, and whatever else it is your trying to figure out. It's a lot to consider," he said as he pulled out his dreadful drink mixture.

"I can still go to the store." I was pouting I knew it, but I was tired and crampy, which wasn't normal, but neither was the work over he gave me yesterday.

He washed his hands and planted them on the counter, glowering. I knew it even before I looked up. He sighed and grabbed the paper and pen.

"All that stuff in your head and then," he pushed the pad of paper in front of me.

Pads and tampons. I read it again and wanted to be annoyed, but I had to laugh.

"Yes, and then there is that."

"Everything will work out," he turned on the blender and watched as it all got mashed up. When it was done, he looked up. "Fridays, Nancy cooks, a lot. We can either eat at home or go out. Message me whatever you decide. I can be home by six."

"Home," I had meant to whisper.

He smiled as he drank down that nasty concoction.

When he finished, he rinsed his glass and then put it in the dishwasher.

He looked down at the list and smiled.

"It's not that funny you know, it's kind of gross."

"I was just thinking."

He walked around the island and turned my stool, "I made you breakfast and I don't get to see you eat it. That's unfortunate. I wish I had time to feed you."

"Tonight?"

"Movie and take out?"

"Maybe I'll cook for you."

"Oh Christ, don't tell me you can cook. I'll fall even harder."

"Southern food. Mostly fried."

"Oh, maybe we'll stick to Nancy's cooking."

"Oh, I see."

"I need to stay in shape. I have this girl who can almost keep up with my needs."

"Do you have a cheat day?"

He leaned in closer and stared at my lips. "I'd never cheat."

"Promise?" I whispered as he leaned closer.

"Most definitely." His minty breath hit my face at the same time his lips touched mine.

His kiss was soft and plenty. He kept giving me little pecks. "Four…"

"Period."

"What?" he laughed as he stood up.

"You call me 'Four' when you're in a sexy mood."

"I do not," he laughed.

"Miss Bassett when you're pissed."

"Fine. You may have a point. But at least you know what you're getting."

"Oh no you didn't." I laughed.

"I have to go." He kissed me again and grabbed my face. "I love you."

"I like that."

"Me too. Have a good day. If you're not too busy, you could stop over and have lunch with me."

"I have a lot to do you know. Busy girl."

"Okay, I will see you when I get home."

He started to walk away, "Abe." He turned around. "I love you, too."

He smiled and nodded his head, "I know."

And then he walked out the door.

***

I walked into The Shore ten minutes before nine. I smiled to everyone who looked up from their computer screens. The front offices housed the secretaries of the advertising executives. It appeared that none liked their jobs. I felt sorry for them. I wished everyone could do what they loved, what they dreamed of doing.

I walked through the double doors into the newsroom. It was always very lively and I loved the energy. I was sure there were some who didn't like it back here either, but I did. I loved it. I walked to my cubical, sat at my desk, and flipped on my computer. As always, I checked my inner office email to see if there was a new assignment. I swear it was like Christmas morning every time.

"You got a minute, doll?" It was Bogart.

"Sure thing."

"Good. Follow me."

I followed him to his office and he shut the door when I sat.

"Look, I'm gonna be honest with you, I found your interview to read more like a college newspaper article. I thought for a few minutes why the hell did this kid who turned in an ass kicking interview with the owner of the Atlanta Braves for her internship application turn in something that read like a kid with a crush."

"To be fair sir--"

"No, to be fair, it sucks."

I didn't like the way he was talking to me or the way he looked at me. He had always given me a creeper vibe, but I ignored it, thinking I was wrong.

"So I drove over to your place last night hoping to find out just what made you change as a writer. To my surprise, a neighbor said you hadn't been around since the incident. Being a news guy, I asked questions. I was pretty shocked that one of my own people would keep something so big and newsworthy a secret from me."

I felt sick to my stomach as he continued.

"So I looked into that too. What I found out shocked me. If you want to be taken seriously, Miss Bassett, you shouldn't be sleeping with the subjects of your interviews."

"To be fair, what happened to me has nothing to do with the Shore. And to be honest, my personal life is none of your concern."

"I'm not running a fucking dating service here, Nikolette! So here's what you'll do. Fix this ridiculous excuse for an article. I know more shit about Abe O'Donnell than you put in this from just a few phone calls I made with, how do I say this, mutual business associates. Don't throw away your career on a piece of ass, understand? Then you'll write a story about what happened at 1273 Park Avenue, it's your duty. Then maybe I'll continue talks with the Giants' press people."

I was sure I was going to get sick to my stomach when I stood to leave

"Don't fuck this up, or I'll ruin you."

When I walked out the door, I swear I heard him say "bitch," and that too, made me ill.

I grabbed my briefcase as I headed to the bathroom. I would be leaving, but I wasn't sure what I would do after that.

***

When I left The Shore I knew where I was going, but once I pulled into Steel I couldn't get out. He had taken care of so much for me that I truly felt I was becoming weaker by the day. I pulled out and headed to 1273 Park Street. I was going to pack up my place and figure out what I would do next. What I did know was that I was bringing in too much drama into Abe's life and that wasn't me.

I spent three hours packing up my apartment and carrying boxes down three flights of stairs in the crazy heat. The entire time I was trying to decide what to do. When I finished, I sat back on the couch and decided I was thankful that my place was furnished.

I looked down at my phone. It was twelve thirty and I had missed two calls from Abe. I decided I better call him back; as much as I enjoyed last night I was pretty sure next time the punishment I received wouldn't be so sweet.

"Nikolette."

"Yeah, sorry, things just got a little messed up today, that's all." And then the water works started.

"Okay. You'll be okay."

"No, I don't think you understand."

"No, I do. Sit still. I'm walking up now."

And then he hung up. I grabbed my purse and decided I better hurry. He thought I was at his place and he was gonna be upset. When I opened the door to leave this place for the final time I saw him standing there.

He wrapped his big old arms around me and rubbed my back as I cried. He didn't say anything, he just held me. When I was done, I wiped my eyes and shook my head.

"You're angry."

"No, just concerned, let's get you home."

"How did you know I was here?"

"Sixth sense I guess."

He opened the door to his SUV, "Get in."

"My car."

"Someone's coming to grab it, should be here any minute. Just have a seat and give me your keys."

It wasn't more than a minute before I dozed off in the air conditioned vehicle. When I opened my eyes, my car was gone and Abe was shaking my landlord's hand.

When he got in he handed me an envelope. "This is your rent money back. The lease is broken and he understands. Says he's sorry."

He backed out of the driveway and started towards his place. He reached up, turned on the radio and the words made me cry even more, *I'll be your keeper for life.* A keeper for life. The song was Guardian by Alanis Morisette, and it was beautiful.

I remember when it scared me that he wanted to own me. It felt wrong, but if I am to be honest with myself, nothing in my life has ever felt so right.

"Abe," I said in a hushed voice. "The Shore knows--"

"I know what happened today. It will be handled."

"Abe?"

"Yes?"

"I want to live with you. I want you to." I swallowed hard, "own me."

"Where is this coming from?"

"I'm scared."

"You don't need to be."

"I'm scared you're going to get sick of me and all the drama I bring to you. Then this morning. God, what a mess. But if you've changed your mind, I understand."

"Have you eaten since breakfast?"

"What? No, but I am trying to tell you--"

"Can we talk later? Can we just be quiet for a while? Just a little while?"

"Uh huh."

"Good girl."

BACK TO BUSINESS

Son of a bitch! Why the fuck couldn't she have said that earlier. Three fucking hours ago I was sending flowers to her at work when the florist called and said she was not there. I called her boss and that son of a bitch told me that she had left for the day. Then the fuck hung up on me. When she didn't answer her fucking phone I went to his office to find out why. After finding out why she had left, I might have made a few threats and then got his ass in a jam. The threat of sexual harassment charges, slander, extortion and any other thing I could think of to throw at him. Then I let him know I had the balls and bank account to pull it off. That made its mark.

Nikolette would not be going back to The Shore, I made sure of that, but I also got her school papers signed off so that her internship was completed and she received the entire semester's worth of credit she was entitled to.

The problem is, I don't trust Bogart Humphrey, seems pretty damn off to me, that's why I set a plan in place to keep Nikolette safe. My privilege, my duty, and I was praying that it didn't blow up in my face. A promise to myself when I first realized fully who I was. A man who would be a man. Not someone who would let his lover flounder or be walked over. A man who took care of what he loved, putting her needs even before his own.

I knew when I found her, the one, my soul mate or whatever you want to call it, she would be my charge in the most cherished and loving way possible. I would put her before me always.

We parked and got out. I had wanted to open the door for her, but she was at my side in seconds. I knew she was seeking approval because instead of calling me, she ran. Not as far away as she did the first time, but she did it none the less. She also did it for comfort. She had been dealing with this for three hours by herself. She chose not to seek comfort in me, but she was now and I would give her what she needed.

We walked in and Nancy had done exactly what I had asked. Candles were lit, food was in the oven, and the shades were down. I wanted her to be able to relax, to rest, to feel like nothing bad would happen to her.

"You did this?"

"I had it done."

"For me?"

"Yes, Nikolette, for you."

She looked at me as if she was confused.

I led her upstairs and brought her into the bathroom. I drew a bath and dimmed the lights. I took my time undressing her; I never wanted to forget what she looked like.

I walked out of the bathroom so she could use the facilities with the privacy I could tell she wanted, and I didn't blame her. I had been a little weirded out by the whole menstruation thing. I'm sure she was uncomfortable because of that. When I heard the toilet flush I gave her a second and walked back in.

I helped her into the bath and I washed her body. There was nothing perverse in cleaning her, I was not looking to gain any sexual satisfaction from it, I merely wanted to take care of the woman I loved while she was hurting.

I let her lay back so she could relax while I grabbed a bathrobe and set it on the counter. I grabbed a towel, held it up as she climbed out, and I wrapped her in it, while I patted her dry.

Again, I left the room and waited for her in the doorway where she could see me, but knew I couldn't see her.

We walked down the stairs, I told her to sit, gave her a glass of wine, and the remote. "Pick something on Netflix."

"Abe, you don't have to stay, I know you have to work."

"The empire won't crumble without me." I winked trying to ease her anxiety.

I grabbed the salad out of the fridge and the bread out of the warmer.

"Nikolette, what kind of dressing do you like?"

"What do we have?"

We? Fuck!

"Italian, Balsamic vinaigrette, ranch."

"What do you like?"

"I like whatever you do, Nikolette."

"Nikki, Abe," she stood up, walked over to me, and sat her wine glass on the island. "I know you're angry."

"No, I'm not."

"Fine, Italian then." She turned and walked back to the couch.

It was quiet for too damn long. I wasn't very good at hiding my emotions from her and I wanted tonight to be perfect.

"What movie did you pick?"

"I haven't. I thought we could decide together."

"I honestly don't care, I'll watch anything." I said as I handed over the large wooden bowl of salad and a few slices of bread.

"I'm really not hungry."

I sat with my back against the corner of the sectional, pushed my leg behind her, and pulled her so her back was against my chest. "We are gonna eat until we can't eat any more, watch a movie, and I am going to enjoy the hell out of just being with you for the next, I don't know how long, but can you please be here with me, please?"

"You're sure that's what you want."

"I'm one hundred percent sure, no, one hundred and ten percent sure. Now lay back and let me feed you."

And that's what we did, all fucking day long. I held her, I fed her, we didn't leave each other's side except to use the bathroom. We watched *Hitch, The Battered Bastards of Baseball,* and *Christmas with the Kranks.* If a giant fucking cloud wasn't looming over our heads, this would be my idea of the perfect night.

She was falling asleep and I would have too if I didn't have issues with dirty dishes on my coffee table. I did the dishes, then I picked sleeping beauty up off the couch. Despite my efforts, she woke anyway. I still carried her up and laid her in bed then I used the bathroom and brushed my teeth. When I came out, she went in, whispering something about garlic.

We kissed a lot before falling asleep. Kissing was always the stepping-stone to sex. I never took as much time as I did tonight to enjoy the intimacy of it.

"I like kissing you, Nikki."

"I love kissing you, and stuff."

"This is good though, right?" I asked as I kissed her again.

"It's great."

"Goodnight, Nikolette Bassett. I love you." I kissed her again.

"Goodnight, Abe O'Donnell, I love being loved by you."

***

I woke in the morning to something hot and wet under the blankets. It felt fucking amazing. Half of me wanted to just stay asleep, or pretend I was just so I could enjoy the hell out of this cause I was pretty damn sure it was gonna be awhile.

"Good morning, beautiful," I flung the covers off me and nearly came right there from just the site of my cock in her mouth. She flicked my head a few times with her tongue and I started scooting up the bed. Damn if she didn't follow still sucking me off. "If you don't stop I'm gonna come and we have something to talk about first."

"That was the idea," she stroked me and ran her tongue down my cock.

"This is gonna kill me. *Motherfucker*. I hate to say this, but please stop, Nikki."

She didn't listen.

"Nikolette, stop!"

She sat up, wiped her mouth and of course, she looked hurt.

"Come up here, please and don't look at me like that. That was amazing but--"

"Why did you stop me?" She crawled up and sat at my side looking at me.

"Look, I really am a good guy."

"I know that."

"Okay, listen. When I made the decision to live this way, to accept nothing less in my life, I kind of swore an oath to myself. Whoever it was that I brought into my life and accepted it, embraced it, whoever I fell in love with would be cherished. I cherish the gift of your submission to me, I hope you know that."

"I do, but I can't give you, you know," she pointed down, "without you telling me to?"

"Yes you can, that was perfect, Nikki, but you need to hear me out. I swore that I would make damn sure to always put your needs--"

"Abe, please just tell me whatever it is you've been stewing over."

"Look, your parents will be here in a couple hours. You're going to go home."

"No, I told you I wanted to live with you. I told you that."

"After you hid for three hours."

"I won't do it again. I promise."

"You have been through a lot lately." She looked away from me. "Nikolette look at me when I talk to you, please."

"Why? What does it matter anymore? I'm not yours!"

"You're wrong."

"No you're wrong. You're a fake, a fraud. Mr. All-powerful dominating BDSM man."

"First of all, I am not a sadist or a masochist. Not like the others."

"I don't care. I don't want to talk to you anymore."

"Good, 'cause I don't want your excuses, I want you to listen, damn it! You don't trust me the way I have trusted you and I have given you no reason at all to mistrust me. I have been an open book and forgiving of every shit thing you have done to me, starting with Florida."

"I told you--"

"Shut up and listen to me, Goddamn it! I love you. I do, but in order to keep you safe I can't have you running around not knowing where the fuck you are when you have some sick bastard who lives next door to you."

"He's in jail!"

"No, he's out on fucking bail, Nikolette. If you had answered your phone I would have told you that. Then you have some piece of shit threatening you and you run. So your problem is you don't trust me, which gives me two pretty goddamn big problems of my own. I can't keep you safe if I don't know where the fuck you are. And the worst part? I don't trust you anymore!"

"Oh really?"

"Yes really. So you are going home with your parents so that you can get your head on straight while I clean up this fucking mess and keep my head."

"You don't get to tell me what to do."

"I just did. You're a fucking mess, Nikolette, and in order to be true to myself I have to admit that maybe I was wrong about what you could and could not handle."

"So this is all my fault!"

"On the contrary. It's my Goddamn fault. I never got inside deep enough to gain your trust."

"Some Dom you are." She huffed.

"You seem to misunderstand exactly what a Dom-sub relationship is. I am not some unfeeling asshole, and if that's what you thought, I wronged you again. You should have respected and trusted me. I have no idea what I did to make you mistrust me. But your responsibility was to surrender not only your body and mind in bed, but your heart and soul always. You should have been willing to devote yourself to me. In this type of relationship my job is to set you free of mistrust and sexual restraints. Yours is to devote yourself to me fully accepting the pleasures I give and take from you. I knew from the first time we were together that you had a submissive personality and that is what I have been trying to find for two years. I have looked for you, so if you think this is hurting you, it is *fucking* killing me."

I had to walk away. I was so pissed. So fucking disappointed that this conversation just ended us when all I wanted was for her to see it was important for me to take away everything that was causing her to doubt. Boy, did I fuck that up.

It was a beautiful fucking day outside. I walked to the window, watching the morning tide. Sadly, inside, it was truly ugly.

"I was going to go home anyway!" she screamed out of nowhere. "This isn't who I am! I don't hurt people! I was going to leave you so that you could get on with your life. So there, Mr. O'Donnell, you don't win the martyr medal today. I do. I have been through some seriously crazy shit in the past few weeks and I have been strong, but obviously not strong enough for you!"

I didn't turn around, "You were perfect for me."

We didn't talk for an hour and then my phone chimed. Her parents' plane had landed they would be here in less than an hour.

"Nikolette, your parents will be here soon. Maybe you should get dressed. I can pack your things."

"I don't want to leave." She said with her face in the pillow.

"Well, I don't want you to either, but what's done is done, isn't it?"

She sat up and laughed, "Yep, it's that easy."

She scooted off the bed, grabbed her bag, and headed to the bathroom. I kicked her tee shirt under the bed. Dick move I know, but I wanted it.

When she walked out dressed, I felt I needed to say something more, "Nikki."

"At this point I prefer 'Miss Bassett,' thank you."

"I love you and I know none of that was your fault. I just want to see you shine again."

She didn't respond. She grabbed her phone out of her bag and tapped the screen a few times.

"Hey Laney, how are you? ... I miss you too ... Actually I'm all done in New Jersey ... Long story but I was thinking I could tell you next weekend. I am in desperate need of a girl's night... Yeah maybe some of that too."

I walked over, pulled the phone out of her hand, and held it to my ear. "Hello Laney, this is Abe, from Florida--"

"Give me my phone back!"

"Interesting story I'm sure when you come to visit Nikki at her place in Georgia next weekend," I held the phone up and walked away as she tried to grab it. "Yeah we hooked up again alright. She's actually in love with me and I with her ... Look the service here at my house, where she's stayed a few nights, sucks," I held it up again as she jumped for it. "Yes, it's quite a story ... But look, she's going through some shit right now. She needs a friend and not a wing man if you know what I mean."

She pushed me and stormed away, slamming the bathroom door behind her.

When I got off the phone she walked out.

"You're an asshole."

"Nikolette, I'm really not in a good mood right now so don't push, okay?"

"That wasn't your place."

"And you shouldn't have rubbed it in my face that--" I stopped, "This is not how this was supposed to go."

"Why Abe, cause you don't do bad break ups?"

"No, Nikolette, because it was never about a fucking break up. It was about a vacation for you from all this shit until I fixed it. Because at the Goddamn time, you were mine! You. Were. Mine!"

"Well now you don't have to worry about it, do you?"

"Would you stop being a bitch? That's not who you are. It wouldn't matter if I never talked to you again, this shit happened on my watch so yes, I will worry about it."

The buzzer chimed on the gate. I grabbed my phone and pushed to let them in.

I grabbed Nikolette's bag and walked toward the stairs as she stood looking out the window.

"Your folks are here."

"Yeah I know, just give me a minute."

When I heard her sniff, I dropped her bag, walked towards her, grabbed her hand, pulled her against me, and held her pretty damn tight.

We stood like that until the doorbell chimed and she looked up at me and gave me the saddest smile I had ever seen. So sad it shattered me and I felt the heat rise in my throat.

I let out a breath, willing my eyes not to do what I felt they may. She grabbed my face and pulled it down to hers.

She took a deep breath, "Please be careful."

I shook my head and kissed the top of her head. I pulled away, took her bag in one hand, and her hand in the other.

We stopped at the front door and she allowed me to kiss her goodbye. I opened the door and her parents walked in.

"This is a very unique place." Her mother smiled.

"Thank you, Mrs. Bassett."

She hugged Nikki and asked where the bathroom was.

I was left standing in the kitchen with her father.

"Thank you for calling us."

"You're welcome."

"It's okay to admit you can't handle the responsibility of another person."

"I could handle her just fine, sir, but in order to take care of the situations causing her pain, she needs to be safely away."

"And we are her parents; we'll protect her better than anyone else could." This guy was a douche, getting jabs in wherever he could, and I was getting tired of it. "It's okay to admit defeat, Abe."

"I could have kept her safely tied to a chair in my garage bound and gagged while I dealt with the situation. And as fond as I am of that idea, I felt maybe there was a different way of dealing with a girl like, Nikki. I love your daughter, so I called you because emotionally I thought she would fare better with you than a chair and a gag while I fixed shit. Don't prove me wrong. Let me ask you something, have you ever spanked your--"

"Okay we're all set," Nikki said loudly as they entered the room. "Mom, Dad, I'll meet you outside."

When they left she rolled her eyes at me, "Did you have to do that?"

"Yeah, I did. Now get the hell out of here before I change my mind."

She looked down, "I'm sorry."

"Me too, Nikki." I opened the door and walked her out to her car. "Drive safe and please let me know when you get home. Nikki that's what that rectangle thing is for, the one that rings and shit."

She mouthed I love you and I mouthed back, I know.

REFLECTION

It had been a month since I had come home and I had plenty of time to reflect on why I didn't trust him, where I failed, and what it would have taken to trust him. I couldn't think of one thing that he did to make me doubt or mistrust him, not one.

I never did call him, I know it was rotten, but I wanted him to hurt like I did. For three weeks I cried every night. I knew how he was because he messaged when creepy neighbor Thomas had "skipped" bail and was brought into custody by a bail bonds man who "found" him five miles over the New Jersey border in New York bound and gagged. His bail was revoked and he was sitting in jail awaiting trial for the crimes he committed against me and the ones against the other women who had previously lived in my very first apartment, the only apartment I had lived in alone.

Yesterday was Tuesday and I received an acceptance letter for an internship in Italy for a soccer club that paid all expenses and I would be doing what I loved. I also could go back to my old school, but I didn't want to. It was yesterday that I realized what was holding me back from trusting him one hundred percent. Steve and Sally. It wasn't Abe, it was them. I still hadn't gotten over that betrayal.

It was also yesterday that I received a letter from Steel Incorporated offering me an internship and a job after graduating from college as a public relations coordinator. I also received a personal note from Carly, Abe's cousin, asking me to consider it. She also mentioned that she wanted me to meet her child.

Today I wanted to go to Italy because I received a text from Abe telling me Bogart was reassigned to a mailroom in Utah for a sister company of The Shore and that he wouldn't dare step foot back in New Jersey. Being in Italy put an ocean between he and I. For some reason that was a comfort. Abe also said it was time for me to come home and it scared me because I knew how long it took me to get over the hurt Steve caused and I had hurt Abe.

He was right, I wasn't me. I lost me for a while but she was back or as close to back as she could be. It scared me that he knew that before I did. Part of me was afraid that no amount of apologies would make things okay with us and no amount of "I love you's" would make him see that I trusted him, I trusted him more than I trusted myself.

I sat on the porch looking at the wind blow through the trees, as the scent of the blooms on the dogwood tress would disappear.

"Sugar plum, what are you thinking about?" Granny came out in the porch, handed me a glass of sweet tea, and a piece of corn bread.

"Trust."

"Trust, huh?"

"Complete trust."

"Very rare thing, sugar plum."

"Yeah."

"You miss that boy don't you?"

"Like crazy. But I said some unkind things before he shipped me back here."

"Fix it."

"Good Lord, Gran, don't let Mom and Dad hear you say that."

"Oh, they'd be fine."

"Gran."

"Okay, eventually they'd get over it. But ask yourself this, sugar plum, will you ever get over it if you don't go see? If you never put yourself out there could you ever really move forward?"

"I don't have a clue."

She stood up and kissed my head, "Don't wait too long."

***

I hopped out of the cab in front of the baseball field and felt butterflies in my stomach. I truly felt like I might get sick. I sat down at a bench farthest away from the game as I could. I held the ball cap little Bella had given me a month ago. The night I told Abe O'Donnell that I loved him and two days before he sent me away. I grabbed my phone and sent my mother a text telling her that I was in New Jersey and that I was fine.

The scoreboard showed a tie game and it was the bottom of the ninth. Two outs and O'Donnell was up to bat. He swung twice and missed, just like he did at the last game. Then he hit it hard. The ball flew past center and kept on going.

Without thinking, I stood up and whistled loud but I didn't think there was any way he didn't hear me from here. As he rounded second, he looked in my direction. When he slid into home he was called out, but with three RBIs, they'd won. I watched from a distance as he picked up the beautiful Bella and swung her around. I watched them start to pick up the equipment and decided to head to the pub.

I walked fast hoping to make it there before he did. His vehicle passed me. I walked around the corner as Abe and three women got out laughing.

I stopped and turned around. My heart raced as I walked fast until I made it around the corner. Once I knew they wouldn't see me, I leaned against the wall and tried to talk myself out of calling a cab and going right back to the airport.

I can't believe I thought a man like him would wait. I couldn't believe I was so stupid to think that after not returning his texts, calling him, thanking him, simply acknowledging him he would wait for me to stop being, I don't know, a freaking freak.

I slid down the wall and sat crying into my knees as I tried to decide what to do. When I looked up a very pensive looking Abe was standing in front of me glowering.

"I'm sorry, I shouldn't have come. Go back, pretend I wasn't here. Ignore the crazy woman," I stood, brushed off my backside, and turned to walk the other way.

"Stop!"

I did, but I didn't turn around.

"I need a cab on the corner of Smith and Donaldson. Abe O'Donnell. Yes, thank you."

I took a deep breath and turned around, "You played well. Two run RBI and won the game. It was a great hit."

He looked past me up the street.

"I'm sorry."

He nodded. At least he gave me some sort of encouragement.

"Did you call the cab to take me somewhere? Back to the airport, maybe? Abe, please say something. I'm dying here and I have been for a few weeks now. I'll understand if you've moved on. I won't cause any problems just—"

"Nikolette, I have to go back to the bar and celebrate a victory with my team. The women with me needed a ride from the field. He reached up and waved to the cab. "You're going to my place, going to my bedroom and locking yourself in there. Do not, I repeat, do not unlock it if I knock. We will discuss this tomorrow after I get home from work."

"Abe?"

"Yes."

"I was scared and depressed okay? A lot happened. Nothing like that has ever happened to me before and I am still a bit uneasy," I covered my face and shuddered, trying not to cry. "I don't want to be alone, but I understand." I batted away my tears. "I love you. I trust you. I need you, and I want you. But don't punish me by not talking to me. This was hard, you know. Coming here was hard, so if you don't want me here, just tell me now."

He looked at me with no expression whatsoever, "Please, do as I ask. Go to my place and get something to eat and go to sleep."

I looked away from him, but did as he asked. I got in the cab and rode to his place.

Unlocked

It was an early night, thank God, because I needed to deal with Nikolette tomorrow, which meant I needed to sleep tonight.

I pulled in just after nine and walked up the stairs from the garage. There were candles lit leading from the kitchen up the stairs to my bedroom. *So much for the door being locked.* She was fucking trouble.

When I reached the top of the stairs I saw her sitting on her heels naked, on the floor with her palms on her thighs and legs spread.

"Nikolette, what are you doing?"

"Waiting for you to do whatever you need to in order to forgive me."

"This isn't what I want with you, Nikolette. Stand up, please."

She stood and looked away.

"Come on, get in bed."

"Will you be getting in bed with me?"

"Nikki, you're butt ass naked, explain to me how the hell I am gonna be anywhere but in bed with you."

"Are you drunk?"

"No, I had two beers and then." I stopped, "Please get in bed."

Fuck, fuck, fuck, and fuck again, even more beautiful than I remember, but no more whole. This wouldn't be an easy fix. It would be hard work, but I knew we were worth it.

She climbed onto the bed and I pulled the blankets over her.

"Nikki, I'm very upset that you never told me when you got home, that you never replied to any of my texts, that you didn't tell me you were coming home. But I am glad you are home. We have a lot to work on. I love you no less than before and I am going to shower because I stink and when I'm on top of you I don't want to smell like a sweaty ass baseball player."

I bent down and was ready to kiss her, but stopped just before my lips touched hers. "I missed you."

"I was mad at you and I shouldn't have been."

"I love you."

"Then please either get in here or go shower."

I got in the shower and was washing my hair when she walked in. I didn't say a word, she just walked straight into me. I bent down and took her mouth, surrounding it with mine. I sucked on her lips and she pulled back. I bent down to her tits and kissed them, sucked them, and bit them. She pushed harder against me asking for more and I sucked harder. She leaned back and kissed down my body. She got close to my rock-hard cock and moved slowly down, capturing it between her tits. Her tongue darted out and she licked off my head, swallowing the pearl that had formed on the tip, and then she sat back on her heels.

"Sit, please." She pointed to the built-in shower ledge.

I wasn't gonna argue.

She wrapped her hand around my throbbing erection and slowly stroked me up and down. She bowed her head and ran her tongue across its head.

"Fuck ..." I hissed, taking her head in my hand, guiding her down again. She opened her mouth wider, taking me as far as she could.

"That's it, baby," I guided her head up and down my throbbing cock.

"You are doing fucking amazing, Nikki, that's it baby, fuck yes."

She moved up and down faster, and I fisted her hair tighter.

"Damn baby, suck me harder."

She continued bobbing faster and faster along my length.

"I'm not gonna last, Nikki, it's been a long fucking time."

She didn't stop. I looked down into her hungry eyes and felt my cock twitch in her mouth.

She opened wide and stuck out her tongue, begging for my cum, as she continued stroking me until I was bone fucking dry.

"I've wanted to do that to you for a very long time. Did I do okay?"

"Oh yeah?" I leaned down and kissed her as I played with her nipple.

"I like how you taste." She moaned as she pushed into my hand.

"You're next."

I picked her up, walked out of the bathroom, and laid her on my bed.

My mouth descended down her body and she was already squirming. I kissed her belly and then went lower. I licked her sweet pussy in slow gently strokes, caressing, teasing and making her pussy become even slicker as I teased her outer lips.

She quivered as my tongue split her open, going deeper. Her knees tensed and I wrapped my lips around her slick lips and sucked gently. She moaned as my tongue plunged deeper.

"Damn," I groaned and rubbed my nose across her hardening tender spot.

"Oh my God," she whimpered.

I licked her harder and deeper ravaging her as she fell apart. I slowed, tugged at her with my teeth, and she screamed out as her pussy clenched. I did it repeatedly until her body had had enough.

I slid up, lay beside her, and pulled her hair away from her face.

"I love you, Nikolette. Don't you ever leave again."

"I won't. Ever."

"Get some rest, I'm gonna be needing you again soon."

Seasons and Change

It had been two weeks since I found Nikolette Bassett sitting against the building after the softball game and crying. The same girl who I found so captivating in Florida, who left me with a note, the girl who walked into my office a week later with poise and confidence and a ere about her that not only drew me to her but pushed me away.

I, Abe O'Donnell, a man who fell into the life I had dreamed of since starting NYU, had been chipped. I was the master of my own part of the universe and dominated every part of it. I never took anything for granted and methodically planned every move, in business and my personal life, until Nikki.

Allowing her into my life went against my better judgment from the moment she followed me in her car and cause me to be car jacked. But some things cannot be helped. She would not allow me to avoid her. She knew what she wanted and went after me hard to get it. That was my weakness, a woman who was so strong on her own, yet so willing to submit.

You see, people have a misconception about the true nature of the D/s relationship. They think they can just become a role, like it's a fucking game you play or a choice you make. But it's not. Something happens in your life to pull you into one of two directions. Neither role is weak, yet both were needy.

Nikki was doing a great job as our PR girl at Steel Inc. It gave her the credits she needs to graduate and a glimpse of what she could do fulltime after school if she wanted too. If she decided not to continue at Steel Inc. after graduation, I will do what I can to help her pursue sports journalism, although I would sway her away from male-dominated sports if I could. Regardless of the path she chooses, I want her happy and strong as much as I wanted my next release.

She and Carly are very close, both have a "sexy smart girl" persona, and both of them loved to read. Love may not even be a strong enough word to describe it. They were obsessed, and together with the three other ladies I met in Florida, they had an online book club that allowed them to obsess over books and authors they loved. I liked that she had a little something to focus on besides me. But her job, friends and book club was enough because I wanted her to myself as much as I could get her.

We sat in the car on our way home from the office. I was driving and Nikki was busy typing away on her iPad when she stopped to look out the window.

"Everything okay?" I took her hand and kissed it.

"Not everything."

She smiled but didn't look at me. I let it go for a few minutes and then being me, well I needed to know.

"Nikki, remember this doesn't work without—"

"Complete trust, I know."

"Good girl. Then let's have it."

"You can't get mad."

"Well I can but I'll try not to." Frankly, I was a little worried about what she was going to say.

"When did you start being this way?"

"Handsome? Intelligent? Great in bed?"

"Modest." She laughed and then looked at me. "I think for me, when I felt broken by betrayal, I let it make me who I was. I was a giver. I was naïve. I was going to be alone and it was fine. I had a great family and friends. But deep down, I felt like an idiot, that I would always be everyone's–"

"Don't talk about yourself like that, Nikolette. You are–"

"Let me finish."

"My apologies."

"When I met you, you didn't see me for what I was to everyone else, or more specifically you didn't see me how I saw myself. You saw what I wanted you to see."

"Who you really are inside."

"Yes I know that now. You made me realize that it was all right to be needy. That it didn't mean I was weak because I let you have your way. You make me feel beautiful, sexy, and strong."

"That's what I see when I see you. Even though everything–"

"Let's not kid ourselves here, Mr. O'Donnell, I've been a bit broken for a while now."

"Bent, not broken. Even still, you're on the mend, which goes to prove I'm right. You're strong, Nikki."

She smiled and nodded. "I've been working on it, thanks to you I feel safe and loved."

"Adored."

"Yep."

"Sexy, so god damn sexy."

Her cheeks flushed and she nodded.

"So sexy I am gonna take you home and ravage your body all night. And since you're so strong, your gonna let me torment, tease, inflict a bit of pain that will intensify the pleasure and –"

"Let me finish?"

"If I must."

"Do you know when your loss of control was taken over by control?"

"Excuse me?" I chuckled.

"The moment that control became so important to you. That loss of control that was taken over by control?"

"When I decided I wouldn't have my life chaos?"

"I like my phrasing better, but yes, that's exactly what I mean."

"Probably forever? I think I was born wanting everything just so."

"Or you were raised with everything just so."

"As were you, I assume. Being only children."

She took a deep breath, "I love you and I know you know that. I will do anything you ask, be anyone you want me to be–"

"I just want you to be you."

She looked out the window again. "We had a conversation awhile back, about your mother. I think that's when."

My mother. It had been a few weeks since I had seen her.

"No. That's not it."

"It's part of it."

"Nikolette–"

"Nikki, and I want you to think about it, that's all. While thinking about it, do so with the understanding that nothing will change for me. But it might for you."

I pulled into the house and tapped in the code.

We walked inside hand-in-hand without words. I gave her a kiss and headed upstairs to change, I needed to work out, blow off some steam, and think about the seed she had planted.

An hour and forty-five minutes later, I was done. I was sore, tired, and yes, a bit emotionally drained.

When I walked up the stairs, Nikki was in the kitchen. "I'm sorry."

"Don't be," I gave her a kiss on the cheek and grabbed a glass out of the cupboard to get some water. "You wanna meet her?"

"Your mother?"

"Yes."

"Of course I do, but when you're ready."

"I'm gonna shower, then we'll go. Then well go grab some dinner. Sound good?"

She smiled and nodded her head.

***

We walked into Mom's room it was evening ,and things was quiet, thank God.

I went over to her bed, bent down, and kissed her head. "Hello, Mom, it's me, Abe. I want you to meet someone who is pretty special to me."

I held my hand out and Nikki walked over. "This is Nikolette Bassett. Nikolette Bassett, this is my mother, Margaret."

Nikolette shocked me when she bent over and kissed her head. "Very nice to meet you, Mrs. O'Donnell. I want you to know your son, Abe, is very special to me as well. In fact, I love him. I love every complicated and uncomplicated side of him." She sat on the bed beside her, held her hand, and just kept talking to her. I swear my heart swelled in my chest to the point that if it didn't feel so good it may actually ache. "I've wondered about you, you know? Wondered who could be responsible for raising such a gentleman. I have met your husband and he is very kind. Now that I have met you and after hearing the story of your struggle and seeing the strength you must have for fighting to stay with your family, I'm even more in awe of you, and your son. You see, if he is half as strong as you, we can get through anything life throws at us. I wish you could give me your blessing and that you could see how genuine I am and just how deeply in love with your son I am. I promise I will make him happy for as long as he wants me in his life. He's helped me a lot. He's helped me realize who I am and he's helped me realize that I can trust and love again. So thank you for that."

I stood taking in all that she had just said to my mother.

"I see you like books. Me too." She picked up the book and opened it to the page I had left off at the last time I was here. I sat next to her and we took turns reading to mom for well over an hour.

When we stood to leave, I asked Nikki to give me a minute alone with my mom. She planted another kiss on Mom's head, then waited for me in the hallway.

"Hey Mom, so the ring, the one that you saved of your mother's for the day I found the one? Well, I found her. Nikki is the one. From the moment I saw her, I knew. She's so beautiful Mom, I wish you could see her. I wish you could just open your eyes and see her, but I know you can't and I know how incredible selfish it is to ask that. She just made me realize you're so much stronger than Pops and I. You've been here for us even though you're not here. Does that make any sense? Well it's been like that since I was born, another thing Nikki opened my eyes too. They talk about the woman behind the man, and you've been the woman behind two, very stubborn, selfish Irishmen who love you. I want you to be selfish for once. Remember my first year playing little league how I struck out almost every time up to bat? It was funny that it came from you and not Pops; but I remember you telling me that at least I swung and you couldn't be any more proud of me for the courage I showed in doing that. I was upset that my teammates were picking on me and you told me when I was up to bat it was my game. They were at my mercy and that if I felt it I should swing, I should without worrying about what anyone else thought. The next game when I was up to bat I had two strikes at the bottom of the ninth inning. We had two outs, were two runs behind and the bases were loaded. I looked at you. You nodded and smiled. That smile told me to go for it. I hit three runners in and we won the game. My point Mom, is that I want you to choose for you and not for us whether or not you wanna play the game for us or for you. Either way if you need to go now, I support you, respect you, and love you always."

I gave her a kiss and walked out.

Nikki and I went to see Mom every other night after that. She said it was cruel not to finish reading her the book. When the book was finished, I started telling her about O'Donnell's ball team and that we had our championship game on Thursday. Nikki was amazing with her and in my deepest most childlike moments, I wished just once she would open her eyes and see how beautiful my Nikki was on the outside even if she could hear it and feel it in everything Nikki said or did.

The night before the game, Nikki and I stopped by and she changed Mom into an O'Donnell's ball jersey. She even painted her toes the same shade of green. Have I mentioned how in awe of Nikki I am? More and more so every day, she was more than I had hoped for or dreamt that she was.

***

After a very close game, O'Donnell's won the championship baseball game and as usual, we headed to the bar to celebrate. Nikki showed Dad the pictures she had taken of me and mom all decked out in O'Donnell's gear. I felt closer to my mom now than I had in years, and it was all because of Nikki. I even allowed myself to hope the next time I saw her she would wake up.

I let Pops take off, He seemed pretty emotional by the pictures of Mom, even though he would never admit it.

He said he wanted to go tell her about the win in person.

I locked up the bar and drew the blinds. I turned around and Nikki was sitting on the bar in a Jersey and nothing else but a pair of matching green thongs.

"What are you doing, Miss Bassett?" I said as I pulled out Pop's stool and sat between her sexy- as-hell legs.

"Waiting for a drink, Mr. O'Donnell."

"Hmm." I kissed her knee.

"Mmm," she moaned.

"What can I get for you?"

"Do you how to make a Lesbian Joy cocktail?"

"You lost me at lesbian, but gained my attention with cock—tail."

"Oh well, it's a great drink. The girls and I had them--."

She stopped talking when I pulled her shirt over her head.

"How about you tell me the ingredients and I'll see what I can do? But let me worn you, the L word is not to be part of your vocabulary anymore."

I unsnapped her bra, pulled it down, and bit on her nipple a little bit harder than she liked but it was definitely earned.

"Now lay back and tell me how to make this cock-tail."

"It was a wild night," she giggled.

"Are you trying to rack up punishments, Miss Bassett?"

"Oh no, Mr. O'Donnell, not me," she batted her eyelashes. "A dash of Amaretto," she said as she lay down. "A dash of kirsch, a dash of whiskey, a few ounces of red—Oh my God." She gasped when I placed an ice cube on her belly and poured the Amaretto onto her belly button.

"Don't move, Miss Bassett. Spilling a drink will be immediate grounds for harsh punishment. Keep going."

"Lemonade," she squirmed a bit with each ounce of liquid I poured. "A slice of orange and a cherry, of course."

"Of course," I said as I placed the cherry stem up in her folds. "Don't let that drop either, Miss Bassett."

"Of course not, Mr. O'Donnell."

"Now the way I see it, this cock-tail needs a different name because even a man would be tempted to drink something that looked this delicious and men are not—the L word."

"Men seem to like—"

I swatted her little bottom, "I wouldn't if I were you."

Her moan and her glazed eyes made me realize she may do it again just to feel the sting of my hand on her sweet little bottom. "You liked that."

"I did."

I grabbed two ice cubes and rubbed them on her nipples. Watching her squirm while her nipples grow more erect than I had ever seen them made me even harder.

"You're doing wonderfully, Miss Bassett."

I ran one cube down her sternum and to the very spot were all the liquid was pooled.

"A taste test, just to make sure it's as good as you say."

"Of course."

I sucked the pooled alcohol and her flesh, then dipped my tongue into her belly button.

She took in a deep breath and her stomach concaved even more.

I drank from her and allowed my tongue to lick her clean.

"It's delicious." I sat back on the stool between her legs and looked at her now swollen lips. They tightened around the cherry holding it in place. "What am I forgetting?"

"The cherry," she gasped.

"Oh. How could I have forgotten that? But I do prefer my cherries cold and by the looks of this," I ran my tongue from her ass up to the cherry, "It's hot as hell. How do you suppose we fix that?" I asked as I stood.

"Abe please," she begged.

"Patience. I want to enjoy looking at the cherry enclosed in the most beautiful pussy I have ever had the pleasure of gazing at. You are incredibly strong and so perfect. Do you know that?"

"You make me feel that way," her voice was husky and filled with need. I wasn't sure how long I could hold out.

I took the ice cube and ran it around the outside of her lips and then kissed her. "I'm going to sit and chill that beautiful little cherry you've been hanging onto for me. Then I am going to take my time eating it, and you. Then, Miss Bassett, I 'm going to pull you off the bar and onto my lap and fuck you until you can't move."

"Please, oh yes please."

I did just what I said I would. I licked around the cherry then under the cherry and sucked her little hard clit until the cherry nearly fell out of her clenched lips.

I pulled her down onto me and pumped into her with all I had as I resisted the urge to come.

I stood, needing more leverage, and pushed her ass up against the beer cooler and pounded into her until her grip loosened form the exhaustion of orgasm after orgasm.

I yelled out "I love you" as I filled her pretty little pussy with everything I had.

"I love you, so much," she panted.

***

We slept in until seven and Nikki jumped up and began to panic.

"We're fine, I shut it off. We had a late night."

"You're sure?"

The phone rang as I nodded.

"Hey, Pops, good morning … Repeat, please… I'll be there as soon as I can."

I jumped out of bed and Nikki followed. I felt sick to my stomach and then confused because I wanted peace for her but more than, that I want her.

I was throwing clothes around in the closet when Nikki grabbed both my arms. "She's gone?"

I couldn't answer because I would not break down in front of anyone, and especially not the woman who I wanted to be the strongest for.

"Abe," she wrapped her arms around my waist and hugged me. "I'm so sorry."

"Thanks," I tried to step back but she held tighter.

"Please don't push me away. You ask for trust and I give it to you completely and without regret. Do the same for me."

"I wasn't ready. I shouldn't have told her I was."

"That was the most unselfish thing I have ever seen anyone do. She knew you loved her enough to let her go and be at peace.

"When we have children--."

"You want to have children with me?"

"Sorry that's a bit presumptuous."

"No, not at all. But If I crack you'll–"

"Love you even deeper."

I stood there, holding onto her, not letting go. I wouldn't break. I wouldn't, because Pops was gonna need me to be strong.

"We should go," she said and stood on her tip-toes and kissed me.

"Thank you."

"No need."

"You can stay here."

"No, I'm going."

We dressed in silence.

***

Nikki said we should stay with Pops, that he needed us, and she was right. We lay in my childhood bed, her asleep in my arms and me awake. I watched her sleep and thought of Mom. I thought about our future children not knowing their grandmother and then I thought of what she'd done for Pops and I.

When I become a father, I know what I would expect from myself. I would be their protector, their champion, and I would be there for them without exception. I would be just like mom had been, even in the last days of her life.

"She waited until she knew you were okay. She waited until she knew you had everything you ever wanted."

I smiled down at my darling Nikki, "I thought you were asleep."

"No, not until I know you have stopped thinking you're at fault for her letting go."

"How can I not?"

"Abe, she waited until you were ready to let go. She waited until she knew she had done everything she wanted to as a mother."

"I know."

"You made her proud."

"I tried."

"Now try to celebrate the most amazing woman you have ever known. The woman who gave you life and fought with all she was to stay until she knew she had finished her job."

"Okay."

"Okay?"

"Yeah. She played her game."

"She did."

"We need to have kids, like now." She laughed. "I'm serious, Nikki, I want them to know Pops, and your family."

"Well me too but--."

"Wait, give me a minute."

I went down to see if Pops was awake.

"Pops."

He looked up from a photo album he was looking at. He hadn't broken down either. Not at the home, not when making Mom's final arrangements, and not now as he looked at the album.

"Everything alright, Abe?"

"Yeah. I need the ring Mom was saving for me."

He nodded, "You sure now's a good time?"

"Not sure, but I know now is when it needs to happen."

"You gonna ask her father, Abe? It's the right thing to do you know."

"He'll tell me no."

"Why?"

"Too soon, but it's not, Pops, she's the one and right now I need a fucking win. We need a win. She wants children with me so—"

He stood up, "Say no more, I've liked her since the first time she walked into the pub and tomorrow isn't a guarantee."

***

I walked into my room and she was pacing, "You're alright, aren't you?"

"Yes. Nikki have a seat." And as always she did as I asked. "You are it for me. I don't want anyone else. I want you. I want you strong, I want you broken, I want you tied up, I want you on a bar. I want you to be my partner and the mother of my child. I want you now and I want you forever." I knelt down on one knee. "Nikolette Bassett, you said that she was the most amazing woman I knew. Well you are no less amazing. I don't want to wait to start our forever, because as Pops just said, tomorrow isn't guaranteed. Marry me, Nikki. Say yes and I promise you, I will give you the moon and the stars."

Tears fell down her face and she nodded and giggled as she wiped her tears. "That's a lot you know, the moon and the stars. I want more than that though, I want your heart, your soul and your promise that no matter what, you will never stop pushing my limits and taking me any way you want."

"Of course, God yes. Fuck could you get any better?" I pushed the ring onto her finger and she knelt beside me.

"I plan to age like wine and cheese, so yes, I can get much better."

"I plan to push the hell out of your limits," I placed my lips to hers, "I'm gonna shatter them."

"Good. I love you, Abe."

"I love you."

Epilogue

It has been four weeks since Abe asked me to marry him, an anniversary of sorts. I am working at Steel Inc. now and love my job. He never demanded I work there, just offered. Of course I was leery at first of giving up on my 'dream' for a man. Abe O'Donnell is not just a man. He is smart, driven, a protector, a nurturer, the keeper of my heart, and the owner of my body.

When I think about the very first night we were together it still takes my breath away. I had never felt so sexual, so free, and so satisfied as I did when I was on the beach with him. He made me feel things I had never felt before, amazing things.

When I thought his control meant giving up mine I ran. When I saw him again, I was sure I was right. Abe O'Donnell CFO was a complete ass. He demanded control. It was his way or no way at all. But when I pushed him without even knowing I was, he gave a little.

A man like Abe, a true Dominant man was not like the ones I had ever read about. He studied me, fought his urges, and looking back I knew he was always putting me first. He sent me away and it devastated me, but now I knew why. It was for protection, it was because he wanted me to be strong, to be sure of us. Not long ago he had admitted, that it was because I needed to be sure of the same, because I could easily break him.

Our days had become quite mundane. He woke early, worked out, and was off to work before I even got up. The first week I got up with him and he insisted I stay in bed. He worked twelve hours a day and if I was asleep for at least three of them, he wouldn't feel as guilty about working so much and not spending more time with me.

The second week I was finally was able to fall back to sleep. My own insecurities that it was because he just needed time away from me dwindled when he met me in the lobby every morning, had lunch with me three times a week, and closed his door before I left every afternoon to talk and really listen to what I had to say about my day.

Week three I had settled in, felt like I belonged. I was even able to stop looking around his home to make sure I had put things back in the exact place Abe would want them. When I realized I was doing this for his attention, for his approval, to regain that part of the connection I thought we had lost due to the events that took place weeks previously, I questioned why.

I realized a couple of days ago why I may feel that way and when it hit me I began making plans for today. It's our four week anniversary of being and engaged couple. What I was missing was the fierceness behind the Abe I met in Fort Lauderdale. He was holding back, not pushing me, not demanding, and in doing so, I felt insecure and less wanted.

I had spent the past couple of days really exploring my new home. The spare bedroom was fully enclosed unlike the room we slept in. It was dark, the windows covered in black out curtains. The bed was made of old beams and canopied from above. A cast iron ring hung on the ceiling; red shear material flowed from it. The headboard and footboard were made of the same beams lying flat, flush with the mattress and on each corner was a cast iron ring.

I walked into the closet and saw a chest of drawers. I stood for a moment trying to convince myself to turn and walk away, but I couldn't.

The drawers held belts, ties, scarves, ropes, cuffs, and even chains. I closed the last drawer and stepped back. I may have been a little shocked. I don't know why, I knew this about him, well I knew, but never truly experienced it's full effect.

My throat was drying and my mouth was watering, I was feeling the same feelings I felt that night on the beach, the pool table, and my apartment, I was getting completely turned on. It hit me then, this was what I was missing, what Abe was missing.

Nikolette was adjusting well. The first week I felt like she was trying to be what I expected her to be, her Dom. I knew she had read about the D/s lifestyle, it was in the history on her computer. Some of the shit that was online was a complete fucking joke. To believe you can put any human being in a category based on other human beings thoughts or experiences was insane to me. No one person is the same. It was illogical. Another reason I liked numbers, facts and things that were absolute.

Had I done that when I saw her the first day on the beach, I would have made the assumption she was a girl out for a good time, a fling, a party girl. I would have assumed she was doing the same damn thing I had set out to do. Get laid, have fun, let lose. I will admit, that's exactly what I did at first, in my own way of course. I had studied her, watched for reactions, clues, for things that would have made her not just a fuck, but something I could control for the few days I would be there.

Control left the fucking building when I felt like she had stood me up, when I felt I had read her wrong, when I felt I had been wrong. When she came to me, I had too much to drink, and I fucked up by not easing into things with her. When she came for me, I knew I had to make her do so again, and again. When she left that note, the one I still had, I was angry at myself because being inside her made me feel stronger.

You see I am not a man to be put into a box, placed in a category, stereotyped, or figured out. That being said, I knew that Nikolette was not a woman who would truly be happy with a man telling her how to behave, what to do, or when to do it. To be honest, I would never be content with that either. The beautiful woman I met was smart, strong, sexy, and at times sassy, and I liked that.

The past two weeks I have seen her strength return. Hell she was even leaving cups in the sink and the cap off of the toothpaste, which was a little annoying but also a welcome sign that she was not just all about pleasing me. She was getting comfortable, seemed happier, less guarded and more open.

These things were necessary for the progression of our relationship. The only part in which control and ownership is an absolute necessity for me, the sexually part. I will own her and she will allow it. We were so very close to that. It was no longer the promise in just words some women give men they wish to please, but the looks, the mannerism, the need I was sensing. Steps away, just steps, from total sexual dominance.

I returned home and called for Nikki. When she didn't answer I set down the bottle of wine, flowers, and the little box that held a gift that reminded me of her, Four.

I walked up the stairs to see if maybe she was in the bath. When she wasn't there or in the bedroom I was getting a little anxious. I called her phone, three times and no answer. I called George and asked him to locate her phone so I knew where she was and he told me it was at my address. I called again and instead of listening for her voice to see if I could hear it in the background. When I did my panic worsened. Was she hurt or had someone gotten to her?

I called again and quickly made my way to the stairs and followed them down. The ringing stopped and I called again. This time I heard it from the back. I walked to the door of a room I hadn't been in for months.

I slowly opened the door and she was sitting on the bed, completely naked, and absolutely stunning. She didn't smile and didn't look shocked to see me. She looked confident and sexy. The way I wanted her, Four, Nikki, Nikolette, my fiancée', my lover, my future wife, my sub to look. "How long have you been in here?" I asked leaning against the doorway.

"A while."

"You shouldn't be in here, Nikolette."

"You shouldn't have been hiding it from me."

"Not hiding, just waiting."

"For what?" She asked the question but I knew she was aware of the answer. "For me?"

"Always." I pushed off the door, walked in, and closed the door behind me. I loosened my tie, unbuttoned my shirt and then shrugged it and my suit jacket off. I laid it over the chair, unbuckled my belt, pulled it off, unbuttoned my pants, and walked into the closet.

When I came back out her eyes widened as she looked at the ropes in my hand.

"Off the bed, please, Nikolette." She did as I asked. "Good girl. Now kneel at the foot of the bed and wait."

"Okay," she whispered.

"No, Nikolette, in here, it's yes Sir." Sir, was respect. Respect was given out of trust and loyalty. In this room that was who I had to be. Her ultimate trust and forever loyalty.

"Did the others call you that?" she asked as she stepped off the bed.

"In here there is only you and I. If you are concerned about anyone else in here, we aren't ready for this step Nikolette." I watched her, gauging her to see her reaction as she watched me. "Nikolette, the foot of the bed please."

She licked her lips and let out a breath, "Yes, Sir."

"Back to the bed, head down, do not look at me. Anticipation. What will he do with me, what pleasure will he take from my body, what pleasure will he give to me in exchange for my submission. Those are the only things you think of in here, do you understand Nikolette?"

I watched her kneel as I instructed, her head bowed, "Yes, Sir."

"Perfect, Nikolette."

I stood on the bed, and attached the ropes to the iron ring above it. "I am going to take you a little out of your comfort zone. This is for my pleasure. I have fantasized about you bound and tied Nikolette. I'm already hard just thinking about how wet your sweet pussy is getting for me. Do you understand?"

"Yes, Sir." The thickness in her voice made me even harder.

Once the ropes were at the right length I stepped down and walked to her. "Spread your knees as wide as you can. I want to see the beautiful pussy that belongs to me." She did without hesitation. "You're wet." I reached down and rubbed between her legs without touching her clit and she rocked slightly into my touch. I pulled my hand away quickly, "This isn't for you. If you do that again, there will be consequences. Do you understand?"

"Yes, Sir."

"Stand up, Nikolette." She stood and looked at me. Taking it easy on her for the first time we were in here I would not demand she looked down. I simply averted eye contact. I bound her hands with rope, "Too tight?"

"No, Sir," she whispered.

"If it is you need to tell me Nikolette. This isn't to hurt you, it's to please me."

"I understand, Sir."

"Good," I leaned in so that I could kiss her neck. Appreciation. She moaned. "Control, Nikolette." I whispered against her collarbone. "You are not just giving me control, you must maintain yours as well. Now, on the bed."

When I helped her up I told her to stand and lift her arms. Once she was strung up I stepped down.

"You are truly the most beautiful woman in the universe. Your skin like caramel, hair sleek, black, thick and sexy as hell. Then the eyes." I loved her fucking eyes. "Turn for me, slowly, in a circle. I want to be able to appreciate the gift that is before me."

She turned slowly, gracefully, beautifully.

When she stopped I knelt on the bed and lifted her leg, kissing all the way slowly up it until I met her moist, bare, swollen lips. I hoisted her leg over my shoulder. "Your arms don't get the weight, my shoulders do," I explained as I started lifting the other. She gasped, "You won't fall," I said between the kisses up her other leg. Once I rested it over my shoulder and she had given me her weight to bear I licked her pussy slowly from front to back and then back again. I then spread her wider so that I could lick inside. I pushed my tongue in and she whimpered. I did it over and over until I felt she was about to come then pulled away. "Not yet, beautiful."

I lowered her legs, one at a time.

She was now standing and I stood off of the bed. Her nipples where erect, her moisture apparent, and I was going to make her even more aroused. Painfully aroused.

I grabbed more rope, bound her ankles, and tied them to the bed rings. I moved behind her and untied the knot above her allowing her arms to hand loosely. "Bend forward, Nikolette, hands on the bed, your ass in the air. As soon as she bent I drove two fingers inside of her, taking her by surprise. I fucked her hard and fierce with two fingers, until she was again on edge. I pulled away and she cried out in protest. I smacked her sexy round bottom, not hard, just enough to tell her that wasn't alright. It was immediately followed by my tongue licking the spot in which I stung her.

I went at her again, two fingers slowly in and out rubbing and spreading her slick fluids around both openings. I couldn't wait to have my cock in her ass, but for now, this was going to have to be good enough. A true Dom pushed limits, but thinks of his sub first, always.

I fucked her harder and she was on edge, her body tensed and her arms began to shake. I quickly moved to the side of her and shoved my legs underneath, "Down, Nikolette."

As soon as the words left my lips she laid down on me. I continued finger fucking her until she was shaking as she tried to not come. "Come for me sweet, Nikolette."

When her breath released I pushed a finger in her tight puckered hole and she gasped.

"Trust, I won't hurt you," I was more gentle. "Trust that this is making me so incredible happy. Trust, Nikolette, that I know how to give you pleasures I haven't even begun to show you yet."

"Yes, Sir," she said as she relaxed a bit.

"That's it. Now back to my last request. Come for me, Nikolette." I fucked her pussy and her ass with my fingers until she screamed out my name.

I slowed as she came down from her orgasm and when she laid on my lap completely relaxed, I pulled my hand away.

"All fours, Nikolette."

Once she did as I asked I pulled her back against me and held her.

"Now lay and rest."

"What about you?" she asked. "Sir."

"I haven't even begun, but for right now, you get some rest."

When she lay down, I covered her, kissed her, and walked out the door.

Playlist for Abe

Guardian by Alanis Morissette

Stay by Safety Suit

Over My Head by The Fray

Make Damn Sure by Taking Back Sunday

Addicted To You by Avicii

Here's To The Night by Eve 6

Rude by Magic

Show me What I'm Looking For by Carolina Liar

ACKNOWLEDGMENTS

First and foremost, thank you to the owner of this copy of Abe.

Thank you to my agent, Marisa Corvisiero, the ambassador of Crazytown, and honorary board member of Steel Inc. She wears each hat with class, a smile in her voice, and professionalism that blows me away. You loved the naughty 'voice' in my writing and you saw the beneath the crude exterior in which all things Steel posses and looked deeper. You believed in me, and for that I am eternally grateful.

To Bobbie, Jamie, Mary, Mary, Renee, KA, Lucy, Christa, Ashley, Laurie, Gloria, Brandi, Michelle, Ellie, Jen, and Stephanie a million thanks is not enough but you have them.

To the F2 crew, BR ninjas, blogs and bloggers who constantly share my work with others via social media and word of mouth, I send you a million virtual hugs and praises. Without you to #sharethelove I would never be where I am today. I <3 U all!

To my family whose support and encouragement does not go unnoticed, even if my nose is buried in the computer, or I am on the phone talking about my books, you are my priority always. Never, ever doubt that. Someday, eighteen hours a day will be more than worth it. I pinky promise.

To Ally B., when you read these books in ten years (or twenty … please) look past the naughty, there's a story of growth and love. Every woman deserves to be loved by a man who protects her and her heart. A man who knows she is a privilege. And she needs to feel the same. Choose otherwise and mommy will kick his ass. ☺

CONNECT WITH MJ FIELDS

Email – mjfieldsbooks@gmail.com

Website – www.mjfieldsbooks.com

Facebook – http://tinyurl.com/mjfieldsfb

Tsu- https://www.tsu.co/mjfields

For more on the Ties of Steel series, sign up for the newsletter on MJ's Facebook page or at

www.mjfieldsbooks.com

Would you like to receive text messages from MJ Fields?

Text MJFields to 96362

Standard texting fees apply

Follow MJ on Spotify and listen to songs that inspired this and many of her other books!

First Chapter Sample of Ties of Steel: Book 2
(Uncorrected Sample)

DOMINIC: THE PRINCE

GRADUATION
~*L*~

I walked out the door with my belongings in hand. It was time to move the hell on. I had made a promise to myself: when it was no longer fun, I would be done.

It was no longer fun. Hell, it bypassed fun four months ago. And after this, well it was over.

James pursued me hard and fucked me even harder. He was a player. You know the type. He smiled, gave a wink, I ended up with a pair of soaked panties before I turned and walked away.

Apparently, I was playing hard to get, so he said, which made him have to have me (his words). After three weeks of him asking me out, I agreed to a date.

Flowers, check.

Dinner, check.

A bottle and a half of wine, double check.

He insisted on walking me into my apartment.

The first time we had sex. Yes that night, but I will never admit that to my girls, we have rules. Rules which my girl Nikki had already broken, that lucky bitch got a hot guy too. Abe O'Donnell is hot as hell and he is one possessive fickle bastard, and she got him. Where were we, oh yes, James and my first time went something like this.

'We've waited long enough, darlin',' with that southern drawl and green-ass eyes boring holes into mine, I caved.

He was big and rough and lasted all of five minutes.

'Its okay," I tried making sure he knew I was alright with what had just happened.

'Better than ok, it that was damn good.'

Uh huh. It's not like it was awful sex. I mean it was frequent and like I said, he was on the larger than average size. I mean seven inches wasn't bad, right?

Apparently, two to three times a day wasn't enough for James. That's what he told me when I walked into our apartment and found him fucking the slut down the hall.

"I need it more, darlin'," he said, as he stood naked, still hard, while she threw her clothes on. "You put out more often and we'll be okay, you'll see."

"Are you kidding me?" I laughed as I chucked all my clothes out of the closet.

"I'll talk to you later?" I heard the bitch whisper, trying to sound sexy.

"You have to have more self-respect than that. Did you not just hear what he said to me?"

"Sex is sex," she rolled her eyes.

"Well, just so you know, you just made it to the top of my prayer list. Bless your heart."

"You too."

"Me?" I squeaked my response.

"You're doing him two and three times a day and I'm in need of prayers?"

"Living together." I pointed between him and I. I stopped when I realized I was arguing with a slut who had been banging my live-in boyfriend. "Get the fuck out."

I bent down, picked up one of my black heels, and hurled it in her direction.

"Oh my God, she's crazy!"

"That's right, skank." I yelled.

I looked over at James and he just looked back at me and smirked. The bastard was smirking, as he held onto himself, naked and hard, and watching the two of us bickering back and fourth.

"You too! Sick bastard." I snapped at him.

"Who me?" He looked shocked and pointed to himself.

Oh. My. God. He was fucking clueless.

I don't know what came over me but I started laughing. It was a cross between a belly laugh and a snort, and then tears started falling as I threw everything I owned into a suitcase and two duffle bags.

Before walking out the door, I looked back at him. He finally had on some basketball shorts.

"You really gonna leave, darlin'? Where you gonna go? Can't go home, can't get back into the dorms."

"Can't stay here with you either."

"If I," he stopped and scratched his head, "If I promise not to do it again, maybe you'll stay?"

How is it that I felt more emotion emitting from James at that very moment than I had in the six months we'd been together? I mean, he wasn't a complete asshole and our first date may have been the last time he showed an ounce of what I would consider a romantic notion.

I shook my head, as he slowly approached me.

"Come on, darlin' give it another shot. Just give me one more try."

I shook my head again, harder this time, as he took my hand, "Where you gonna go, Laney?"

"I'll find a place?" *my voice cracked.*

He shook his head, "Not that easy darlin'."

At that moment, the dam broke. I fell apart, and at that moment, James hugged me, which was the second nicest thing he had ever done. He slid the duffle bag strap off my right shoulder and the other off my left. And I stood there and let them drop to the ground as I sobbed against his bare chest.

He wrapped his arms around me and rubbed my back.

It was probably the sweetest moment in our entire relationship—until he popped wood.

Before pulling out of my parking spot, I looked up hoping to see him coming after me, hoping that he would fight for me. I gave it two minutes. One hundred twenty seconds waiting for a man to beg me to come back, a man that I just caught fucking another woman.

Pathetic. That's what I was.

***

Mel opened her dorm room door, and I held up a bottle of wine. "Wanna help me drink this?"

She smiled and stepped back, "I'd never say no to you."

"Paige here?" I asked, as I walked in.

"She's on a date."

"Cool," I set the bottle down and wiggled my jacket off my shoulders. Mel had that look, the one of concern and question. "What?"

"Spill it," she said and turned her back to grab two cups out of the shoebox-sized cabinet that housed their dinnerware. Red Solo cups.

"It wasn't fun anymore." I began.

"Oh come on, he's what the third one in three years? It's not always about fun, Laney."

"Don't you judge me," I said pouring the Red Cat into my cup.

"You--"

"I caught him in bed with the whore down the hall."

"No," her mouth dropped open.

I took a long drink and nodded as I swallowed.

"I thought you and he had a great sex life."

"Great. Yeah I wouldn't say great. Frequent, but apparently not frequent enough." I took another drink as she filled her cup.

"You can stay here as long as you want, okay?"

"Mels, I can't be a fucking mooch for--"

"You'd do it for us."

"What if you get caught? Get into trouble? I won't put you in that situation. I was stupid to move in with him to begin with."

After the bottle of wine was finished and we had male based for a while, I stood up, and yes I stumbled.

"Where are you going?"

"I don't know, my car, the Y, the ... "

"At least stay here tonight. I don't think Paige will be back, so you can have her bed."

I didn't want to, I mean I really didn't want to be someone else's burden.

"You're drunk Laney, just stay."

I ended up staying from February until May in Mel and Paige's tiny dorm room. After that night, I never heard from James again.

***

I hadn't spoken to my parents in months. They had a fit when I moved in with James and I was adamant that I was an adult and could make my own choices. But they banded together, for once in my life, and stood their ground. If I moved in with him, I would not get their support. I told them to take their support and shove it. That night, James lasted a bit longer than his normal five minutes and said, 'I'm proud of you, darlin'.'

I stayed out a little later the few nights preceding graduation, not wanting to face my friends, not wanting them to find out what I had been hiding for the past six months.

They didn't know that my parents and I were at odds. I knew they would be pissed when they found out. I know I messed up by not telling them, but honestly, it hurt. So what if I didn't want to share the hurt?

I even pretended to be sick so I would miss the deadline to fill out the online registration for the commencement ceremony. But my friends weren't haven't it. Me? Miss graduation? Hell no. Paige rushed through her finals prep class and brought home chicken noodle soup so I'd feel well enough fill out the form. At one point, she even offered to feed me right before placing an order for my cap and gown.

I was so fucked.

Nikki and Abe arrived two nights before graduation, and stayed in a hotel. The three of us were supposed to meet up for dinner and drinks, but Abe would be staying in to get some work done.

Outside Nikki's hotel room, Paige and I anxiously waited to be reunited with our friend. But the moment we laid eyes on her, it was like old time, and in typical *us* fashion, we hugged, laughed, and she even cried. She was excited to be back. She'd spent the last year of school doing an internship and Abe O'Donnell, CFO of Steel Incorporated.

You should have seen the look on Abe's face when the tears started rolling down her cheeks. I'd swear he thought she was upset. He immediately was at her side in protective alpha male form and seemed to enjoy the attention. Hmmm. He was even hotter than I remember.

"Happy tears, I missed them," she explained.

"You're sure?" he asked he rubbed his knuckles down the side of her cheek and she nodded.

"Now don't you have something to do? We are about to embark on a four-hour conversation about all I've missed in the past few months," she looked at us again. "Almost year."

After he placed a chaste kiss on her lips, he disappeared into the suite's master bedroom.

"You guys don't mind if we stay in and eat? Order room service? We have so much catching up to do," Nikki asked.

We ordered sushi and went through several bottles of wine before the conversation centered on my break up with James.

"I'm fine. Honest to God. I mean really, what was I gonna do, stick around here? Marry him and move to his hometown where his life will be consumed by his family's ranch and weekend rodeos? Shit, I was an idiot not to think about the future anyways. What would I be, Mrs. JD Farnsworth the second? The minute his little brother graduated high school last year, his mom ran for the hills. His dad JD Sr." I air-quoted his name, "Was a complete ass. So let's talk about something else shall we?"

"His dad beat his mom?" Nikki looked at me the same way she would at a wounded bird.

Paige laughed, "Hey at least she gets it now, can't save them all. Remember Heather? You two tried so hard to help her after her break up. Crazy is crazy right, Mel?"

"I'll drink to that," Mel raised her glass.

I forced a laugh, excused myself, and retreated to the bathroom. The mere mention of that girl's name made me sick to my stomach. I hated that bitch, hated her! The girl everyone in high school shunned, the girl that Nikki and I tried so damn hard to help was fucking my father. Not just fucking him, living with him. My mom was on the road with some cross-country hillbilly-riding bitch in a fucking tractor-trailer. My life was turned upside down last year, but with all the things Nikki and Abe had gone through, I'd kept quiet until now. If I'm being truthful, I didn't want them to know anyway. It was embarrassing.

The door opened as I was sitting on the cold tile floor. Abe walked in.

"I apologize. I didn't know anyone was in here."

"It's fine, Abe."

"You alright?"

"I'm fine, emotional you know. Graduation, all the pomp and circumstance," I stood and tried laughing it off. "Females, *pfftttt*. You live with Nikki, I'm sure you understand. Please don't mention it."

He nodded and walked out, closing the door behind him.

Not two minutes later, the door opened and Nikki walked in, and shut the door. "Spill it."

"What?" I tried to act like nothing was going on.

"You don't get emotional. Abe said you were upset."

"In front of them!"

"Abe? No. He would never."

"Why?"

"Because he's amazing. He gets it. He-" She put her hand on her hip. "You're deflecting."

"Am not," tears stung my eyes.

"Are too." She grabbed my hand. "It's me. The girl who you talked out of making the biggest mistake of her life not too damn long ago; now talk to me Laney."

"I'm not ready," I stopped when the door opened and Mel and Paige walked in.

"Not ready for what?" Mel asked and walked over and sat on the counter.

"Nothing, God. Can't someone just be emotional? Can't someone just not want to sit through a stupid ceremony in a damn green gown?

"Time to spill the beans, Laney," Paige piped in. "For a long time, I thought it was James but now I know damn well it's something else."

"My parents are getting divorced okay? They're both assholes too. I haven't talked to them in months and I don't want to talk about it."

"Why haven't you said anything?"

"Cause its embarrassing, alright?

"It happens. My parents divorced when I was ten. It's not embarrassing; its part of life," Mel smiled. "We're here for you."

"You can't just walk away from them either. I mean family is family, messed up or not." Paige interjected.

"Yes I can. And if you three keep pressuring me, I will walk out of here too."

None of them said a word. They knew I was serious.

***

I sat on a bar stool looking at the clock. An hour before graduation, and I was shit faced. I sent the girls a text telling them I wouldn't be there. Ten minutes later James walked in, alone. He pulled a bar stool up beside me and ordered two shots of tequila. He pushed one over to me and I shook my head.

"It's graduation, darlin'. We're gonna celebrate."

"Why are you here?"

"You know damn well why I'm here. This is my spot. So now ask yourself why you're here."

"Because I'm pathetic."

"No you ain't." He held up his shot glass. "To graduation and what the future holds."

I gave in. Twenty minutes and four shots later we were in the bathroom.

"You gonna come with me?" he asked as he pulled my skirt up.

"No."

He pulled down my panties, "Step out, darlin',"

I did and after he pulled them off, his jeans hit the floor.

"You ready for a ride?" he asked in that damn drawl as he ripped the condom open and rolled it quickly on.

"No." I closed my eyes. I was being fucking ridiculous.

His fingers ran up my seams and he moaned, "When things hurt, this always makes it feel better darlin'. You sure you ain't ready? You certainly feel it." He pushed a finger inside me and everything came alive.

I reached down and stroked him.

"That's right, girl." He pinned my arms to the wall above my head with one hand.

"Tell me you want a ride," he hissed against my lips, as he pushed another finger inside my wetness.

"I want a ride." I was ashamed by the need I heard in my voice.

In one hard swift move, James was inside me. He lifted me up. "Wrap 'em around me."

As I wrapped my legs around him, I glanced at my watch. He laughed. "You got somewhere to be?"

"Nope." I said as my back hit the wall.

"Good answer, now hang on."

He was brutal, which is exactly what I wanted right now. I wanted to feel his cock hitting as deep and as hard as possible.

After I came, he let go too. I glanced at my watch again. *Seven minutes.* He was up by two minutes.

"Feel better now?" He asked as he handed me a wad of toilet paper.

"Nope." I cleaned myself up, pulled my skirt down, tossed the toilet paper, and started to walk out of the bathroom.

James grabbed my arm, "Bullshit. Nothing feels better than an orgasm, darlin'."

"Maybe not," I said pulling my arm back, "But you didn't deserve me again."

"I just need more than you. Didn't mean I don't feel it in here for how bad I fucked up." He hit his chest for emphasis.

"You have a fucking problem, you know that?"

"Sure do. Just wanted to make sure you knew it wasn't you that I had a problem with."

"What the hell is that supposed to mean?"

"Means I didn't enjoy hurting you, okay? Means I still wish you were under me everyday. Means. Hell, give me another shot, maybe?" He scratched his head, "Come home with me."

You have got to be kidding me. "Why?"

"I won't fuck anyone else. Hell, this summer's circuit is crazy. I'll be getting my ass thrown around by bulls," he smirked, "Tell me you wouldn't enjoy seeing that."

"No, I wouldn't."

"Cause you'd be worried about my safety. I promise you could doctor up my wounds after each rodeo. Plus where else you gonna go?"

"I have friends, a degree, big things in store."

"There's jobs on the ranch, some in town. Busy place, you know, not a lot of downtime."

I huffed, "Meaning you won't be passing time by fucking the neighbor?"

"No I won't be."

"Why is she ugly?"

"Hideous," he chuckled.

I tried to push past him, but he pulled me back, "This is an olive branch, Laney. Take the damn thing and let's see where it leads. I said I would try. Never done that before. Just. Try."

About the Author

MJ FIELDS

MJ Fields's love of writing was in full swing by age eight. Together with her cousins, she wrote a newsletter and sold it to family members. She self-published her first New Adult romance in January 2013. Today, she has completed four self-published series, The Love series, The Wrapped series, The Burning Souls series, and The Men of Steel series. The Norfolk series has one title self-published so far and Ties of Steel, which was acquired by Swoon Romance in June 2014. MJ is a bestselling erotica author and former small business owner, who recently closed the business so she could write full time.

MJ lives in central New York, surrounded by family and friends. Her house is full of pets, friends, and noise ninety percent of the time, and she would have it no other way.

How to Tie the Four in Hand Knot

Step 1: Start with the wide end of the tie on the right and extend a foot below the narrow end.

Step 2: Cross the wide end over the narrow, and back underneath.

Step 3: Continue around, passing the wide end across the front of the narrow once more

Step 4: Pass the wide end up through the loop

Step 5: Hold the front of the knot loose with you index finger; pass the wide end down through the front loop.

Step 6: Remove your finger and tighten the knot. Draw it up tight to the collar by holding the narrow end and slide the knot up snug.

MORE BOOKS IN THE STEEL SERIES

TIES OF STEEL SERIES

ABE

DOMINIC (January 2015)

SABTATO (April 2015)

MEN OF STEEL SERIES

FOREVER STEEL

JASE

JASE & CARLY

CYRUS

ZANDOR

XAVIER

JASE & CARLY SUMMER LOVIN' PART "DUE"

Steel Christmas (coming soon)

The Norfolk Series

Irons

Irons 2

Irons 3 (March 2015)

The LRHA Legacy Series

A collection of series that follow the Links, Ross, Abraham, and Hines families through several generation.

Each series can be a standalone but is so much deeper read in order.

The Love Series

Blue Love

New Love

Sad Love

True Love

The Wrapped series

Wrapped in Silk

Wrapped in Armor

Wrapped Always and Forever

Burning Souls Series

Stained

Merged

Forged

And the latest release

Love You Anyways

Ava links story will be coming out in winter 2015

KINK VS. CLASS

BFBS SERIES 0.5

By:

V. Andrews

H. Harbour

And

M. Roberts

This book is intended to be read by mature readers over the age of 18

Table of Content

Chapter 1

Haylie

I inhale a deep breath and allow my eyes to take in the place where I grew up, hopefully for the last time. Although it's not much it's a far cry from what I remember the room to be as a small child.

A few years back, before I won a scholarship allowing me to attend Saint Anne's high school, I didn't care what it looked like. This room holds a piece of me that was gone. I took comfort in the memories made here.

After attending Saint Anne's and meeting my best friend, Tori Andrews and seeing how she lived and how full of life a person could actually be. I changed things here a little.

I managed to find an actual frame for my twin size mattress that once only set upon the bare floor of my small bedroom and the bare walls have since been splashed with color, a beautiful cherry blossom pink. Tori helped me pick out the color when I could no longer stand the discolored and stained walls.

I wasn't living in this room, I was existing long enough for this day to come. The day I could walk away and become my own person leaving this all behind, like so many others had done in the past.

I had two boxes and a duffle bag. That's all it took to carry everything I owned. I carried them out and set them on the counter looking at the clock I decided I would make some coffee. It was only a two hour drive but I am sure my mom would need a quick pick me up in order to function this early in the morning.

When the coffee was done I determined it was time to go wake her up. I was hoping to give her enough time to shower before we left.

I could have taken the bus, but I wanted her to take me, to see what I had worked so hard at all through high school. I earned a scholarship to UNC, a full ride, based on my grades and test scores alone. I wanted her to see how hard work could pay off. Because deep down, regardless of what had transpired in our past she was my mom and I loved her. I wanted better for her.

I had sold my school uniforms from Saint Anne's to pay for gas to and from my new home, so there was no excuse. She had the money so she had to go. I had also saved every penny I had ever found, earned, been gifted, so that I could buy a cell phone. One more step towards blending in.

I knocked on her bedroom door, "Mom it's time to get up. We need to leave soon." When she didn't answer I knocked harder, "Mom, rise and shine."

When there was still no answer I turned the knob and opened the door not sure of what I'd be opening it up too.

I don't know why it surprised me, or why I let it hurt as bad as it did but when I saw she hadn't come home I was pained. Then when I looked in the coffee can in the freezer and found that one hundred and eighty seven dollars was gone, I was devastated. Now I wouldn't even be able to pay for a bus ticket.

I sat on the floor crying, praying she'd walk in the door, when she didn't I knew the only thing I could do was sell my cell phone.

I called the bus station to see how much a ticket was. Seventy dollars. There was no other choice, I would have to walk down the block to the pawn shop and hope to God they would give me that much for it. I had saved all my life for a phone and I was going to get less than a quarter of what it cost me. Being it was a pre-pay I would lose even more.

I decided to call Tori and let her know I would be late, to not wait around for me at lunch as planned and that I wouldn't have my phone.

I told her that I was taking the bus and I heard her cover her phones receiver and then she uncovered it. "We can be there in thirty minutes."

"No, I don't want you to go out of your way for me Tori. You and your parents have done enough."

"Well we're going there anyway silly. It's no problem. Did your mom get stuck at work?"

Something like that, I thought. "Yes."

"Well cool, now I get to see your place. I can't believe in four years I have never been to your house."

"Actually I am already at the bus station," I lied as I hurried back to my house. "How about you just meet me there?"

When she agreed I was so grateful. I didn't want to lie too her about anything. But I never wanted her to see what I came from. If she saw who I really was, what I came from, she would never look at me the same and I could never allow that to happen.

The car ride was interesting. Her parents were talking away, her mother especially, which wasn't like Mrs. Andrews. I knew she was nervous and would miss Tori. I felt bad intruding on this moment for them. But it was nice to see love, even if I never felt that kind of love, I could see it.

When we got to her dorm it was beautiful. This place cost a lot more than mine a semester but Tori knew she would be in a sorority as soon as she could be and out the door. Her parents indulged her, they always did. The thing with Tori was that she had everything a girl could ask for but never acted snobby or spoiled. She truly was the nicest person I had ever met. Having been permitted into their home for the past four years and watching how they were with each other made me realize where she got it from. Her parents loved, respected, and cherished one another. That was exactly what I would have one day. I wouldn't settle for anything less.

Their goodbyes started as soon as we pulled up to her place. It continued through the whole unloading and unpacking process.

When it was time for them to leave, I watched as Tori fought to be strong. Something she had never had to be.

"You ready Haylie?" Mr. Andrews asked.

I looked at Tori and shook my head no. "If it's alright I would love to stay here for the night with Tori. My roommate isn't expecting me until tomorrow. I called her and told her I would be late before I called y'all."

"Thank you," her mother hugged me so tight it almost hurt. "You two will still be there for each other every day right?"

"Of course we will."

"You are an angel Haylie Harbour."

She was wrong I was not, but to these people who didn't know of my home life and past indiscretions I just may have been.

"She's been mine for years." I told Mrs. Andrews.

Tori cried for over an hour, which of course made me cry too.

"It's a good thing she had a private room," she told me, "these girls may think I'm crazy otherwise."

"Do you think I'm crazy Haylie, because I already miss them? God I am being so rude. Your poor mother had to work, didn't even get to bring you, and here I am acting like a baby. Forgive me won't you?"

"Of course. Tori we're only two hours away. We will be fine. Plus we have each other."

"And our books," she yawned.

"Always our books."

"What are we reading next? You get to pick this time."

"I've heard a lot about Beautiful Disaster, by Jamie McGuire. Can we try that one?"

"Of course we can."

I had an iPhone now with a kindle app. I was so excited to be able to read on it just like Tori had been for two years now.

Tori had given me a gift card for graduation and what did I give her? A photo book that I made from dollar store materials. She acted like I had given her the moon and actually apologized for being so impersonal. She vowed someday she would make me something with her own two hands like I had for her. Secretly I wished she wouldn't. I loved the gift she gave me. I could buy close to twenty books if I chose ones when they were on sale. And then there were the freebies. My books were personal to me. There never could have been a better gift than what she gave me on graduation, except of course her friendship, that gave me even more than I could have imagined.

Two girls from two different worlds, and best friends forever.

When she fell asleep I laid wondering if I would like my roommate or if she was going to be a snob, or a slob, or to pushy, or just plan mean. I didn't sleep for beans that night as I lay and wonder what tomorrow would bring.

Chapter 2

Tori

Haylie and I shared our first breakfast at the college café', which was a nice way to say cafeteria. I guess it gave off the vibe that we were now more mature. Looking around I noted that in fact some of us were. Then I saw a table full of girls chuckling and laughing, one actually snorted and yes, milk spilled from her nose.

My instinct was to get her a tissue and then leave. I certainly couldn't imagine eating every meal with people who didn't even have the slightest clue of what table manners were. Didn't their mother's teach them right?

We walked outside and Haylie started laughing. "That grossed you out huh?"

"Certainly did. That was disgusting. I do wonder how some of those people passed the entrance exam."

We walked down the street a bit watching the gathered groups outside of dorms and private housing, all laughing, all smiling, all having a great time.

"Can you believe we're actually here Haylie? Me and you, students at UNC together, it's a dream come true."

"Sure is." She smiled as she looked around.

Out from nowhere a Frisbee hit Haylie, in the side of the head, almost hitting her in the eye, and I heard it. It was so loud. "Geez Haylie, are you alright?"

"Yes." She whispered and held her hand over her eye.

I looked up and a sandy blond hair boy was in front of her.

"Let me see." He pulled her hand off of her face and held it. "You alright?"

"I'm fine thank you," she said looking away.

He smiled, "You sure? I could take you to medical. It wouldn't be a problem."

"No I really appreciate it but I'm alright."

"I have to be sure, since the offending Frisbee was mine. Let me ask a few questions, if you can answer them, and your friend here can confirm they're correct I will let you walk away. If not I'm gonna have to insist on taking you to medical immediately, okay?"

She nodded.

"Name?" he asked.

"Haylie Harbour."

"Freshman?"

"Yes."

"Where's your dorm?"

"Two blocks down, first building on the right."

His smile grew.

" I truly am fine," she began to blush.

"One more question?"

She nodded.

"Phone number?"

She started rattling it off and I nudged her. She stopped and looked at me wondering what I was doing.

The blond boy laughed and then Haylie caught on.

"The Frisbee was fate Haylie Harbour, that's how we met. Next time it will be well planned out. My name is Rex, and I live here. If you had a pen I would give you my number."

She was grinning from ear to ear, "Sorry I don't have one on me."

"Well next time we run into each other I promise it won't hurt so bad." Then he leaned forward and kissed her head. "See you around Haylie Harbour."

I grabbed her hand and walked quickly away.

"You should tell security about this. He knows where you live, your name--."

"He was sweet." She giggled, "And cute."

"Haylie, have you never watched Lifetime television? He could be dangerous."

"I'm sure he wasn't."

I wasn't sure what to say to her. The boy was extremely forward and probably had ill intentions.

"You don't have to walk me the rest of the way. I know you have things you need to do."

"You're safety is more important."

"Oh my gosh Tori, he was just being nice."

"That time! What happens next time? Will he knock you over the head with a bat and drag you into the bushes somewhere? You have to watch out for people like that."

She smiled and nodded. "I know, but really you have to go. I'll be just fine."

She was right. I had appointments to keep and after eating in that café' I knew they were important. I couldn't wait for a kitchen of my own to cook meals in.

"Text me when you walk in your dorm and then after you meet Miss Roberts?"

"Of course. I'll have to come by and grab my things anyways. Maybe the three of us can meet up tomorrow."

After a hug goodbye I was off and when I looked at my watch I realized I had no time to spare. I was supposed to head over to a couple sorority houses. They sought me out since my aunt attended UNC, so technically I had a family member that was alumni which made me prime target for all the sorority houses. Alumni equaled possible donors.

I received three different invitations requesting me to attend their social function for the same night.

The first party I went to was at the Alpha-Chi Omega house. The house was ranked at the top of the sororities to join based on their grade point average being the highest. Schooling was very important to me so it was at the top of my list as well. I walked into a house full of girls dressed in beautiful Sunday dresses, hair and makeup done to a T. They looked pretty much all alike. They were beautiful and very affectionate. I went into the living room where most of the girls were. There were trays of food and music playing softly in the background. The president of the house jumped up and came right over to me. Overall I got the feeling they were caring but they had to be made up every day from head to toe. I enjoyed my Sundays just lying around, so I'm not sure that I was going to fit in well, so I was on to the next house.

Next came the Kappa Delta. They were ranked right behind the first sorority and showed a lot of potential when I entered the house. I liked that all the girls wore whatever they wanted. One of the girls had walked straight up to me and stated that she loved my shirt. Right there, I thought I could fit in nicely with these ladies. There was some music playing and it was country, my favorite. A couple more came over and gave me a hug and told me about how the house was ran, what they did for the local charities and for fun. I was sold, this was the house I would pledge. I mean unless the last house was amazing.

The last house had the lowest grade point average between all three of them. Alpha Kappa Alpha's were partiers, I could tell. They were all walking around with drinks in their hands and none of them were dressed up. I mean they seemed like they could be a lot of fun but nothing more than that. A few girls just walked by me like they didn't even see me. To tell you the truth they probably didn't. They were too busy drinking and talking. I looked around and then made my way right back to the front door.

After four hours of social gatherings I was exhausted and ready to crawl into my bed and fall asleep. Haylie and I had a big day planned tomorrow. I couldn't wait to meet her new roommate. I hope she likes to just hang out like we do and read. Oh, maybe we can get her to join our book club.

Chapter 3

Marley... the night before

The first night here in Carolina, my new roommate's car had broken down and she was going to be here in the morning. Haylie Harbour, I liked her name, sounded like a party girl. I hoped like hell she was cool, if not, no big deal, people of the female persuasion never really liked me anyway. Quite frankly I didn't like bitches either. I promised my little sister Happy that I would try to get along and play well with them. So I suppose I had to. She promised me she wouldn't let the parents drive her crazy and to help keep them at a distance so that I could finally show the world who I was and that I was not my parents.

I decided that I would try, and honestly was a little disappointed that I had to try to make friends on the first day without my roommate in tow. I had seen signs about a blue and white scrimmage at the football field. When I was carrying the last box from my car up three flights of stairs in my all girls dorm (Yeah that sucked) I was handed one of said pamphlets by a sweet little southern girl.

"Make sure you come show our boys support now won't ya?"

"I will try," I faked smiled as she set the pamphlet on top of three boxes I was lugging around with no offers of help in site. I held it there with my chin as I climbed the stairs.

When I finally reached the landing of floor one my arms felt like they would give out.

"Need some help?"

I looked up and saw, Jacob, or a guy who had that same smile as Taylor Lautner did in the Twilight movies. I flashed him my own smile.

"You sure you have time?"

"Just got my little sister situated in her room," he pointed to the doorway. "It wouldn't be a problem at all."

"In that case, I would love some help."

He took all three boxes and his muscles flexed under his white tank top and all I could think about is what kind of beast this man could turn into when provoked.

"You go ahead, I'll follow."

Oh yes you will little wolf boy, like a lamb to slaughter. I pulled my already short skirt up a little higher and made sure to exaggerate the shake in my ass.

As luck would have it the door opened on the second floor and breeze blew the flyer off the box over my head, landing at the top of the next landing.

"Shit can you get that?" He laughed. "By the way, what's your name?"

"Bella."

"I like that. Mines--."

Pause, I didn't want to know his name, son of a bitch, he was Jake to me.

"Taylor."

SCORE!

"You go to school here?"

"Nope. Senior at V Tech. Just dropping my sister off on my way through."

"Perfect."

I leaned over slowly without bending my knees to grab the pamphlet. I was damn sure to give him a show.

When I looked back and held it up, "Got it." He looked stunned.

"You okay?" I asked as sweetly as I could.

"Yeah, no, sure."

"That's good."

I unlocked the door and walked in while holding it open for him.

"My roommate won't be here until tomorrow, go ahead and set those on her bed."

He did and then turned around.

"So maybe I could introduce you to my sister, at least you'd have someone here that you kind of knew."

"That's awfully nice of you," I said twirling my hair purposely. "But I have a lot of unpacking to do still. "Just wish my roommate were here. I mean, I wanted her to hold this chair while I put some things on that shelf, but it'll have to wait. I don't want to fall in here all by myself."

"I can put whatever you need up."

I looked at his broad chest and then reached over rubbing his arm, "I bet you could. Just hold the chair for me, I wouldn't want you to feel like I have taken advantage of your kindness."

I slowly looked down and saw a pretty decent size tent being pitched in his basketball shorts.

"You've got permission to take advantage. I just need to be on the road in a couple hours." His voice was gruff and thick.

I smiled, turned around grabbed my Jack Daniels clock, a graduation gift from my parents, don't ask, and stood on the chair.

"You got me?"

"I certainly do," he all but groaned.

I looked down at him and saw the tent had gone from a one man to a possible three or four man tent.

I reached up and leaned forward making sure to stretch and arch enough so that my ass was in his face.

When I felt his tongue lick my cheek I looked back over at him, "Did you just lick my ass?"

"I did," he grabbed my hips and I arched again and he responded by licking me a bit harder.

"Did I give you permission?"

"You certainly seemed to be."

I carefully pushed his hands off my hips and then climbed down off the chair holding his shoulders for stability.

"Next time ask a lady before licking her ass."

"Really?" He gasped.

"Of course really."

He started to step back and I held firmer. "Ask me."

"You gonna say no? Because if you are, just save me the embarrassment. I must have read you wrong which I have no clue how an ass in the face twice, three times if you count the stairs isn't a god damn signal. Fuck you aren't even wearing panties."

"You done rambling?" He nodded yes. "After you ask me are you going to make damn sure I come before you?"

"I sure will try."

"No, I know how to get myself off, so all you have to do is follow instructions. Now ask me."

"Christ Bella, can I lick you again."

"Where?"

"Everywhere." He growled.

"You start with my pussy and you make her purr and the answer is yes."

"Oh fuck, I am going to eat you till you come twice."

I walked over to the bed and sat.

"You wanna lay down Bella?"

"No, I want you on your knees," I said as I spread my legs wide and pulled up my skirt.

"That's where we'll start," he groaned right before dropping down and licking my pussy.

After I came, and it took awhile, he wasn't as skilled as the ex. He stood and so did I.

"Thank you," I said pulling my skirt back down.

"Thank you?" He laughed as he pulled down his shorts.

"Yes thank you. I have a football game to get to so," I walked to the door and started to open it.

"Fuck, Bella what the hell?"

I didn't say a word I just stood holding the door open as he pulled his shorts up.

"I didn't think it would take so long. Maybe I will see you next time you stop in."

He walked towards the door and stopped, "Not worth my time. That was a bitch move."

"Sorry to hear that," I wiped his chin, "You got a little on you, " licked my finger, "Mmm, taste well worth it to me."

His jaw dropped and I gave him a little push and shut the door behind him locking it.

So I bet you all think I'm a bitch, a whore, trashy, and dirty. Go ahead and admit that's what you think, I will take no offense to it. Hell I will admit it, yes I am all of the above and I don't give a fuck what anyone thinks.

I was burnt once. Gave it up to a boy who showed me how good sex could be and then he fucked me over.

So now I was in the driver seat of my sexual life. The choices were mine, all of them, no one would control me, or my pussy again.

I love sex. I love to come, I love to hear desire in a man's voice, and see it in his eyes. I love to have my pussy licked and fingered until I come in waves.

I also love cock. The boloney pony, beaver basher, the cum gun, beef whistle, the deep V diver, the dong, the custard cannon, the flesh flute, fun stick, the heat seeking moisture missile, the piss weasel, the one eyed trouser snake, the purple headed love warrior, the joystick, the microphone, the pecker, the pork sword, whatever you fancy calling it doesn't matter, it's all the same. I love to suck it, swallow the come of a worthy stick and feel it between my legs.

I looked out the peep hole hoping he was gone and he was. No it didn't bother me one bit that he wasn't outside the door looking like a whipped puppy, that's not what I wanted. I wanted a man who could handle my terms, which were simple. One, I don't want your name, I want you to lick me, fuck me, and leave. I want no promise and to give you no hope that this was anything other than an exchange of orgasm. You cross the line and you're out. Taylor crossed the line, not really sure what it was but hey, who cares. I was chalking it as Marley one Carolina zip, sucker.

I grabbed a freshen up wipe and cleaned my jewel, threw my knee-high leather boots on and headed out the door. I paused briefly considering whether or not I would wear panties and I decided fuck it. This may be football but in baseball terms, I wanted a double header and I was gonna find a pumped up hard bodied muscle head to ride until I passed out.

Holy hell I hit the mother load. There were about thirty athletic hot men on the field, and a bonus, the game was almost over. Ten minutes was all I had. Hell it wasn't like it was a bad thing. I was kind of digging the pants.

I heard two girls behind me talking about one of their brothers who said there was some girl on the third floor that was a real slut. Her name was Bella. I knew immediately who they were talking about, but fuck I wasn't Bella. Judgy bitches, didn't they watch the damn movie, Bella didn't fuck the wolf boy, and hell I wasn't going to screw that up.

"I am gonna text him and find out the room, I would love to give her a piece of my mind. I mean seriously he helped her carry boxes and she bends over revealing her bare ass? Who does that? Then asks him if she can thank him by giving him a blow job."

"What a pig," The other girl snarled.

"Yep, I will find out who she is and make sure everyone knows too."

"Let's do it tonight," the other twat giggled.

I stood up and walked to the pop machine, grabbed a mountain dew and came back.

"Are you new here?" Snatch one asked.

"First year, go Tar Heels," I gave them a fake ass smile.

"You a football fan?" Snatch two asked.

"Who isn't?" I didn't give two fucks about football, I liked to watch the boys.

"Number 45 is mine," she giggled.

I smiled, "You meet him here?"

"Yep, last year. Actually one year ago today. It's our anniversary."

Anniversary? Really peppy ass Pollyanna of the, protect the pussy pom-pom squad. Gawd, I already hated that bitch.

"Congratulations." Yes I threw up a little in my mouth.

"Everyone goes down to Four Corners after the game you should come."

"You and your man gonna celebrate there?"

"It's a start," she winked.

"You enjoy that."

I looked out on the field for number 45 and he was a big guy. Tall, check, good ass, check, able to pound one home, damn he tackled one of the guys in blue, fucking hard to, double check.

Hmm, I thought to myself. Nah.

I went back to my room to grab some cash, I felt like it would be a taxi cab kind of night. I also grabbed a fistful of condoms, ribbed for her pleasure. No that's not being selfish. Check this, make a circle with one hand, use your other and point out that finger. Now make the fucking motion. Which feels better the circle or the finger? Exactly, so yes, I wanted a little more friction, can't blame a girl.

I was sitting at the bar minding my own business when a guy who, although was not wearing football pants, looked like a football type guy.

He was standing in line and smiled when I looked back again, "You wanna order for me. I'm sure he'll pay a hell of a lot more attention to you than me."

He was hot, like too hot for me. I am not typically impressed with pretty boys, short black hair, blue eyes, and perfect smile. Don't ask, I have issues but I want hair I can hang onto you know.

"Slide up here Friday Night Lights," I said scooting over and then waving to the bartender whose smile faded when he saw Friday beside me.

"Busted, he thinks were together."

"Bullshit," I laughed, "Hey buddy," I lifted my shirt up and flashed him.

"Holy shit," Friday laughed. "You just flashed that guy."

"Say thank you, he's on his way over."

After ordering Friday was standing their shaking his head. "I can't believe you just did that."

"What's a pal for huh? Plus you bought me a drink."

"I would have bought you one anyway." He smiled a one hundred watt smile and I laughed, "What?"

"You and I can be friends. I will sit here all night, show the bartender my tits and get your drinks. But please don't be one of those guys, not with me anyway. A serious waste of time."

"Those guys huh?"

"The ones who think they have to buy a girl a drink to get laid. You and I have the same parts buddy."

His jaw dropped.

"No, Jesus Friday, keep your shit together. By the looks of that bulge in your pants you have a nice size ride. I have a dick to, smaller, and attached to more brains then most men have. It's called a clit."

He chuckled, "And my cock isn't attached to brains huh?"

"Not sure, don't really care. I'm not looking for a boy to buy me drinks or pretend to be interested in me. You all are physical and even though I have tits and a pussy doesn't make me a sloppy mess of emotions and expectations that when I cum, you did that for me. Cause truth be told I can do that all by myself, and I do pretty often."

"Is that so?"

"It is, so as long as you understand, me and you are cool. You wanna tap me on the shoulder when you need a drink ordered I will flash my tits for you. Cause we're cool right?"

"Hell yes we're cool. What's your name?"

"Saturday."

"Interesting, what made you chose that?"

From behind me some drunk fuck slurred, "Whore."

I turned around, "Who the fuck do you think you're talking to?"

"You. Fucking showing your tits for beer."

"She's gonna sit on your lap and let you poke her in the ass with what I assume is a midget sized dick for a draft and I'm a whore?" I laughed.

"She's my girl." He snapped.

"Jesus honey, I'm sorry if you've gotta put up with Sloth, just to get your drink on."

"You bitch!" She screeched.

"Okay maybe I'm not sorry."

Sloth pushed me and all of a sudden Friday, my new buddy was diving on him. Four or five guys, who must have been on the football team pulled him off and dragged me behind them out the door.

"Sloth?" Friday laughed.

"Hey you guys!" We both said and laughed at the same time.

"Saturday?"

"Yes Friday?"

"I like you."

Damn it now his ass was off limits. "I like you too Friday."

We all hit a bar down the street and danced, drank drafts, and did shots. I was having a blast. These guys were cool. I even pointed a chick out for Friday, who had been checking him out.

"You should buy her a drink."

He laughed and looked at me funny.

"Don't confuse drunk lust with love. Today is not our day Friday, its only Wednesday."

My back hit my dorm door as what's his name was hiking up my skirt. I fumbled in my bag for my key as he pushed against me. Son of a bitch, this guy was huge.

I unlocked the door, pushed it opened, he lifted me up and I wrapped my legs around him as he kicked the door shut.

His tongue and mine fought for control until we found our grove. He sat on the edge of the bed bringing me down hard on him and then leaned back as he reached in his pocket for a condom.

"I have some."

"No babe, I use my own."

I was wasted and truly didn't give a shit at this point. I knew there would be a hell of a lot of friction. Did I mention this guy was a fucking horse?

As soon as he wrapped it I knelt above him and took as much as I could and he worked out the rest. *Mother fucker!*

I woke to the stallion under the sheets, spreading my legs and his tongue was just as magical as his cock. I came a few times before he popped up and planted a kiss on my lips.

"Breakfast of champs."

I licked my lips, "Not bad. Now roll over so I can ride you and then kick your ass out."

He laughed and did as instructed.

"You broke a rule of mine." I said as he reached down and grabbed his jeans producing a condom out of his pocket.

"Oh yeah, what's that?" He asked as he rolled it on.

"No sleep overs." I said as I straddled him.

Holy hell I was gonna be walking funny for a few days.

His mouth was on my tits as he and I were going hard and I was right there when I heard the door open.

"Stop," I said pulling my boob out of his mouth and grabbing the covers.

"You okay?"

"Oh. My. God. I am so sorry."

"You must be Haylie," I stuck my hand out and she covered her eyes and came over and shook my hand.

"Jesus, babe," the Stallion whispered.

"You better keep that shit up BABE," I scolded him. "Haylie, give us just a few more minutes. Put some headphones on or something."

"No, no I'll just go out to the lounge and read," Haylie stammered while trying to exit gracefully.

"It's okay this Stallion doesn't mind. Do you?"

Haylie yelled goodbye over her shoulder as she all but ran out the door.

Chapter 4

Haylie

I couldn't believe her, but still I thought, wow. Was I jealous, well maybe. As I walked into the lounge there were a bunch of people playing pool and talking. Noticing a couch free, I sat down and pulled out my smartphone. I observed a few people looking over at me, I didn't know any of them personally. I mean I had seen them and said hello as I passed by on the way to my room but that was about it.

After about forty- five minutes in walked Marley smiling ear to ear, "You really could have stayed you know."

"I didn't want to interrupt or make you both feel uncomfortable with me in the room."

Marley laughed out loud, "I was already uncomfortable he was fucking hung."

I snickered at her, she was crazy and I think she was just who I needed in my life right now. The polar opposite of Tori, who I love, but sometimes I wondered if she wasn't a little bit better than me you know. Tori and I were best friends. We always would be. However she and I didn't go out much, our Friday and Saturday nights consisted of reading together in our two person book club that we formed years ago. We decided that even though it was just the two of us in it, it was still a club.

"You wouldn't think I was awful if I crashed for a few hours would you?"

"Not at all. I can just read out here. I'll unpack later."

"You can unpack now."

"I wouldn't want to disturb your nap."

She smiled and laughed out loud, "It's your place too. Plus, I could sleep through a war. Come on."

After unpacking I sat and read until Marley woke up.

"You feel like dinner?"

"Absolutely."

We were about to leave when there was a knock on the door.

"You make friends already?" she asked.

"My best friend goes here too but she was going to visit some sorority houses."

I opened the door and two girls were standing outside glaring at me.

"She's blond, you think it's her?" one asked the other.

"You Bella?" The other girl snapped at me.

"I'm sorry you must have--."

"Look, my brother told us about you and we wanted you to know--."

The door opened wider and Marley stood beside me, "What's up ladies?""

"Hey it's you, from the football field yesterday."

"It is me, and this here is my friend Haylie. She just got in this morning, so if there's a problem here than maybe it's with me."

Their jaws dropped, "Oh no. No, we're sorry it must be a different girl. You know the slut we were talking about at the game. The one who tried to get my brother in bed."

"So you just think going door to door and being," she stopped. "How do I say this nicely? Oh, I don't. Bitches to everyone who answers the door is going to do what?"

"Well my brother said," her face started to turn red.

"Maybe he's full of shit, did you ever consider that? Maybe he hit on this, Bella girl and she said no. Or maybe they fooled around and she, I don't know, decided she was done."

They both laughed, "You don't know Taylor. He's beautiful. He could have--."

"Dicks dick ladies." She looked at me, "And foods food. You ready to go get lunch?"

I smiled and she grabbed her bag. We walked out and the girls apologized over and over again.

"No big thing," Marley laughed it off, "Come on Haylie, I'm starving."

We got outside and she looked at me and started cracking up.

"What?" I started to laugh too which caused her to laugh even harder.

We stood like complete idiots laughing for a solid three minutes before she wiped her tears.

"Sorry about that. I almost got you in trouble. I swear I'll try harder next time."

It took me a minute, "Wait, did you?"

"Haylie Harbour," she reached her hand out and shook mine. "Nice to meet you. I'm Bella."

I was confused and then she laughed again.

"Not really, but that's what her brother thinks. Like I'd give him my real name."

"Oh. Well I don't really know what to say."

"He's a damn liar too, son of a bitch wished I sucked his dick. All that happened was he was served pooty on a platter, or on my bed anyways. After he ate me I told him to leave. Fucker thought he was in control. I don't play that way."

"The guy from this morning?"

"No," she laughed, "Hell no. I liked him. I didn't like the wolf boy."

"Wolf boy?"

"Reminded me of Jake from Twilight."

"Wait you read? Tori and I love to read. Oh I am so excited you will have something in common…"

"Hold up there sister I don't read." She giggled.

"But you said--."

"I'm a movie buff. I like movies."

"Oh," well there goes that. One thing in common was hopeful but now I had no idea what I would do to make them friends.

We sat in the café' and ate. She was hysterical and so much fun to be around. I didn't feel like I did when I was around Tori. I didn't feel like I had to live up to her expectations. Now Tori, never made me feel like I had to be perfect but just being around her I wanted to be a better person, all the time. Sometimes it was exhausting.

The next few days flew by. I met Tori, every day for breakfast. She was a morning person and I ate dinner with Marley. She was not a morning person.

"So, it's Friday night what do you want to do for fun?" Marley was up for anything.

"I was just about ready to head out and meet up with Tori. You are more than welcome to come but I need to stop and grab the pizza along the way. We are reading a book by Jamie McGuire it's called Beautiful Disaster. It's an amazing book."

"Is it a movie?"

"No, but I'm sure it will be someday. Travis Maddox is a bad boy. Kind of sleeps around a lot until he finds the girl. The stuff he does to make sure she's around him is so sweet. But she's hiding a secret."

"I don't know about this nerd girl thing." She laughed, "No offense."

"None taken."

"Are the sex scenes hot, like naughty hot?"

"We only just started the book, so I'm not really sure how it is yet. But I'm sure its coming."

"Coming?" she giggled and wagged her eyebrows suggestively. "Or cumming?"

"Do me a favor, try it. I really want you two to get along. We could have great fun together."

"Fine, I'll give it a shot. If all else fails and I'm miserable I'll just hit the bar and bring home something to play with. You could come too, or cum too."

I laughed and then wondered what the hell I had just done.

"Ok, let's get going because we need to stop and get some wine to go with the pizza. I'm buying."

"You sure?" I asked giving her the option to back out. I was anxious and honestly wished I had given it some time. You know, to prepare Tori, for what was to come.

"Anything for you Haylie Harbour. I kind of dig you."

I shot Tori a text and let her know I was bringing my new roommate. In an attempt to let her prepare for what was about to happen I also texted her that Marley was bringing wine. Marley bought 3 bottles of wine, three different kinds, stating she was in the mood to mix it up a bit. I had drank before, but Tori well she was a different story. I don't know if she was ready for Marley, nor would Marley be ready to meet someone so pure. Oh, Lord it could be an interesting night.

Tori met us at the door and was all smiles as usual. She leaned forward and hugged me like she always did then she embraced Marley too. I chuckled at the look of horror on Marley's face.

"Tori, this is Marley."

"It's so nice to meet you" and once again Tori hugged her.

Marley gave her a slight squeeze and then turned and walked into her private and spacious dorm room. "So this is how the other half lives."

I couldn't help but laugh and Tori blushed a bit.

"Our room is small. You'll have to come over and check it out."

"Next Friday we do book club at your place then."

"I brought the wine." Marley wasted no time opening the bottle and taking a drink. Then she handed me the bottle. "Now show me this book that you ladies are reading."

"Well it's pretty great, I've already read the first 4 chapters and am very surprised that this Travis, character has some very redeeming qualities."

"Is this Travis guy hot, like I want to rip his clothes off hot?"

"Ummm, he's getting better. Using his manners at least."

"That's not what I asked. I want to know does he make you want to screw the next guy you see and call him Travis?"

"I really don't know what you mean and I umm, don't do that?"

"What, screw?" Marley was laughing out loud.

I could tell Tori was getting upset and it wasn't worth it so I jumped up and spoke. "Hey let's eat. I'm starved."

"Some wine Tori?" Marley handed her a bottle, "House warming gift."

"Thank you." Tori took it and looked at it.

I saw Tori blush. The first bottle of wine came and went easily between Marley and I while Tori, just held the bottle Marley had handed her.

I was starting to feel a buzz and I could also see Marley, got a little bit looser lipped when she had alcohol in her system. Shocking because I didn't think it could get any looser than Marley.

She told us things that I had only read about in books and clearly Tori, had never heard about based on her facial expressions.

"Tori, have you ever drank before?" Marley, took the bottle from her, opened it and handed it back.

"Umm no not really."

"Not really or you never have, which is it?"

"Well, no then."

"Oh, girl you need to live a little. Now take a drink and let's have some fun. So what's this book club thing you ladies were talking about?"

"We find a book that looks good, we read it and then meet to talk about it," I said before Tori, had a chance.

"And how are the boys on this campus? I mean based on what I just rode at the beginning of the week they have to be better than these book guys. I could go for another ride now actually."

I looked over at Tori, giggled and even though I could see she was a bit wide eyed she was smiling so maybe that wine was taking hold of her.

"Marley, you are going to be trouble, aren't you?" I was smirking at her.

"Stick with me chic, and I'll get you a fine piece of ass. I'll even find little Miss Princess, someone that will make her scream."

Tori and I both looked at each other and laughed. There was nothing left to say. So this is how the night went. Marley, said things we never would have while we sat there blushing. Before we knew it the night had passed and decided we'd just crash at Tori's seeing we had a bit too much to drink.

Chapter 5

Tori

I didn't know Haylie liked to drink, we never drank before or at least I never had. Clearly Haylie did more than I knew of. I found out she had actually had sex before we met. I was shocked, very shocked because we met when we were fourteen. It didn't matter. I just wished she had told me before and I had a sneaking suspicion that she wouldn't have ever had it not been for Marley going on and on about not wanting names, she just wanted to pretend they were guys she got Hot for in movies. (Her words, not mine)

The girls thought it was funny that I started talking more and giggling a lot. I mean I could tell I was feeling different after just the first couple sips, but after I saw how much I had drank I knew it was time to stop. My head was spinning just a little and I had to hold on to things just to go to the bathroom. Marley and Haylie downed the rest of the second bottle then went right on to the third. They were pretty funny, the music was going, we were dancing and stories were flowing out of Marley, all about her sexual experiences.

Meeting Marley was a treat. I kept thinking she is nothing like us. I was wild and way more carefree than we were. She definitely spoke her mind and wasn't afraid to say whatever she wanted. The way she spoke of sex like it was no big deal. Didn't she understand it was supposed to be between two people that loved each other? I guess that's not the way for everyone.

I sat up and had a slight headache and looked to my left, Haylie was still sleeping. I looked to my right and Marley was laying in the lounge looking intently at her phone. When I stood up she looked over and smiled.

"Morning how are you feeling?" She asked.

"A little head ache. What are you doing?"

"Travis Maddox. Love his fine ass. I want more description in the sex scenes but—."

I covered my ears, "Don't spoil it. You can't talk books unless we are all on the same page."

Haylie, sat up and giggled and I uncovered my ears.

"You like it huh?"

"Shh," Marley said. "You may have created a monster. You can damn sure bet next guy whose under me is gonna have to agree he's Travis."

"Welcome to our world." I said as I walked into the bathroom.

When I came out Haylie, was verbally giving her a list of books to read and she was making notes on her phone.

My headache was worsening the louder they got.

Haylie seemed fine, how could that be she had more than me last night?

"Haylie, remind me again why I let you two convince me to drink not just one, but two glasses of wine?" I said as I groaned.

Marley smiled, "Practice makes perfect you know. Now tell me is it your stomach?"

"I have a slight headache. How do you this all the time?"

Marley stood, stretched, and laughed "You should have taken two aspirin and drank a bottle of water before heading to bed."

"Now you tell me," I groaned again.

The girls headed out as I had plans with the Sorority that I was pledging. Marley, said that she and Haylie, had some stops to make so they could join one as well. Later that night I called them and it went to voicemail.

I tried not to be jealous of their friendship but I didn't want to lose Haylie, because I wasn't as fun as Marley.

I dove into my book that night to escape how silly I was feeling. Haylie, and I were soul sisters.

As the weeks and months wore on we got into a groove, all three of us. Many times Marley, overstepped and many times I told her she was doing just that. But we were friends.

I won't say I didn't look forward to going home for winter break. I was so excited that Haylie, agreed to stay with my family after the holidays. Her mother worked all the time so Haylie, said she would understand, that she would probably insist being that she wouldn't want her to be alone. So Haylie, and I would have time to hang out and read and be, well normal again.

Normal. Something she needed more than me, and it all became clear just how much she needed that. I went to meet the girls for breakfast and they were late and not answering their phones. Their new sorority, one which I would have never considered had a huge end of semester party. I knew they must have partied harder than I ever would so I dropped by their dorm to wake them up.

Nothing prepared me for what I walked in on that morning. The door wasn't locked so I opened it and yelled, "Rise and shine party girls."

I grabbed the blanket and gave it a tug, uncovering a naked man with a girl's head between his legs, doing, well that thing with her mouth.

"Oh dear lord, Marley, I am so sorry," I turned around.

"Marley?" the man who I recognized from somewhere laughed. "You change your name and not tell me?"

I took a couple steps toward the door and it opened shielding me from seeing who was coming in and thankfully to the atrocity that I had walked in on.

"Haylie, we got company coming. You better get your ass dressed and out of here with Rex, before Tori, walks in and freaks the --."

"Marley," Haylie whispered.

"Oh shit," Marley whispered back.

That moment I realized they had been hiding things from me. I won't say I wasn't crushed because I was. I thought being accepting of her lewd behavior would make my relationship with Haylie stronger and accepting Marley wasn't hard but now I wanted to run.

The door slowly closed and both Haylie and Marley stood looking at me. Both looked like petulant children who had gotten caught by their parents smoking cigarettes.

I plastered a smile on my face and walked quickly by them, "Call me when you're free."

Haylie, was at my door half an hour later telling me she was sorry. That she didn't want to disappoint me. She cried and I acted like it was no big deal.

Our winter break was great it was just like old times and when we returned to school things quickly fell back into place. Like that incident had never happened.

When I agreed to attend a party with Haylie and Marley at the end of the spring semester something equally as awful happened. I walked into the bathroom with Haylie and Rex, the man whose penis was in Haylie's mouth at the end of last semester, was in the bathroom with one of the Haylie sorority sisters on her knees doing the same thing to him.

Having had two glasses of wine, I myself was a little lose lipped.

"Isn't that your boyfriend?"

Haylie quickly turned away and walked out of the room.

"You are a horrible man! I hope that thing falls off you- you-son of a --."

Marley, walked in and grabbed my arm, "Let's go there Betty-bad-ass."

I didn't understand why she wasn't freaking out on him. But when we had gotten outside and I saw Haylie, wiping away tears I knew immediately that she needed me.

"How could your boyfriend do that to you?" I hugged her.

"He's not my boyfriend, he's just a friend."

"Nonsense. Now he's neither. He's a piece if garbage. So unworthy of you."

"Haylie!" I looked up and Rex, was walking out the door still buttoning his pants.

"Fuck off Rex!" Marley, snapped at him.

"No you fuck off bitch!"

"All of you stop." Haylie said looking at us.

"We need to talk," Rex walked quickly towards her.

"No we don't. Its fine Rex, go back."

"Baby--."

"Don't," Haylie started walking away, "Just don't."

"We were never exclusive. If that's what you wanted you should have said something."

"Rex, have you lost your fucking mind. Look here Romeo, you don't ask a girl out when you get busted getting your dick smoked in a bathroom you fucking-tard," Marley laughed in his face. "Haylie, you and Tori, go ahead I'll make sure dumb fuck stays put."

"You look here bitch." I heard as Haylie and I walked down the sidewalk followed by and whelp and a thud. "Fucking cunt."

"Yeah, yeah, I've been called worse by better men." Marley said sarcastically.

In two seconds she was on Haylie's other side.

"I kicked him in the nuts," she smiled. "We'll find you a new toy soon. Bigger and better model."

"Are you serious? She just had her heart broken."

"No it was a wake-up call, right girl?"

Haylie looked up, "I'm fine. Just have to be stronger."

The next two years blew by. Things changed around us but the three of us stayed strong. Our friendship wasn't one that was bound by childhood memories or the closeness of our families. It was formed by the need to broaden our horizons, to grow and change with peers, people who had similar interests. What kept us coming together every week, regardless of our obvious differences was books. We read and we laughed. We even held each other up when we were down. I don't think there could ever be a stronger friendship than ours.

Marley and Haylie, had an apartment together. They decided against moving into their sorority house. It just so happened that the girl in the bathroom on her knees was very influential in their sorority.

Marley, got an apartment after her family came into some money and asked Haylie, to live with her. Haylie, wouldn't until she could contribute. Luckily my father was close with a man who ran a country club close by. She worked a lot but loved it. She always talked about all the seemingly happy couples that came there every week. I loved that regardless of what happened with Rex, she still dreamed of, and admired the happily ever after's in life.

We had gone to several different events, as I liked to call them, even though Marley and Haylie, called them parties and laughed at how I always tried to make them sound more respectable. They were fun, but I really tried to stay away from the alcohol and all the other *extra-curricular* activities that took place at such events. When the girls were giving me grief about going to another one of their sorority parties, I tried to say no but they wouldn't take no for an answer.

"Come on Victoria, really you can just hang out like you always do. We have less than a year left here. We need to live a little." Haylie, was trying to make me feel guilty, I could tell.

"Why do I have to go, it's no big deal."

Marley piped in, "Look, Tar Heels just won the championship and we need to celebrate."

"Fine, if I go you two need to back off. Honestly I don't need to go out all the time and I am fine with you two doing so. It doesn't upset me at all. If I go that means tomorrow night I'm staying home. I want one night to relax. We've been going out a lot lately. I'm exhausted, now couple that with all the activities that the sorority has going on lately, please understand."

"Agreed, now get your sexy ass moving and get prettied up. We've got some little boys to tame," Marley and Haylie, giggled at the same time.

We were all getting along famously, and together all the time. It was as if we were connected at the hip.

As we walked up to the door of their Sorority house I looked at what both Marley and Haylie, were wearing and then down at my own.

Marley, was dressed in a very short jean skirt with an American flag low cut tank top. But it was the high wedge heeled sneakers that made her outfit stand out. They made her legs look incredible.

Haylie, stood there adjusting her little red skirt. She matched it with a black shear shirt with a camisole underneath. I thought she looked adorable and those red heels brought it all together.

I smoothed my hands down my dress, it was tight and I wondered how I even fit in it. It was a dazzling designer piece and it fit me like a glove but was it too much for a college party? The dark purple shade with a splash of rhinestones around the neckline matched my new lace up silver stilettos. I never had a chance to wear them so the choice was easy.

When we walked through the door the party was in full swing. The music was loud and had everyone dancing. Marley immediately disappeared and left Haylie, and I standing to the side of what was being used as a dance floor.

I watched her return carrying three cups. She handed each of us one and I took a sip. It was sweet but it did have a hint of something in it, something that wasn't wine. I took another tiny sip and asked her what it was.

"For God's sake Tori, loosen up!" Marley lifted her drink in toasting form. "Down the hatch."

"Fine," and I started drinking it.

I had set the large red solo cup down and turned to talk to the girl walking around with a tray full of Jell-O and pudding shots to let her know I was all set. When I turned back around my cup was full. Marley and Haylie each had a shot.

Haylie turned and handed me one as well. "Tori, it tastes like chocolate pudding, just try it."

"And exactly how do you expect me to eat this with no spoon?"

"Like this!" Marley swirled her tongue around the inside of the little cup, smiled and grabbed another. Then I heard the whistles and catcalls that came from across the room. I turned to see three guys all raising their glasses to her and she bowed.

"I can't do that," I whispered.

With them nodding their heads at me as if to say do it, I rolled my eye in frustration. I dipped the tip of my finger in the cup and I licked it off. Wow this is good. It really did taste like chocolate. Needless to say I kept sticking my finger in the cup, scooping pudding out until it was empty.

One thing led to another and before I knew it, I was licking them out of the cup just like Marley did. Truths be told I lost count of how many I had but I knew every time they came around I grabbed one. They were good!

We started dancing and singing to the music. We were having so much fun. I'm sure I was doing things that were completely out of character but I didn't seem to care. We walked into a room where a group of guys were doing keg stands. It looked like so much fun. I started to walk to the line to participate, and that's when the girls pulled me to the next room.

Smoke filled the air and it smells sweet. Not like cigarettes but like the smell of Marley's car interior. I liked it and wondered where they sold that fragrance of air freshener. We hung there for a moment before Marley and Haylie tried to stop me from doing things that they knew I'd regret in the morning. That's when I turned to them and told them to loosen up. *Crazy right?*

Then in walked Jake Wyatt, he was beyond hot. I had seen him for years around campus. He was always well groomed, smelled delightful, and smiled at everyone. He was talking to Marley. Just another admirer that no doubt thought she was beautiful. He turned and looked towards me. I couldn't help but smile.

He was built, not overly big but just enough to know that he took very good care of himself and his looks insinuated very good genes. The fitted t-shirt and the jeans that sat low on his hips showed that he was incredible from head to toe. Clearly the alcohol was getting to me because I couldn't stop staring or smiling at him. *Geez Louise Victoria, look away!*

He strolled over to me and started dancing extremely close. Marley and Haylie, started dancing next to us with two guys that were pretty hot as well.

The room was warm and the music was loud. It spun a bit. I wasn't sure if the spinning was caused by the alcohol or by Jake. He was talking to me and I was nodding and then before I knew it he was holding me close to him. All I knew was that he was beautiful and I would probably do anything he wanted to at this given moment.

Chapter 6

Marley

One year and two months later

I stood in my empty apartment looking at all the boxes. I had a few weeks before I would be moving out. I wasn't sure what I would do or where my life would take me once I was handed that piece of paper but I knew it wouldn't lead back to New York.

Over the past four years I had a handle on who Marley Roberts was. I wasn't my parents, my hometown, my shitty circumstances or the things people called me behind my back.

I wasn't someone whose heart could be broken or toyed with and I wasn't alone. I had two best friends, female friends who may not agree with all my choices but they accepted me for who I am.

I sat down on the couch and grabbed my trusty little bowl and sparked it up. I took one hit, then two, and then hell yes I took a third. I sat back listening to some Bob Marley and waited until I heard a knock on the door.

When I opened it I couldn't help but look at him, take in the beauty of the guy I had been calling Edward, for the past week. I had grown up a bit, so I didn't say yes the first five times he asked if he could come over. I actually was studying.

Okay so that's bullshit. I was trying to finish the damn series I promised Haylie and Tori I would finish, the one that brought them together to begin with.

"Are you going to invite me in?"

He was tall and on the thin-ish side. Not scrawny, but not a man who worked out at a gym seven days a week. He had eyes that could melt panties, a bluish gray color and thick hair that begged to be held onto.

His features were chiseled and the way he stared at me made me squirm.

"Of course."

I shut the door and turned around. He was standing not two inches from me. His stare was intense and hungry, exactly what I needed right now. A hunger, a thirst, and a desire that was unmistakable. With him, I would allow control this would work better that way.

He turned my back towards him, lifted my shirt and unsnapped my bra. Then he kissed between my shoulder blades as he pushed my bra strap gently off my left shoulder before my right. He kissed up to my neck and then across and down the other side. His teeth scraped down across the same area he just kissed.

Fuck, I wanted him to bite me.

I felt a million goose bumps spread over every inch that he kissed or his teeth grazed. I felt my body warming to his touch, my pussy getting wetter by the second.

Every time his teeth scraped my skin, my back arched and I pushed against him. He kissed, sucked, and scraped his teeth down my back and across my hips slowly. I felt his tongue dip down between my waistband and my bare skin. His hands gripped my ankles lightly and he slid them slowly up my legs past my knees continuing up as he nipped at my flesh.

"Oh God yes," I praised him.

He pushed my skirt up and his mouth left my skin briefly only to return to my body. I felt the heat of his breath as he kissed and bit lightly on the strap of silk covering, barely anything. His fingers slipped between the thin string at the waist of my panties and then he slowly pulled them down as he continued grazing his teeth in the tingling trail his fingertips had left. He nipped just above my knees and I felt his tongue and lip kissing, licking, tasting my skin.

"Oh Edward," I whimpered as I felt his tongue dip lightly following the line down my ass.

He turned me around and hitched one of my legs rubbing his erection that was hidden by denim, against me. I fumbled and reached inside to see what treasure I would uncover today.

"Damn," I said as he reached in his pocket and pulled out a condom.

Yes I finally finished the Twilight series by Stephanie Myers and tonight my treat, my reward, my orgasm, would be given to me by Edward Cullen. I thanked my lucky stars that I read the series. I had never rooted for Edward because of the movie, but now, today, I was all team Edward, and I had a wet thong to prove it.

Fuck you wolf boy.

What's next?

Glad you asked.

Check out our first full length Grinding in Greenville available now.

Hang with us at:

https://www.facebook.com/BoyfriendBookstand

Check out our website:

http://www.boyfriendbookstand.com

MERCILESS RIDE

A Hellions Ride Novel
Hell Raisers Challenging Extreme Chaos

By

Chelsea Camaron

<u>Merciless Ride</u>

1st Edition Published: September 2014

Whiskey Girls Publishing

Cover Design by: Jessie Lane

Images by: | Magnolia Ridge Photography | Shutterstock

Cover Model: Jacob Sones – Photo taken by Scott Hoover

LoveNBooksBoys ~ Ellie

Editing by: Asli Fratarcangeli and C&D Editing

Intended for mature audiences only

This book contains strong language, strong sexual situations, violence, and rape. Please do not buy if any of this offends you.

This is not meant to be a true or exact depiction of a motorcycle club rather a work of fiction meant to entertain.

Although part of a series, Merciless Ride can be read as a stand-alone novel.

CHAPTER ONE

Unexpected

~*Tessie*~

No, no, no, don't die, dammit. Fuck my life.

It is two in the morning, I just got off work from the bar, and tonight has already been a long damn night. We have been busier since the Desert Ghosts Motorcycle Club arrived in town. They must be working with the Hellions on something to be here, returning as often as they do.

Staying in this small place, they only have two options for a spot to grab a beer. *Tiny's,* where a man that is far from tiny will be serving them, or find me and the girls at *Ruthless.* Since they are in business with the Hellions, they come to *Ruthless.* Although not Hellion owned, it is known as their place to grab a drink and unwind.

I am on my way to pick up Axel, my son, when my little Honda Civic begins dying a slow, painful death as my dashboard lights up like a Christmas tree. I have just enough time to pull it safely to the side of the road before it shuts off completely.

No! This can't be happening, I think to myself as I try to restart the car.

Turning the key over in the ignition, I am left with silence surrounding me. Click. Click. Click. Nothing.

Looking over at my cell phone, I think of my limited options for aid. Who can I call at two in the morning to come give me a ride?

I don't want my mom to have to get dressed and then get Axel dressed to come out here. Plus, I am still going to need to have the car towed. I knew I should have signed up for one of those automotive clubs, but damn that would be another bill. A bill I certainly can't afford.

Picking up my cell phone, I dial the one person I know that can help me get a ride and get my car towed all in a quick manner as well as keep it within a reasonable budget.

"Hey, Doll, sorry to call so late," I say when she answers.

"No problem; what's wrong, Tessie?" she asks, the sleepy tone in her voice reminding me normal people don't keep my kind of schedule.

Shit, I woke her up. I feel even more guilt now, but she is one of the few friends I have. Plus, she will come get me, no question, since Tripp and Rex are away on a transport. I would've been tempted to call Rex; however, I have promised myself no more. Luckily, he is away, so the urge is gone, leaving me with Doll. If they were home, Rex would've been at the bar tonight, either to troll for fresh pussy or give me an orgasm in the stock room before the night was over. Rex and I have a fucked up history - one centered around sex, sometimes a little more, but mostly it is just about getting off. Well, that was until recently when I made the decision to cut him out of my life as much as possible.

"My car broke down out on Miller's Hill Road. It won't start back up and I need to get home. I'm sorry for bothering you. I didn't know who else I could call," I say as I hear a noise in the background.

Doll is mumbling something, but I can't bring myself to focus on her as my blood runs cold when I hear Tripp's voice say *his* name.

Shit, Rex! He can't come get me. No. No. No. He cannot come with me to get Axel. Panic is setting in as I run through how this night is going. He will ask me where my son is. He always asks me about Axel. My plan was to get Doll on her way and call my mom to keep him overnight. If Rex is too close, I won't have time to make the call. Then he will wonder why we can't go get him.

"No worries, Tessie, Rex will be there shortly to get you," I hear her say his name, snapping me out of my thoughts.

"Rex? I th… thought they were on a transport," I stammer, questioning why he is back.

"Oh, they got back about an hour ago. Tripp heard you talking so he called him while we've been on the phone. He'll pick you up and get your car taken care of. Do you need a ride tomorrow?"

"No, Doll. Thanks, you've done so much already. I gotta go. I need to call my mom so she's not expecting me right away for Axel." With that, we hang up.

Making a quick call to my mom, I ask her to keep Axel overnight for me. Since he's already asleep, this works out better for him anyway. Regardless of who comes, none of the Hellions are going to lay eyes on Axel.

Knowing my son is settled, I have to prepare myself to see Rex. I seem to lose all self-control when he's around. I always have. Boundaries, I have given myself mental boundaries with him. He is never going to grow up, so I have stopped holding out for that. He is also never going to commit to me or anyone else, for that matter. I have given up on that pipe dream. With that said, I have to set the boundaries for my body more firmly. No more allowing lust to takeover.

Rex is sex walking, period, end of story. He has shoulder length, dirty blond hair. Eyes that are piercing blue, a body that's got defined muscles, and ink that makes you want to lick every inch of his skin. The thing about Rex, he knows he is the whole package. He knows he looks good. He's confident in his bedroom abilities, as he should be. There is also this edge to him. The same edge that all the Hellions carry. The thing that draws the barflies to them like a man lost in the desert to water.

Headlights coming my way draw my attention. Then a wrecker pulls up in front of my little car. I hold my breath as the driver side door opens, my mouth dropping open when it's not Rex who climbs out.

At six feet tall, with broad shoulders and all muscle, the man coming to me is another example of the edge all the Hellions carry.

His long-sleeved, black T-shirt pulls tightly against his well-defined chest, abs, and arms. His normally spiked blonde hair is hidden under an old, worn out, baseball hat. The jeans he is wearing are well washed and fit him like a pair of broken in shoes, comfortable perfection. Black motorcycle boots stop in front of me, drawing my attention back to my situation.

"Hey, Tessie, let's get you loaded up and home to your boy."

"Shooter," is all I manage.

"Yeah, baby, you get me. Rex called. He couldn't make it, but didn't want you on the side of the road."

This is the moment my heart should sink a little that Rex isn't coming to help me. What surprises me, though, is I don't feel short changed in the least bit. I don't feel let down. For once, I feel absolutely nothing for Drexel 'Rex' Crews.

~Shooter~

Damn him! Brother or not, right now, I want to kick his ass. I swear I heard him speaking to someone else as I answered the phone, *"Suck it harder, bitch."* Instead of dropping the barfly, he calls me to pick up his woman off the side of the road. Only Tessie isn't his ol' lady; she's just his back up pussy; the pussy he doesn't want to hold onto yet won't let go of, either.

Tessie is beautiful. She deserves so much better than Rex or any man the likes of us. She's petite, maybe five-feet-four, with dark brown hair and brown eyes that dance when she smiles. Her perky breasts are what most may consider small, but they fit her body perfectly. She has a round ass, but not overly large, just enough to really grip as she rides you. With Tessie, though, it's more than that. She is genuine, caring, and sweet. Loyal to a fault sometimes, she puts up with a lot of shit, not only from our club, but all the guys going into the bar.

I won't lie to myself; I have watched her for years with Rex, envious as hell. Tessie accepts him as he is, whatever he gives her.

I have never met a woman who can easily understand and take a man truly at face value the way Tessie does, not only with Rex, but all of us.

I have been a patched member of the Catawba Hellions MC for five years now. My boss, Ryder, introduced me to the club after he patched in with the Haywood's charter. His wife Dina's father was an original before he passed away tragically in a car accident years ago.

I make the almost hour commute daily to work at Ryder's Restorations in Charlotte. Most days, I paint cars for him. Occasionally, I step in on some fabrication, but it's rare. The pay is good, business is good, and the guys at the shop are good. I could relocate to a place closer to work, but I don't want to be in the city. I like being close to my club and not having neighbors close by. This life is simple and calm compared to what I have seen in my past.

I am going through the routine of hooking up Tessie's car to the wrecker. My buddy here in Catawba has a towing and recovery business. He said he would come get her, but I couldn't do that to Tessie. She's a single mom, by herself on an old road in the middle of nowhere, and it is beyond late. A familiar face might make things a little better, especially since I don't know how disappointed she is over Rex not coming personally.

Glancing over my shoulder, I see she's watching me.

"Need help?" she asks, sticking her hands in her jean pockets.

"Nah, baby, I got it. Go ahead and get in. I'll be a few minutes, and then we'll get you home."

She nods at me before proceeding to get in the truck. The 1993 silver Honda Civic she has been driving certainly has seen better days. Once we get this to the shop, I'm going to give it a complete over-haul. She has a kid to get home to.

Jobs here are few and far between. The bar is really the only place she could go right now without leaving her mom behind to work in the city. It's a small town, people talk, and Tessie hasn't had an easy life.

With the car secure, I climb in behind the wheel to tow it back to my place. Looking over to the passenger seat, I see she has fallen asleep against the door already. Reaching over, I buckle her in, and she startles and wakes.

"Shooter, thank you."

"Anytime, baby. You need me to take you to your mom's or your place?" I ask, wondering if she needs to pick up her son.

"My house, please. Mom didn't want me to wake Axel."

The exhaustion is written on her face, but more than that there is loneliness in her eyes. I don't know why, yet I feel the need to apologize that it's me that came to get her.

"I'm sorry Rex couldn't make it."

"I'm not," she says, gazing out the window into the dark night.

How do I respond to that? Rather than involve myself in another man's business, I stay quiet. Her phone rings from her purse saving me from continuing our conversation.

"What, Rex?" she answers with a dull tone. There is a pause for him to speak. "Yes, Shooter came. I'm on my way home." Her brows draw together in frustration, but her voice remains impassive. "No, you can't come over tonight." She sighs deeply. "Rex, I told you, no more." Another pause. "You couldn't come get me because you were doing who knows what to some barfly. I'm not stupid. Rex, I told you, I'm done. The fact that you want to come over tonight shows the complete lack of respect you have for me. We're over and have been for years. Hell, we weren't actually ever officially together, so there is nothing to be over."

Her voice never raises, never sharpens. She is calm, cool, and detached as she continues after allowing Rex to reply. "We're nothing more than friends. Move on, Rex. I'm going to. Goodnight." And with that, she swipes her thumb across the screen to end the call.

She lightly bangs her head against the window as we pull up to her house where she starts to unbuckle. Quickly, I reach in my back pocket and get my business card out of my wallet.

"Look, Tessie, if you need anything, I don't care the time, call."

When she looks at the card then up to me, a slight smile crosses her face. "Andy 'Shooter' Jenkins. You look like an Andy."

"What?"

"In all the years you've been coming to the bar, I've only know you as 'Shooter' and 'Jenkins,' never Andy. You look like an Andy."

Sexual Awakenings: Volume One
The Walz

By

Angelica

FALL

I lit candles all over the house in only the scents he would tolerate. I covered our topiaries with soft, clear lights, and arranged fall flowers and large cornstalks into vases around the living room and porch. I loved fall, and by the way the house now smelled and had been transformed, it showed. Grabbing my pumpkin spice latte, I sat in my reading chair on the porch, watching the leaves sway in the cool breeze. I was already cold, but refused to go inside, soaking up the last of the sun as it made its way behind the trees, basking in the feeling in the air. Everything seemed clearer, crisper, and cold days were rare in the south this early in the season. Receiving an incoming message on my tablet, I tapped it, finding nothing new. He wouldn't be home for dinner. It was a good thing I hadn't bothered to cook. I knew better. A year straight of eating alone will do that to a woman. I opted for another night of wine and my vibrator.

Once inside, I chose my favorite bottle of red and poured a healthy glass. Surveying my beautifully decorated home, I rolled my eyes. What was the point? Maybe he was right. The last time I had decorated for the holidays, my husband had asked that same question.

"We don't have any children. We hardly have company. Why even bother?"

Prick. We didn't have children because he had a vasectomy three weeks after our wedding without telling me, only for me to find out in the first of many viscous arguments that ensued. We didn't have company because he was too occupied keeping his own, busy with his constant need to stick his dick in their throats. It wasn't enough for my husband to have one affair; he was in the midst of two.

I was not a woman scorned. Fuck that. I was a woman who had been freed, and too lazy to leave him, having no desire to start another relationship or leave my beautiful home. Alex was never here, ever. What was the point of giving up my life for a ghost I barely lived with? I took my wedding ring off months ago. He never noticed because, in all honesty, I couldn't remember the last conversation we had.

And then I remembered.

"You never loved me did you?" I asked as he entered the house after another late meeting.

"Sure, I love you. Why are you acting so out of sorts?" He ran his hands through his hair, a signature move on his part that I used to find sexy. A stranger to me at that point when we had originally been so close, he stared at me as if I disgusted him, and I returned it. We had been best friends before we were lovers. We'd shared everything. I didn't even recognize the man who now took his place. There was not a damn thing wrong with me or the way I looked. All of his fucked up issues of infidelity were his own.

"I'm not an idiot. Don't play innocent, Alex," I snapped.

"Drink your wine, honey," he said dryly, pushing past me.

That was our last conversation. When he was home, he called his mistresses from his office. I heard every word, because I listened. I listened to strengthen my resolve. I had already decided to ask for a divorce after Christmas. New Year, new life, I guessed. He would let me keep the house and I would let him keep most of his money. He had plenty of it, due to old money passed down from his parents, and his newfound success at his advertising firm. I supposed he thought that since I wanted for nothing, I should just accept my circumstances as a good little wife, go shopping, get pampered. The truth was, I mourned my relationship with my husband, or at least the man I knew before things fell apart. The most frustrating aspect was he refused to admit anything was wrong; the man that had proposed to me knew something was wrong with me before I did at times. He was attentive and nurturing and...human. My tears saddened him, my smiles and laughter fueled him. He'd loved me.

I shook off the small amount of pain making its way into my chest. I had no more room for self-pity. I had done it all. I had worked out, tried new hair, new clothes. I had even gone so far as to get Botox. The only conclusion I came to after a few months of being refused in the skimpiest of lingerie was FUCK HIM. FUCK HIM. I had tried to make my marriage work. He was more interested in seeing it fail. Our relationship was too far gone from what it used to be. There was no trust, and definitely no lingering love. I had spent hours crying over him, now I just wanted my freedom. And freedom was becoming more important than comfort. I had to get out of this and soon.

I sipped my wine, thinking how completely unsatisfying it all was. I had waited until the age of twenty-nine to get married. It seemed the sensible thing to do after a few months of dating Alex. I couldn't even remember the last time we had made love or fucked. My last attempt to keep the home fires burning had failed miserably.

"We aren't a couple of fucking horny teenagers living out a fantasy, Vi. We aren't making a porno, and what the fuck are you wearing?"

I gave up that day, throwing every single negligee I owned away and burying any remaining hope. Sex with Alex was never exactly hot. It had been enough because I had honestly loved him.

Drinking the last of my glass, I poured myself another. Sex, now there was something I was tired of living without. I had my trusty toy. God, how I loved that thing. Battery maintenance promised endless minutes of pleasure. The thought alone had me wanting to reach for it.

I was thirty-two years old, sitting in a big, beautifully decorated house, imagining the next session with my vibrator. I heard the shatter of the wine glass before I realized I was the one who had thrown it in anger.

This is not my life! This is not who I am. This shit…this waiting, much like my marriage, was over!

Things were about to change and change today. First, I had to come up with a plan.

Sex, or lack thereof, was what set me off in the kitchen. I missed it. I wanted it. I needed it, but why? I'd never really had sex like most adults. Well, those adults who I envied, which included pretty much anyone who was having their needs met at this point. I abstained from having my own affair because, for a short time, I held out hope. Now that my mind was made up on divorce, I no longer had to justify my reasoning. Sex was a necessity for me. I had waited long enough. My body was starving for touch, my lips bankrupt from a lack of kisses. While a relationship didn't appeal to me, at least not immediately, the thought of a good hard fuck made me insane with want. Not that I'd ever been satisfied sexually.

My experience consisted mainly of missionary, with a few sporadic moments here and there in various positions. Alex was not well endowed and had by no means made up for it throughout our years together. I wondered what it was like to be with a man with a big cock. I moaned at the thought, never once having an orgasm from a man's dick. My girlfriend Molly told me that without a vibrator I may never have one. She insisted girls who came with men inside them were either porn stars with amazing acting skills or had been divinely gifted in that department. It was a myth to me, an orgasm from a man's cock. I'd had fantasies for years about the possibilities of sex. All of it interested me, especially the kink. Alex would look at me as though I was insane when I suggested anything out of our norm. I would get hot and bothered reading all of my dark erotic romances and begged him to try some scenarios with me. Looking back now, I can kind of see his point on why that might seem a little strange. It just wasn't realistic.

Do these people really exist, the people that explore the forbidden? Of course they do, but where were they? Certainly not on the outskirts of Savannah, GA. I laughed at the thought. I'd do good to find a decent looking, well hung, hardworking man in this area period, let alone one that would explore my sexuality with me. Then again, what if? I mean, surely the insatiable and erotic sexual cravings of people are not limited to only large cities.

Where in the hell would I look for something like that here?

Of course there was the web, but some, or most, of those sites had a virus attached. I'd delved into porn a little when my imagination couldn't do it for me and I needed a little extra something. That got old as well. I was tired of watching. I wanted the experience. Pouring myself another glass of wine, I ignored the shattered glass on the floor. Who the hell would care about the mess anyway? After all, it was only me here.

Hours later, after watching Jimmy Fallon, my curiosity brought me back to the web. Fuck it; I'd been the well-behaved, jilted wife long enough. I wanted to know what was out there, especially those like me who shared the same curiosities. I would love to know if any other women in Savannah had a fascination with kink. After a few hours of searching, I stumbled upon a site advertising a local adults only page. There was a large triple X on the screen and a flashing advertisement of what looked like a bar in or around Savannah, but my excitement was stifled when I realized there was no address. After a quick Google search for the bar, named The Rabbit Hole, I came up empty, and gave up. Yawning, I threw my tablet beside my pillow and laid my head down to watch Nightline when I heard a ping.

I looked at my tablet to see an incoming message asking for the password. After careful thought, I had nothing. I typed my plea.

Hint?

Rabbit Hole.

Not helpful at all. Shit. The possibilities were endless. I studied the XXX on the screen and saw an Alice in Wonderland cartoon encased in them. Inside the rabbit hole, in the middle X, was Alice kissing another Alice on the cheek as she held her pointer finger to her lips.

Making the best guess I could, I keyed it in.

Don't kiss and tell.

I was immediately brought to the homepage, asked to create a username—Blue_Alice—and started navigating my way around.

It was a chat room, and from the subject matter floating in boxes around the screen, it was definitely a no holds barred kink fest. Perfect! At least the curious vixen inside me wouldn't have to show her face for now. I sat for hours in the various chat rooms reading the conversations. Most of them consisted of people hooking up and then agreeing to email in private. Great, hours on the site and I had only gotten a little hot reading what appeared to be an open and unashamed twosome having really kinky message sex. I could read a book and get hotter than this. I was just about to grab my trusty silver bullet and a new erotica book when I got an incoming message.

MadHatter: What are you doing here?

I froze, feeling completely busted. I shook my embarrassment off quickly. I had knocked on the damn door, so far so good, why the hell not? I typed my reply.

Blue_Alice: Looking.

MadHatter: For what?

Blue_Alice: Anything but what I'm doing.

There, honesty. Honesty was good.

MadHatter: Why so blue, Alice? Bored housewife?

Blue_Alice: Fuck you.

MadHatter: So I'm assuming I'm correct?

Blue_Alice: Maybe, what the hell does it matter?

MadHatter: We don't do married here.

Blue_Alice: I am getting a divorce.

MadHatter: That's not a new one.

Blue_Alice: Keep your boring ass chat room.

MadHatter: Temper, temper.

Blue_Alice: I could do a better job turning people on than this bullshit.

MadHatter: Wow, you really need a thick cock in that sassy mouth.

Blue_Alice: And I suppose you're the one who will be giving it to me?

MadHatter: Why not me?

I felt my cheeks grow hot and took a deep breath. Okay, now we are talking here.

Blue_Alice: Fine…talk to me.

MadHatter: Why are you here?

Blue_Alice: You already asked me that.

MadHatter: And you didn't give me a good enough answer.

I thought about it. Going into this with honesty would be the only way I would truly get what I wanted. But is this what I wanted? What if he was some nasty, fat perv with bad skin and greasy hair? Then again, he may have thought I was some nasty troll with a huge gut and overgrown forest in my pants. I shook my head, indignant at my own stereotyping. *Not cool, Vi.* This whole scenario meant taking a chance. I had been teetering on the edge of this for years, if I was honest with myself. I wanted to be fucked ruthlessly, worshipped and tortured, brought to levels of sexual awareness I'd only dreamed about. I was sure, no positive, I had an undiscovered fetish or two. Honest, I'll be honest.

Blue_Alice: I want to explore a part of me I've kept hidden.

MadHatter: Why?

Blue_Alice: Because I don't have anything to lose.

MadHatter: That's dangerous.

Blue_Alice: That in itself is why I am interested. I want to be fucked in ways I've only imagined and I'm tired of only feeling half full. I have cravings and I'm ready.

A few minutes later, I was sure the conversation had ended, then a ping.

MadHatter: I'll be in touch.

Blue_Alice: Wait!

Okay that seemed a little desperate.

MadHatter: What?

Blue_Alice: Who are you?

MadHatter: I'm the guy with the thick cock you'll be wondering about tonight while you play with your toys.

Blue_Alice: Charming.

MadHatter: I can be.

And he was gone, if it had even been a he. For all I knew, it could have been a she. This too fascinated me. I thought of women and my sexual boundaries when it came to them and decided one leap at a time. Although women appealed to me from the waist up, I had no desire to explore the waist down. Then again, I'd really never had the opportunity.

The next day, I brought my iPad on every single errand with the chat room queued up. He could see me, he knew I was waiting. I looked desperate, but I needed this! I felt it in every part of me. I needed to be sexually free. I'd slept with six men in my thirty-two years. Two one night stands, one when I was in college and the other right before I met my husband Alex. The rest were boyfriends and not one of them was a freak, well not in the sense that I wanted them to be. A few got me off with their mouth, but it wasn't earth shattering. It was more or less a struggle and an enormous amount of effort with constant murmurs of "Are you close?" during what seemed to be rigorous work. So I rarely got off.

I had, as the mysterious messenger predicted, taken my toy to bed last night, imagining the man behind our brief chat. I was hot in a way I hadn't been in months at the possibilities alone. This had to be explored. I felt like I was a sexual creature on the verge of finally introducing myself. Once I was home, I unpacked my groceries, praying for the fucking iPad to ping. Just ping! When I got nothing, I decided to forgo cooking and treated myself to dinner at Tubby's, a nearby seafood restaurant on River Street. I sat on the balcony watching the boats glide down the river while the sun set. Couples passed by below me on the busy street holding hands and smiling while I dined alone. Minutes later I got my usual message from Alex letting me know he wouldn't be home tonight and I rolled my eyes. Why did he even bother at this point? God, how I hated him.

Later at home, I thought about looking up some listings to show. I had a real estate license I rarely used and knew it was getting close to time to put it back to use. I was good at it, and I enjoyed it, but when my marriage fell apart I dropped it completely. I had stayed at home for a month solid after hearing Alex's first conversation with one of his mistresses. I didn't need to see anything. The prick had no issue talking openly with her behind his office door. If you are going to cheat, at least have the smarts and decency to hide it. The devastating thought that he didn't care enough to hide is what really drove the knife into my heart. A few months after I had questioned him about his distance, I realized he had no intention of revealing his indiscretions to me. He was simply that fucking stupid. I heard every word he uttered to those women. It was eerily close to the way he used to speak to me. It hurt me horribly at first, now it just made my stomach turn. Why the fuck was I still here? What more reason did I need? He cheated, our marriage was over. I hated him. Why didn't I just ask for a divorce? PING!

A wave of adrenaline shot through me as I looked at the screen. It was an address. It was obvious why. It was an invitation and one that came way too soon for my comfort.

Well that would be a hell no. I wanted to at least have a conversation longer than a few short sentences before I agreed to a rendezvous.

Blue_Alice: Hello?

No response came. I already knew the address would be my only message tonight. It was a challenge. He wanted to see what I was made of, if I was willing to step out of my comfort zone. All the reasonable reactions raced through me.

What kind of person barely introduces himself and then gives an address to a total stranger?

Then again, what kind of person tells a complete stranger they want to be fucked six ways from Sunday?

I stared at the address for what seemed like an eternity. Okay, I could drive by. What's the harm? I would just look around, scope the place out. I could do this. Throwing my blanket off my legs and retiring my yoga pants, I took a scalding hot shower. I Googled the address with a towel wrapped around me, fear creeping into my thoughts. My search, of course, showed only results with possible directions. It had to be a home address. He gave me directions to his home? I shook off the towel, covered myself with scented lotion and took in my body. I had long legs and curvy hips, a little extra weight made them even more pronounced. My breasts were pushing a C-cup, and though they weren't perfectly proportionate to my hips and ass, I was fine with them. I pulled out a thin black sheath dress that collared at the top, hugging my neck snugly, slipped on my spiked red heels and put on my best face. Thick eyelashes and perfectly painted red lips later, I ran my hands through my dirty blonde hair that I'd ironed straight. I was ready.

Two small glasses of wine and a mini-breakdown later, I corked my bottle and made my way to my car. *You can do this, Vi. You can also back out at any time.*

My cell had no issues navigating the address. My screen map timed my trip to thirty minutes, and in thirty minutes I could be in the midst of possibly the best or worst situation of my life. Then again, I couldn't imagine anything worse than the one I was already in.

I had enough heart left to give, I just didn't give a damn enough to use it. This wasn't about my heart; this was about a thirst I'd fought long enough. This would be good. This could be my something to look forward to.

Come on Violet, divorce is not death and you've got a lot of living to do.

The Sexual Awakenings serial should be read in order: